A Past Best Forgotten

A Harry Bennett Mystery

Helen Wills

LSK Publishing

Texas

First paperback edition September 2022

ISBN 979-8-9870063-2-0 (paperback)
ISBN 979-8-9870063-1-3 (hardcover)
ISBN 979-8-9870063-0-6 (ebook)

Cover design by Mike Cochran
Man's photograph by Drew Hays on Unsplash

Published by LSK Publishing

Acknowledgments

My thanks to Dr. Milton Altschuler for providing insights into the world of psychiatry and the West Houston/Texas Writers' Group members (Shela, Mike, Jean, and Fred) for their patience, guidance, and enthusiasm in reviewing my writing.

I am extremely grateful to my husband, Don, for vetting plot ideas with me and reviewing endless versions of this novel. Thanks also to my family members (Luvoid, Bret, Stephen, Melissa, Aiden, and Abby) and my best friend, Carol, for their encouragement to finish the book and to my hairdresser, Penny, who never tired of listening and discussing whatever version of this story I brought into her shop.

In Memory of Nancy

1

Black leather pants, a white silk shirt, and lacy lingerie trailed from the end of Harry's bed to the closed bathroom door. He recalled opening a bottle of scotch, but not sleeping with a woman. Based on the clothes on the floor, she didn't seem like the kind of female he would forget.

Harry studied the clothes and wondered where he had met the owner. Living in downtown Houston, brought him close to all the action, both for his private investigation work and extracurricular activities. Women in the area ranged from hookers to wealthy socialites. He shook his head. No way had he slept with someone he just met unless she had drugged him.

A quick glance at his dresser confirmed his cell phone, keys, and wallet sat in their usual place. He checked the wallet. All his cash and credit cards were still there.

His ex-girlfriend, Candy, enjoyed playing games. He smiled. She reminded him of those cinnamon candies which burned his tongue but left a lingering taste of spice. A treat he both loved and hated.

If only Candy hadn't swapped him out for that rich guy.

Maybe she had given up on Richard and returned.

Harry stared at the bathroom door. He hated interrupting whoever was in there, but his bladder couldn't wait much longer. He shoved aside a pair of red stilettos blocking his path to the bathroom, then twisted the doorknob in warning.

He cracked open the door. "You about done in there?"

The toilet paper holder rattled as she reeled off tissue.

"I'll give you a few minutes," he said.

He shut the door. If it wasn't Candy, perhaps a hot blonde waited on the other side or a sexy brunette. Harry looked down at his boxers. No matter what he had on, he was probably wearing more than his mystery guest.

Something clattered on the floor.

Waiting much longer wasn't an option, he had to pee. Harry opened the door a fraction.

"Are you okay?" he asked.

Inch by inch, he widened the crack. No one stood at the sink, no steam fogged the mirror. His nail clippers rested on the floor as if she had used them, then missed the counter. Like her clothes, she hadn't even bothered to pick them up. No one sat on the toilet, but paper sprawled on the floor as if she had pulled too much tissue.

He eyed the walk-in closet at the end of his bathroom and peered beyond the entrance, but only saw racks of shirts and pants.

If he pushed the door farther, he could see the shower. A vision of a woman standing in the glass enclosure waiting for him flashed through his mind. He looked around the corner.

The shower stood empty, and no water droplets rested on the glass. Maybe she enjoyed playing games and hid behind the clothes in the closet. His bladder reminded him of a need more urgent than locating any woman.

He walked past the shower and faced the toilet. Something rubbed against his legs.

Harry jumped, knocking his shin on the porcelain. "What the hell?"

An orange tabby stared up at him. One ear looked like something had taken a bite out of it. Bits of fur were missing like a mink coat chewed by moths.

"How did you get in here?" Harry wasn't a fan of cats. Like women, they were unpredictable.

Candy picked up stray cats like she picked up stray men. The felines tracked litter everywhere, got hair on his clothes, sunk claws into his flesh, and ripped up the furniture. Candy pulled pranks but leaving a cat at his place was way beyond her usual shenanigans.

He snatched his robe off a hook and cinched the belt. In the closet, he shoved suits, shirts, and pants aside, but no woman hid amongst them. The cat followed him as he moved through the rest of the apartment. The front door was locked. The coffee table in front of the brown leather couch held no glasses or anything else.

Candy had always nagged him to decorate the space with personal photos. He promised he would but knew he'd never do it. Some people enjoyed reminders of the past, he preferred living in the present.

No dirty dishes waited in the sink. A litter box sat on the floor along with two small bowls, one containing food pellets and the other water. A zebra striped pet carrier blocked the laundry room door. In front of the dryer, a trail of kibble led to an opened bag. He picked up the bits and closed the bag.

Harry shut his eyes and massaged his pounding forehead. Pets and women, neither fared well with him. Now a woman had disappeared, leaving her clothes, a scruffy cat and all its stuff.

Whoever it was, wouldn't have left here naked, so it must be a pre-planned joke. Perhaps the clothes would give him some clue as to the owner's identity. He returned to the bathroom and chased a couple of aspirin with some water, then examined each piece of clothing. The buttonless silk blouse mirrored the shape of the bell-bottom sleeves. The material felt soft against his calloused skin. A scent of gardenias and cigarette smoke teased his nose, intensifying the ache in his head. The leathery smell and suppleness of the pants implied money. None of the clothes had a store or laundry label, except for the padded bra, Victoria's Secret.

Two women had keys to his place, Candy and Charley. He glanced at the clothes, definitely not Charley's style. He grabbed his phone, pressed Candy's number, and waited. His shoulders tensed tighter and tighter with each ring. When she answered, a tingle raced along his spine. Her voice was low and raspy as if she'd smoked away the years. Yet he had never seen her with a cigarette.

"Did you drop off a cat at my place?" He would bring up

the clothes later.

She laughed. "I wouldn't do that to a cat."

"You should take the cat." Harry didn't want it.

"I already have two."

Harry wondered if cats traveled in packs like dogs. "What's one more?"

"One more and Richard leaves."

That worked for Harry. "This cat is cuter than Richie." From what he remembered anything looked better, but then he didn't know what she found attractive.

She laughed. "But is it richer?"

Harry reflected on his recent inheritance. "Maybe."

"In that case, bring him over. I'll take good care of him."

Harry fought the temptation to see her again. "I'll find him another home." Besides, the owner of the clothes had first dibs on him and the cat.

Within minutes of hanging up, the phone rang.

"Harry, it's Buddy."

He hadn't heard from his old partner since Harry had resigned from the force. Either someone had died, or Buddy needed something.

"What's up?"

"Do you know Lisa Angel?"

Harry kept client information private, even from Buddy. "Why?"

"She's dead, stabbed last night." He paused. "I shouldn't be telling you this, but I owe you. They discovered your fingerprints at the crime scene."

"Shit." He didn't even remember last night.

"Drake's been assigned to the case."

"Shit." Drake hated Harry.

"Yeah. Age hasn't improved him."

Harry ended the conversation. He needed time to think and figure out who left the clothes. If he was lucky, she could alibi him.

He stood still and widened his eyes. His breathing stopped for a moment. What if he had it all wrong? What if the woman from last night was Lisa?

The cat rubbed around his legs. Harry didn't have time for a cat. He had to find out what happened last night.

As Harry knocked on the door next to his, he recalled the first time he'd met Charley and smiled. Second grade at a new school was tough but joining a class in the middle of the year added extra stress. Lunch time found him sitting at a table in the cafeteria with only his sack lunch to accompany him. Kids passed by his table but never stopped.

He had focused on his food until a voice said, "Can I sit here?"

Harry looked up at a girl's round smiling face. Blue eyes matching her bright blue t-shirt sparkled at him. Her brown hair fell in waves to her shoulders.

Harry smiled. "Sure."

She slid her tray of food on the table and sat across from him. "I'm Charley."

He squinted. "Charley? Isn't that a boy's name?"

She frowned. "It's short for Charlotte." Her eyes narrowed. "But don't ever call me that." Like the sun splitting through the dark clouds, her eyes widened, and a smile returned to her face. "What's your name?"

The memory faded as the apartment door opened. "Harry. I haven't seen you in a while." Wrinkles formed at the corner of her eyes when she smiled. Some grey strands intermixed with the dark hair pulled into a ponytail. A few extra pounds had gathered around her waist over the years. Time had changed her, but the smile was the same as the girl who'd welcomed him that first day of school.

"Come on in." She motioned him inside.

Harry stepped over a pair of flip flops and maneuvered his way around cardboard boxes stacked around the room.

"Are you moving?" He frowned at the thought of a stranger moving into her place. When he looked for an apartment during a rough patch in his life, she let him know the one next to her was available. He had gotten used to having her next door.

"Are you kidding? That's way too much work." She waved toward the direction of the boxes. "I order a lot of stuff online." She shrugged. "Who has time to go to the store? Anyway, I haven't had a chance to take them for recycling."

"Have a seat." Charley waved toward her living room furniture which consisted of three beanbag chairs sitting in the middle of the room facing a TV hanging on the wall. On the other side of the room, she had a desk with three monitors and an ergonomic chair.

"I can't stay long." Harry always struggled sitting in the beanbags and getting up from them was even harder.

She lifted a mug off her desk. "Want some coffee?"

Harry shook his head. "Want a cat?" The cardboard boxes would be nirvana for any feline.

Charley stopped walking toward the kitchen. Her mouth fell open. "Did you say a cat?"

"It would only be for a while. Just until I find its owner."

"You picked up a stray?" She squinted at him like she didn't believe he did that kind of thing.

He shrugged. "I like animals."

"Then you should keep it. I like cats but I wouldn't get any work done with one. They like to sit on keyboards. Plus look at this place."

Harry took in the pens and papers on the kitchen bar and spread across the round breakfast table.

"My last cat shredded my papers and knocked everything onto the floor." Charley rolled her eyes. "I was constantly picking up stuff." She shook her head. "It just wouldn't work."

Charley grabbed the coffeepot and topped off her mug. "What's really going on, Harry?"

He couldn't keep much from her. She knew him too well. Besides, he wanted her take on what had happened.

Charley's eyes widened as Harry gave her a shortened version of the morning's events. He didn't mention the woman's clothes. Some things he couldn't even tell Charley.

"So, you don't remember anything from last night?" She blew the steam off her coffee.

Harry shook his head.

"Sounds like someone's playing a trick on you." She frowned. "Did you ask Candy?"

Charley had never liked Candy. Harry figured it was because they were exact opposites. Candy wore the latest in fashion, kept her nails painted, and every hair lay in place as if scared to move. One look at Charley said she had different priorities.

"She denied knowing anything about it." Harry rubbed his jaw. "I know Drake will try to pin Lisa's murder on me."

"If you just told him the truth about his sister, he wouldn't harass you anymore."

"It wouldn't make any difference. He would say I was lying. He always had a blind spot where Beth was concerned." Harry shrugged. "If I had a sister, I might feel the same way."

Charley sipped her coffee. "I might be able to find something on Drake. Something you can use on him." She glanced at her computer.

"I don't want you to get caught hacking." He knew she worked magic with systems, bypassing security, and gleaning information without leaving a trace. It was a game for her, but he worried one day she might lose and end up in jail.

She tilted her head and smiled. "I never get caught."

Harry looked up at the ceiling, then at her. "Look, I don't think you'd find anything on him anyway. He's clean."

She gave him an assessing look as if measuring him for a coffin. "Everybody's hiding something."

Harry picked an imaginary piece of lint off his shirt.

Charley walked toward her computer, then said over her

shoulder, "Leave it to me."

Harry took that as his clue to leave. As he headed for the door, he wondered what Charley might be hiding.

2

Charley heard the door close behind Harry, then got up and locked it. Ever since Harry's aunt had passed away, he had been different but not so much that he forgot things. Perhaps Candy leaving him for another guy had pushed him over the edge. Charley never understood his attraction for Candy anyway. The few times she had met Candy, the woman didn't come across as that bright.

Charley sat down at her desk and stared at her monitor. She would take a few minutes trying to hack into the Houston Police Department System. After all, it wasn't her first time to break into it.

A couple of hours later, she had hacked into the employee records. Drake's career was marked with positive comments and high ratings. The only anomaly was early in his record when he switched from the Narcotics Division to Homicide. Probably, someone presented him an opportunity and he took it. A few weeks ago, Charley's manager had offered her a chance to move from a cryptographer role to a cryptanalyst. She had accepted it for no other reason, than she wanted a new challenge. Perhaps the same was true for Drake. Still, it might be worth digging deeper into his transfer to see if there was anything shady about it.

Adele's "Hello" sang from Charley's phone. She looked at the ceiling and debated answering, but like the lyrics in the song, her mother wouldn't stop calling. Unlike the song, her mother never apologized for anything.

She decided to answer. "What's up, Mom?"

"Your birthday is Wednesday."

Charley wondered if her mother was reminding herself or Charley of the event. As she waited for her mother's next revelation, she contemplated her nails. She really had to stop biting them.

"I wanted to schedule a spa day for the two of us. Or a spa weekend." Her voice contained more enthusiasm than Charley could muster for the idea.

"We could get your hair colored and trimmed. I noticed some grey in it the last time we were together." Before Charley could interrupt, her mother continued talking. Her voice increased in speed and excitement like a county fair ride going faster and faster until it brought on nausea. "We could have a mani-pedi. One where they soak your feet and rub fragrant lotions into your skin."

Charley pictured her mom sitting on the edge of a chair, gripping her phone, leaning forward like a runner ready for a race. As always, she would be dressed for a day on the town whether she went anywhere or not. Every bit of her highlighted hair would be sprayed in place around her unlined face.

"Oh, and a facial might slow down your wrinkles." Her voice rose to a fevered pitch. "We could do Botox!"

Needles weren't Charley's idea of a birthday celebration. She had to shut it down.

"Mom, work is really busy right now. You know, I just switched positions."

"You can't work all weekend. We can go shopping, get you some clothes and shoes."

Charley and her mother had different ideas of what she should wear. The shopping trip would either end in an argument or result in purchased items that remained in the back of Charley's closet until the next charity drive.

"Thanks for the offer, but I can't spare more than about an hour. How about lunch?"

Charley would have to listen to her mother discuss the calories in each entree and the importance of diet and exercise, then Charley would get an inquisition on when she was getting married. Since no appropriate answer would be given, she'd lecture Charley on ways to attract and capture a man which always brought to mind black widow spiders. For some reason, her mother didn't consider a woman complete without a man. While Charley wasn't opposed to marriage, it had to be someone who liked her for who she was and not for her physical appearance.

A call alert buzzed on her phone. It was her new boss, Derek. Her stomach clenched.

"Mom, I've got to go. My boss is calling. Let's talk later."

Before her mom could disagree, Charley switched to Derek's

call. "Hi Derek."

"Have you cracked the email from Mexico?" He wasn't one for greetings or idle chitchat.

"Not yet." It would help if she knew what the previous guy had tried. "Did the guy working on this leave any notes? Or could I give him a call?"

"We haven't been able to locate him," he said.

Charley wondered how someone lost an employee. Did he go on vacation and just never return?

Derek cleared his throat. "The FBI wants to arrest these guys while they are in the states. All our intel tells us they should arrive in a couple of weeks." He paused. "Can you decode the message by next Wednesday or do you need someone to help you?"

That gave her a little over a week to finish. "No. That's ok. I'm sure I can crack it by then." She didn't want her boss to think she couldn't handle the job.

He hung up. Charley downed her coffee, then refilled her mug. Researching Drake's past and birthday plans would have to wait. Working for the CIA left little time for either.

3

Harry clenched the carrier's straps as he stepped into the animal shelter. Getting the cat in the carrier had been a fight. Harry glanced at the scratches on his hand. A fight Harry had almost lost.

The place reeked of bleach with an underlying trace of urine. Dogs barked as if they sensed strangers entering their territory. The tabby growled in the carrier.

Harry didn't want a cat. Besides, Lisa rescued animals and this one looked like a prime candidate. Someone else could have left the varmint in the apartment, but he couldn't be sure.

A brunette stood behind the counter smacking gum. Her hair hung past her shoulders and framed a narrow face with a nose as long as a greyhound's.

"Are you dropping off an animal?" She blew a bubble, then sucked it in with a pop.

Harry nodded. She opened the carrier and peered inside. The cat backed into a corner and hissed, immediately dropping his adoptable index to zero.

"We need to complete some paperwork first. Is it a male or

female?"

"A male." He paused, then added. "You're welcome to check." She might want to grab some gloves or a tranquilizer gun first.

"I'll take your word for it. Name?"

He didn't want to give his real name in case the cops searched for the cat. It was doubtful they would, but still. "Josh McClain."

She rolled her eyes. "I meant the cat's name."

The cat snarled providing Harry inspiration. "Evander."

The woman squinted and frowned.

She was probably a baby at the time of the Holyfield/Tyson fight ear incident. Rather than explain, he made it simple. "Van for short."

She pointed at Van's lopped off ear and laughed. "I get it. Van as in Van Gough."

"Yep." If that interpretation helped get the cat adopted, it worked for him. Harry finished the paperwork and handed over some cash as a donation.

Van's wide green eyes peered through the mesh at him. The rascal moved towards Harry with his motor running as if he sensed his fate.

As Harry drove away, Van's eyes haunted him. They had glistened as if moist with tears. He shook his head. What a sucker he was. Cats don't cry, or do they?

Harry didn't need a pet, especially a cat, maybe a dog, a Rottweiler, muscular and intimidating, the perfect beast for a PI. Harry eyed the red claw marks raked across his hands. Still,

Van was no pussy.

No one would adopt him with his torn ear and missing fur. They had probably already added him to the kill list. One more death chalked up to him.

"Damn."

He turned the car around, arriving at the pound only minutes after leaving. The carrier still rested on the counter.

The brunette wadded her gum into a wrapper. "I was just about to take him back."

"I've changed my mind."

Harry grabbed the carrier and returned to the car. As he placed the container on the passenger seat, Van growled.

"You're only staying with me until someone claims you. If no one does, then I'll find a home for you. Although, I'm not sure how with the way you look right now. It would help if you didn't claw people."

He could drop the cat off at Candy's. Like a drug addict, he looked for any excuse to pick up old habits. Candy wasn't old, but she was a bad habit. He mentally slapped himself and turned in the direction of home.

When Harry arrived at his apartment, a police car sat in the visitor parking lot. Holding his breath, he pulled closer to view the man approaching the lobby. The man turned to open the door for a couple of ladies behind him. Harry recognized the stocky frame, the thick black hair, and the angular shape of his face. *Drake.* He whipped his car around and drove away. The crate slid. The cat meowed.

"Time to find a hideout, Van."

The sun glinted on the star hanging above the red letters announcing the Star Motel. Dingy white railing rimmed the balcony of the two-story grey building. Numbered black doors probably covered a multitude of stains and sins. Harry navigated past the craters in the asphalt and parked in front of the main entrance, then grabbed the carrier. Van snarled.

"I agree. The place is a dump, and the rooms probably aren't any better. At least you can sleep in your carrier."

The squat man behind the counter stared through strands of brown hair. His dilated eyes and sweaty skin indicated a possible amphetamine addiction. A name tag pinned to his white shirt spelled out Sam. Harry knew calling someone by their name brought a familiarity. Not that he wanted this guy for a friend, but he wanted special treatment.

Harry smiled and leaned on the counter. "Sam, I need a room for a night, possibly longer." He pointed to Van. "You take pets, right?"

Sam nodded. "It's a little early for check in. Let me see what we have available."

Based on the number of cars in the parking lot and the state of the place, Harry doubted the motel was fully booked.

Sam clicked on the keyboard. "Do you have a room preference?"

"I'd like a room off the back parking lot."

Sam smirked. "Hiding from the law?"

Sweat beaded on Harry's forehead, but he kept his smile. "Isn't everyone?"

"Ain't that the truth." Sam rolled his eyes.

Harry completed the registration paperwork, then paid in cash. He kept his wallet out, ready to provide a fake driver's license that matched the information he had provided.

"Your room is behind the building, first floor, on the end."

Interesting, the motel required no ID. If he ever needed to stash someone, this was the place.

Harry parked his car in front of his room. He opened the door and saw the interior lived up to the exterior. A king-sized bed rested on green indoor/outdoor carpet. No doubt the dirt-brown bedspread covered a party of bed bugs. A mirror cracked in one corner hung over a chest of drawers missing a knob. He checked the bathroom. The welcome smell of bleach infiltrated his nose. The tub and toilet were white, the beige tile and grout grit free, the shower curtain without mildew, only the dingy white towels marred the room. Perhaps he'd sleep in the tub.

Returning to the car, Harry pulled out the throwaway litter box, and added the other purchased bags on top. The trip to the pet store wasn't one he would repeat. Van had growled and hissed at every passing dog. The customers had looked at him as if Van was a toddler pitching a fit.

Harry dragged everything inside his temporary home, then unzipped Van's crate. The cat stayed scrunched in the corner.

"You can come out. It's just you and me."

Van crept toward the carrier's opening. Harry's phone rang. The cat scooted back inside as Harry answered, "Bennett Investigations."

"We need to talk."

He recognized David Angel's gravelly voice, a voice straight out of a mafia movie. It was hard to believe he would call with his wife murdered. At this point, did it really matter whether Lisa had cheated on David? Maybe he hoped Harry was tailing her last night and saw something. If only Harry could remember what he'd done.

Harry gripped the phone but kept his tone casual. "Ok, let's talk."

"Not over the phone."

David wasn't much for phone conversations. Harry suspected he liked the added facial cues and body language of a face-to-face meeting. He checked his watch. "I can meet you in a couple of hours."

David's voice boomed down the line. "A couple of hours? Who's the customer here?"

Silence worked best with David, so Harry didn't answer. Instead, he watched Van chase a roach across the floor, then toy with it.

David sighed. "All right. Raphael's. Two hours from now." He hung up.

Harry stared at the phone and wondered why David never mentioned Lisa's death. The cops must have already told him. Maybe he wanted to break the news in person. After all, he would no longer require Harry's services. The cops wouldn't have told David that Harry's fingerprints were discovered at the scene of the crime, at least, not this early in the investigation.

It paid for Harry to have a cop for a friend. He would wheedle out of Buddy exactly where they found his prints. Someone must have picked up something with Harry's prints and planted evidence. Probably Drake grabbed something he knew Harry had touched.

Any idiot would know stabbing Lisa, or anyone wasn't Harry's MO, too messy, too close, and too risky. He preferred guns.

Harry rubbed his forehead. His shrink would have plenty of material the next time they met. In the last twenty-four hours, Harry had lost his memory, a woman, and a surveillance gig. He had gained a pet and Drake probably had him down for murder. Like a snowball headed downhill, accumulating snow, his life gathered trouble, but instead of a soft landing at the bottom, the hard floor of a jail cell waited for him.

4

Dr. Janet Worth opened the door to her office and looked around the room. Eight years of practicing psychiatry had proved rather dull. Nothing really challenging had walked through her door yet. The room itself spoke ordinary. Two light grey chairs faced an off-white couch. She wiped some dust off the glass-topped coffee table separating the chairs from the sofa, then picked up her coffee cup sitting on the small white table between the two chairs. Perhaps this year she'd get a challenging case.

There was the erotic transference case, but that was more of an aggravation than anything else. Her mind wandered to a phone call two nights ago, a voice whispering her name, then the unlisted number went dead. She'd checked the locks on the doors and windows and pulled the shades in case the creep stood outside her home. Janet resisted calling her ex-husband. Either his latest girlfriend would answer, or he'd think she made up an excuse to call him. Instead, she watched TV in bed with a 9mm Glock by her side. Snuggling with cold metal wasn't her idea of a bed partner, but sometimes it was easier.

Janet could think of no one with any reason for harassing her. Well, perhaps one.

She walked to her desk, tucked off to the side of the room, and checked her calendar, then pulled out a chart and moved to her usual chair in the sitting area.

Minutes later, the receptionist ushered in the next patient. Janet noted the dark hollows under Harry's blue eyes, the disheveled black hair as if each strand fought against the other. As he sat on the chair close to hers, she noticed his white shirt hung loose on his athletic frame. Everything indicated he struggled, but his straight back and direct stare showed he would beat the hell out of whatever demons he faced.

Janet smiled. "How have you been doing?"

He frowned. "I think the antidepressant caused a blackout."

It had taken her a long time to convince him to take it. Like many men, he believed only the weak needed medications to cope. Yet somehow alcohol was considered an acceptable form of coping.

"Blackouts aren't a side effect of the medication." She flipped through his paperwork. None of his test results indicated any physical problems. "Have you passed out before?"

He shook his head.

"What were you doing right before it happened?"

He stared up at the ceiling as if visualizing the previous night. "The last thing I remember was opening a bottle of scotch." He stared into her eyes with a blank look. "But not pouring a drink."

Other patients admitted drinking straight from the bottle, usually alcoholics or slobs or both. She'd pegged Harry as neat bordering on OCD. It was possible he hated dirtying a glass. He had mentioned before that he enjoyed a nightcap, but never any addiction. With his prescription, he should avoid all liquor.

"You're not supposed to mix alcohol with anti-depressants." Janet had explained this to him, and it was listed in the directions. She wondered if anyone ever listened or just did whatever they wanted to do. "Perhaps you nodded off."

Harry broke eye contact with her. "I don't think so. This morning a woman's clothes were on my bedroom floor. I don't remember inviting anyone to my apartment."

She wasn't sure which bothered him more, the memory loss or the woman's clothes. Perhaps they were equally frustrating.

"Did you ask her what happened?"

"She wasn't there this morning."

Janet leaned closer. "Was anything missing?" A hooker could have spiked his drink, then robbed him. Although, paying for sex hadn't come out in previous sessions.

"Nope." He raised his eyebrows. "I deal in crime. I don't bring home strangers."

"Who do you think it was?"

"I don't know." Harry rubbed his chin. "Weird thing is all the labels on the clothes were missing except for one: Victoria's Secret."

"That is strange. Maybe she left it as a clue to her name. Do you know anyone named Victoria?"

Harry looked up at the ceiling, then returned his gaze to her.

"No. At least not one that I remember." He frowned. "Whoever it was left a cat."

"A cat? That's odd. Are you keeping it?" A pet might help him get over the death of his aunt.

"Just until his owner shows up."

"If his owner returns, you can always get a dog." Dogs needed walking. Harry would meet people and possibly develop relationships. Some sort of social life other than work would help him through this phase of his life.

He shook his head. "I don't need a pet. I'm fine except for blacking out."

She figured he had downed one too many drinks.

"The most common cause is excessive drinking, but it could be a medical issue. Nothing in your records indicate anything serious. If it happens again, we'll run more tests." She made a note in his file.

"Discounting the memory loss, has the medication helped?"

"It has, but I don't think I need to take it anymore."

"So, you're over the loss of your aunt?" No one really gets over the death of someone close, but his pain would diminish with time.

"Well enough to stop taking the medicine."

Doubtful, but she couldn't force him to take the pills. "Are you sleeping better?"

He shifted in his chair. "Most nights."

"Have you finished going through your aunt's things?" Janet worried he was avoiding memories of his aunt.

Harry looked down at his hands. "I haven't had the time.

Her house sold so fast, I had to dump everything into storage. Furniture, clothes, books." He looked at her. "Just one more thing to deal with."

She wondered if he would ever deal with it or just continue paying the storage fees. "In previous sessions, we discussed the guilt associated with your aunt's death. How do you feel now?"

Harry rubbed his fingers across his eyebrows as if hiding behind a mask. "Fine. Just wish I'd made her see a doctor sooner."

Janet knew only time and friends would ease his loss and regret. "We talked about reconnecting with old friends and socializing more. Have you made any progress?"

"I've spent some time with Charley this week, but work has kept me busy." He looked at her and smiled. "If I'm lucky, the woman from last night will visit me again."

She had never seen him smile. Lines crinkled around his eyes and deepened lines in his cheeks, giving him a rakish look. The room felt warm. Janet tugged on the edges of her jacket, then gripped her pen and wrote some notes in his folder.

Janet checked his chart. "Do you want to talk about your parents?"

He folded his arms. "Not much point. They've been dead for thirty-two years."

She resisted rolling her eyes. Every time the subject of his parents came up, he dismissed the topic as if he were flicking away a wasp before it plunged a stinger in his skin. Just like a wasp, she persisted. "Do you remember much about them?"

"Not really."

Janet stood a better chance of fitting into her high school jeans, than getting any information out of him. She wondered why he bothered coming to see her. Perhaps mentioning the car crash would stir some emotions.

"You were lucky to survive the accident."

Harry frowned. "Even luckier if my mom had survived."

"Just your mother?" She kept her face neutral so he wouldn't feel any condemnation from her question.

His eyes widened. "Of course, my father too. I was just closer to my mom. Probably true of all eight-year-olds."

Janet scribbled a note to approach the subject again next time. "Is there anything else you'd like to discuss?"

He shook his head.

"For now, continue taking the anti-depressant." She raised an eyebrow. "Stay away from the alcohol." Janet closed his folder. "Have the receptionist schedule an appointment for next week."

After the door closed, Janet drummed her fingers on Harry's chart and smiled. Harry might prove to be her first real challenging case.

5

As Harry drove away from Dr. Worth's, he regretted scheduling another appointment with her. Rehashing history didn't help anything. Better to forget the past and move on with life. Harry had followed this motto until his aunt's death. Now, his past wouldn't leave him alone, waking him at night and haunting him during the day. Capturing and tossing the daytime thoughts was doable, but he couldn't control his dreams.

If Dr. Worth knew his life story, she would think less of him. Maybe he would reveal more if the doc wasn't so attractive. He was a sucker for brunettes with green eyes, especially ones with great bodies. Her suit hid some of her attributes, but when she'd pulled on her jacket today revealing a well-endowed silk shirt, his mind had blanked.

Harry knew information increased the likelihood of solving a crime. Without providing Dr. Worth a complete picture of who he was and the events of his life, he was limiting her ability to help him. Next time he would try to do better. His problems probably paled compared to some of the other patients. At least, he hoped so.

Harry checked his phone as he arrived at Raphael's. He was only a few minutes late for his meeting with David Angel. Harry parked the car under the shade of a tree, then walked to the restaurant. As he stepped from the sun's heat into the place, a blast of cool air welcomed him. His eyes took a moment to adjust to the dim room. As the hostess led him to a back corner table, the thick carpet absorbed their footsteps. Lighting sourced from table candles and wall sconces left faces concealed in shadows. Harry knew within these walls, society shared secrets, illicit lovers lingered over food, and people closed questionable deals. He had tailed wayward spouses, employees, and politicians here watching them from dark corners while he enjoyed a meal on his client's tab.

David stood and welcomed Harry with a handshake. The buttons on his white shirt strained against his belly. Fewer brown strands covered his scalp. Harry wondered when he would give up and just shave it.

They ordered drinks, then David leaned across the table breathing stale cigar smoke in Harry's face. He resisted the urge to pull away from him. After all, he was the client. Instead, Harry locked on David's faded blue eyes like every word was of interest.

"My wife is dead." His voice cracked. "Someone stabbed her."

Harry studied David's drawn face, the puffy eyelids, and the red nose. Was he a man upset over his wife's death? Or had David killed her and the fear of getting caught brought its own kind of grief?

A vision of Lisa alive flitted through Harry's mind. The sun hitting her blonde hair as she exited a dress shop carrying bags with a smile on her face and a swing in her step. Death came too soon for her like a song stopped in the middle of a jaunty refrain. A sadness crept over Harry. He focused on David's bloodshot eyes. Harry's instincts said David hadn't killed her, but he had been wrong before.

"Is there anything I can do?" Harry asked.

David hit the table with his fist. "I want you to get the son of a bitch who killed her."

"I'd like to help, but it's a police case." In David's place, he would want justice too, but the police resources far exceeded his. Harry fiddled with his napkin. "I can't do any more than they can."

"They'll try to pin it on me. Don't they always suspect the husband? If they find she was cheating on me, I'm a goner." David looked around the room, then fixed his eyes on Harry's. "Did you keep any copies of the pictures you gave me?"

David was right. The cops would suspect him. Although, if Drake had his way, Harry would be the one to go down for Lisa's murder.

"You have all the prints. I have digital copies," Harry said.

"I'll destroy mine." He pointed at Harry. "You delete the images."

"Hold on. What if her lover killed her? You might need them for the cops. Just hide them. I'll delete my files." No way would he delete them, but better to lie than lose his license and serve jail time for destroying potential evidence.

They halted their conversation as the waitress deposited their drinks on the table and took their order. Afterwards, she disappeared into the shadows.

David took a swig of his Bloody Mary. "Were you able to find out the guy's name?"

"Not yet. I'll need to keep a picture of him if you want it."

He narrowed his eyes and leaned in closer. "I told you, delete the pictures."

Harry held up his hands. "I'll only keep one of his face. I can't get his name if I don't have a picture."

"Ok. Just delete everything else." He drummed his fingers on the tablecloth. "Will you search for her killer?"

Harry picked up his water glass, took a sip, and wondered what he'd done last night and how his fingerprints wound up at the crime scene. He needed to find the killer before he landed in a cell. He might as well get paid for it. Before he could answer David tapped his arm.

"I'll pay double your going rate plus expenses."

Harry did the math, then said, "Where was she killed?"

"Alessandra Hotel."

Harry's aunt had taken him for lunch at Alessandra's to celebrate his thirtieth birthday. It was an upscale-five-star hotel with a price to match, very different than the one-star motel he shared with Van. No way he would forget visiting Alessandra's last night, but somehow his fingerprints had ended up at the crime scene.

The sun slid behind the clouds as he exited Raphael's. Only empty cars sat outside. At the rear of the building, he located the worn path leading through the trees and brush to the parking lot of the dentist's office where he had left his car. Honeysuckle grew in a patch close to the trail. Its scent welcomed the bees who moved from flower to flower savoring the sweet nectar. Halfway down the trail, a snap of a branch stopped him. Harry slipped his hand underneath his jacket. He grabbed a gun from his side holster, then hid behind the thick trunk of a live oak. Sweat trickled down his sides as he watched for any possible movement. Birds called to one another. A horn honked. A moment of silence, then he heard the crunch of footsteps. Within seconds, Drake appeared.

"Give it up Harry. I know you're here."

Harry looked around for a better hiding spot, but the other trees and knee-high shrubs offered even less coverage. Drake would find him no matter what he did. He couldn't run fast enough to get in his car before Drake got him. Besides, running from a cop never ended well. Harry holstered his gun, stepped out from the trees, and faced him.

"What do you want?"

Drake thrust his chin forward. "Where were you last night between the hours of ten and midnight?

Harry mentally noted the time frame of the murder and glared. "What's it to you?"

"Lisa Angel was murdered, and your fingerprints were found at the scene." He moved in on Harry. "So, I'll ask again, where were you?"

Harry reviewed last night's timeline in his mind. He had opened the scotch within minutes of arriving home around seven. The woman, whoever she was, arrived after that. Without a name, Harry had no alibi. If he said he blacked out, Drake would think he was hiding something or worse assume Harry had killed Lisa.

He kept eye contact with Drake and forced himself not to blink. "At home alone."

If the woman alibied Harry later, they would want to know why he hadn't mentioned her when questioned. Harry would make up a story which wasn't a problem. Storytelling was a requirement for his profession.

Drake's eyes narrowed. "How do you explain the fingerprints?"

No lie or speculation would work. Drake might produce witnesses or video of him arriving and leaving Alessandra's.

"I don't have to explain them."

He leaned into Harry. Years of pent-up rage burned in his eyes. His breath reeked of garlic.

"You son of a bitch. I'll nail you for this one." Each word hit Harry like a punch in the face.

Harry's shoulders tightened. His neck strained as he drew closer to Drake.

"Go ahead and try," Harry said.

Harry prepared for spit or a fist in the face. Fighting with a cop was stupid. He took a deep breath and stepped away from Drake.

"Unless you're arresting me, I'm leaving." Harry turned and

left.

A push landed him face down on the trail, rocks dug into his skin. Part of him had wanted Drake to push him. Walking away from a fight wasn't Harry's style. He rolled over and stared at him.

"That was a cheap shot."

Drake smirked. "Looks like you tripped. You always were a klutz."

He got up and brushed off his clothes and gave Drake a second chance. "I'm going to forget this happened."

"Like you forgot Beth's death." Drake clenched his hands. "I'll never forget. If it weren't for you, my sister would still be alive."

Drake's emotional punch hit him harder than any physical blow.

"We each make our own choices. You had as much influence on her as I did, probably more."

Drake's face turned a deep shade of red and his eyes bulged. He balled up his hand and rubbed it in the palm of his other hand like he was polishing a stone.

"You never did take responsibility for your actions. This time I'll make sure you do," Drake said.

Drake went for the gut. Harry blocked it but missed the jab to the cheek. Pain exploded through his face. He punched Drake's nose. A crunch of bone was underscored by a cry of rage and blood spilling toward Drake's lip. Drake's fist shot across Harry's mouth, snapping his head sideways, then Drake slammed his hand into Harry's chin. Everything went black.

6

Charley's butt had gone numb. She stood, stretched out her arms, and pulled her shoulders back, emulating a posture worthy of her mom's approval. A walk to get the mail would improve her circulation and give her some much-needed exercise.

She grabbed her keys and locked the door. With all the neighbors' doors facing the hallway, it always felt like she lived in a hotel. One day she might have a house with a front and back yard.

The smell of sizzling onions seeped into the shared space reminding her of fajitas and margaritas. After five years in this apartment complex, she still didn't know any neighbors well enough for more than a casual greeting, except for Harry. She walked past his door and the elevator, opting for the stairs.

When she exited the building, a man passed by her. She looked up to see if she recognized him, but he looked the other way as if interested in the cars in the parking lot.

As she followed the sidewalk to the main building, she watched a couple of squirrels chase each other across the green space, then race up a tree. The sun and the humidity had her sweating by the time she reached the lobby. Charley yanked open the glass door. A wave of cool air sent goose bumps across her arms. Elevator music stopped anyone from loitering in the area, so Charley had the place to herself. She unlocked her mail slot, opened it, and emptied the box. As she walked back to her place, she sifted through the flyers and bills, stacking them in order of importance.

When she approached her door, she noticed a white envelope laying in front of it.

"Someone didn't want to pay postage." Charley mumbled as she picked up the legal-sized white envelope and examined it. On front, her name was hand printed in black ink. She looked up and down the hall, but none of the other doors had an envelope. She hadn't missed a rent payment, had she?

When she opened the door, her computer dinged. Probably her boss checking to see how far along she was on decoding the message. If he would stop pestering her, it might actually get done.

Charley tossed everything on her kitchen counter, then checked her email inbox and frowned. A calendar notice for a video conference was scheduled for Tuesday. The agenda listed her name for an update on her project, so she had to attend. A video conference would require fixing her hair and face and wearing something other than sweats that day. She could block the camera, but it probably wasn't a good idea for her first meeting with the team. Just the thought of talking in front of a group caused her palms to sweat.

After several hours of trying different encryption keys, Charley's stomach complained. She fixed a sandwich, then sat at the kitchen bar and ate. The stampless white envelope with its black lettering caught her eye. She ripped it open and pulled out a folded sheet of plain letter paper. The same writing spelled out the message: "Stop what you're doing or we'll stop you permanently." She stared at it for several minutes, then let the paper fall from her hand onto the floor.

Who would leave such a message? What did they want her to stop? Decoding the message? Only the CIA knew the work she was doing. It could be someone who had discovered she was digging into Drake's past, but she'd only started looking at his records a few hours ago. Charley grabbed her phone and called her boss.

"Derek, this is Charley. I just got a threatening message telling me to stop what I'm doing, or they would stop me."

"What? What kind of message? Was it a phone call? Email?" His voice held a note of concern.

"It was in an envelope outside my apartment door. The letter was handwritten."

"It's probably a prank. Do you have any friends or family members who might have done it?"

Harry played jokes on her, but nothing like this. Her dad had left the state after her parents divorced and, as far as she knew, he wasn't in town. Besides it wasn't something either he or her mother would do. All of her friends were too busy with life to email a message much less handwrite a note.

"No. They've got better things to do," she said.

"Could it be related to something other than your work? Is a neighbor upset with you?"

Charley rolled her eyes. "I don't interact with them enough to cause any trouble."

"People are crazy. Some get upset if you take their parking spot," Derek said.

"I've parked in the same place for the past year."

"We can check it for fingerprints. I'll send someone over to get it." He paused. "Or would you rather drop it off at the office?"

She didn't want to leave her apartment. Someone might attack her.

"It's probably better if someone picks it up so I can focus on decoding the message. Just let me know when they're coming."

An hour later, Charley hadn't had any luck in determining the encryption key. With the message being one between Mexico and the U.S., it could be in Spanish or English. Maybe reviewing the information she'd gathered about the individuals involved in communicating the encrypted email would help her come up with the right key.

Someone knocked on the door. Charley's heart banged around in her chest like bullets from a machine gun.

The phone rang. She checked it, recognized the number, and answered it.

Before she could say anything, her boss said, "The guy at your door is legit. Give him the envelope." He hung up.

Charley turned toward the front door and yelled, "Hold on just a second."

She snapped a picture of the letter and envelope with her phone, then using some tongs stuffed them both in a sealable plastic bag.

She picked up the bat leaning against the frame of her door, then asked, "Who is it?"

"I'm here for the envelope."

Charley looked through the peephole. The shaggy haired blond man wearing a dark business jacket looked safe enough. She left the chain on and opened the door just wide enough to slide the envelope to him. No point in taking any chances.

The envelope disappeared. She shut the door and locked it. A quick look through the peephole confirmed the man had left. She exhaled, placed the bat back in position, and returned to her computer. The sooner the message was decoded and out of her apartment, the safer she should be.

The end of the day found Charley no closer to deciphering the message, but at least she'd eliminated a lot of possibilities. She looked out her bedroom window for Harry's car. Just knowing he was home would bring her some comfort, but his usual parking spot was empty.

If only she could show the letter to Harry. He might glean some information from it and track down whoever it was, but he didn't even know she worked for the CIA. If they were married, she could tell him, but what were the chances he would even ask her on a date much less marry her?

Charley checked out a ketchup stain on the front of her grey sweatshirt and sighed. Harry went for glitzy women. He believed all that glittered was gold. Although from her perspective, he had dated a lot of pyrite.

7

When Harry woke, the sun's rays peered underneath the canopy of the trees and into his eyes. No Drake stood over him or welcomed him with a taunt of how he had beat the shit out of him. The last thing Harry wanted to see was Drake's mocking smile.

Birds chirped and in the distance cars hummed. His head pounded and his face ached. The taste of blood salted his mouth. He ran his tongue over his teeth, all there, none loose. The muggy air weighed on his body like invisible hands pushing him into the ground. He moved his arms to prop himself up, then something bit his hand. *Ants.* An army of them crawling on him. As he raked them off, Harry wished he hadn't bothered getting out of bed that morning.

As Harry drove to the Star, his stomach growled. He moved his mouth in an imitation of eating, then grimaced. Tomorrow chewing might work, but tonight a smoothie was on the menu. Waiting in the drive-through, he replayed his fight with Drake, trying different moves. By the time he'd finished his liquid meal, he had a strategy in mind. Next time he would beat the shit out of Drake.

If he couldn't recall what he'd done last night, fighting wouldn't matter. Drake would arrest him. Even the sleazebag Star was better than jail. Since Drake had already found him, there was no need for hiding anymore. He would pick up Van and head home. The thought of sleeping in his own bed, lifted his spirits which brought to mind other spirits. He recalled a liquor store near the motel where his friend, Johnnie Walker, waited for him.

Harry yawned and rubbed his eyes while he waited on the traffic light to turn green. By the time he had parked in the Star's lot, Harry wondered if he could drive home without falling asleep. His head throbbed as he grabbed the Johnnie Walker and dragged his body out of the car.

When he entered his room, the pungent smell of bleach greeted him, but not Van. The cat was probably sleeping somewhere. Still, he had hoped the varmint might give him a rub around his legs or some indication he cared. After all, he had gone back to the pound and gotten him. A dog would have run to him, wagging its tail. The thought of so much motion made him dizzy. Maybe a cat was the better choice.

Times like this, he missed having a partner, missed the camaraderie. When he was on the force, Buddy shared taking the bad guys down with him. They were always there for each other and had remained friends even though Buddy's new partner was Drake.

Once Buddy married and had kids, he had even less time for Harry. He shrugged. One day, Harry might find the right woman and marry… However, it was better to not marry, than marry the wrong one. Although the wrong ones were all he seemed to attract, or he was only attracted to the wrong ones. For now, if he needed to talk, he would visit Charley or call Buddy. After he figured out who killed Lisa, then he would take on a partner. Perhaps Buddy would ditch the force and join Harry's agency.

Once the door clicked shut, Harry selected a paper cup, poured some scotch, and reflected on his situation while downing the gold liquid. All the cops had on him were fingerprints. They couldn't arrest anyone on that alone unless the prints appeared on the murder weapon too. If they had, Drake would have handcuffed him already. He poured another drink.

Someone had framed him. That woman last night could have drugged him, then wrapped his fingers around an object and left it at the scene of the crime. Drake hated him enough to pay someone to incriminate him. Others hated him too, people he had arrested and testified against. No one liked detectives, except victims and their families.

He needed to know exactly where they found his fingerprints. Maybe Buddy would tell him. He picked up his phone and listened to the ringing until voice mail clicked over. It was simple and straightforward like Buddy.

"Leave a message."

Harry hung up. He had left Buddy voice messages before

and sometimes it took hours for him to respond, but he answered text messages in minutes. Harry didn't want any evidence typed on a phone, but a lunch invitation was innocuous enough.

Meet me for lunch tomorrow at 1:00 - Willie's Grill?

Harry watched and waited.

See you there.

Harry's mind filled with possible suspects, but none were nuts enough or had the brains to go after him. His money was on Drake.

He massaged his forehead. If he could find the woman from the last night, she could alibi him unless it was Lisa. That didn't make sense. She didn't drive to the Alessandra naked. She could have changed clothes before she left his place, but why leave the clothes and a cat in his apartment?

In a drunken stupor, he might agree to watch someone's cat, but he wouldn't sleep with a client's wife. It wasn't the way to run a business or build clientele.

If he had murdered her... His body shook. The thought of physically hurting a woman repulsed him. Killing one was unfathomable, but then so was forgetting an entire evening.

Harry's shoulders slumped and his eyelids grew heavy. Maybe if he took a quick nap, then he'd have enough brainpower to figure out who had killed Lisa and even remember what happened at his place last night.

8

The moon glowed on the buckled and cracked sidewalk guiding Dr. Janet Worth home. In this area, empty houses waited for destruction, the teardowns turning into commercial property or apartments. Trash littered the gutters and the smell of urine mixed with her perfume.

A block away, light glowed from a twenty-four-hour convenience store. A couple of guys lingered outside smoking cigarettes. On one, muscular arms extended from his dingy undershirt which ended just shy of his beer belly. His friend's long hair and toothpick frame reminded her of drug addicts she'd treated, patients to whom food was no longer as important as the next fix. Their conversation stopped as she grew closer.

Janet hated this. Anytime a strange man watched her, the amount of unease multiplied by the number of men leering. It was like their eyes were hands visually touching her, assigning her body a score. She could cross the street to avoid them but had as much right to this street as they did. Looking straight ahead, she focused her eyes away from them, forcing a normal stride, a pace too quick showed fear, a pace too slow invited confrontation.

She should have called a cab, but only a mile separated her home from her office. The mechanic promised to return her car tomorrow. One time walking wouldn't kill her. She needed the exercise after sitting all day and it hadn't seemed like much of a risk.

If only she'd left before dark, before creeps settled on doorsteps searching for prey. She recalled her mother's advice when Janet had expressed her fear of rats: "It's not the four-legged rats you need to worry about it's the two-legged ones."

Unfortunately, her mother gave good advice, but didn't follow it. Janet learned about men from the stream of bad choices her mother dragged home. She recalled one in particular, a depressed man driven to drinking. A tall man with broad shoulders, double the size of her pre-teen body. He'd hit her mother once. Janet had gone after him to prevent any further blows, but her mother stopped her. He had laughed, but never hit her mom again. From then on, his interest in Janet increased. So much so, her mother believed he liked Janet more than her. Yet, she continued to date him. Janet learned to avoid any situations where she might be alone with him.

Some women, like her mother, ran on emotion and chemistry, a concoction destined for failed relationships. Janet fought her desires for bad boys and risk takers. Instead, she wrote a prioritized list of the top ten traits expected in a good companion. Her ex-husband had fulfilled the top five, but she should have waited for the perfect ten.

As she drew closer to the men, the cigarette smoke irritated her throat. She suppressed a cough.

"Hey pretty momma, you want a ride?" Mr. Beer Belly's voice sounded as filthy as the stains on his T-shirt.

She visualized punching him, crunching his nose underneath her fist, then whipping around with a jab for his friend. Instead, she popped the clasp on her shoulder bag, her fingers poised to grip her gun.

"I'd like to give you a ride," said the other guy. Both men laughed.

As she passed them, one of the men whistled. She moved along as if no one existed on the street. The men resumed their conversation. Janet let out a breath she hadn't realized she'd held. She continued along the path, their voices fading with each step.

The next block held apartments under construction, the framing reaching upwards like matchsticks. The ping of a phone interrupted the quiet. She checked her phone, nothing. Someone was close, too close. She glanced from side to side but saw no one. Maybe one of the men had followed her. Turning around would slow her down, possibly invite conversation or worse. She kept a steady pace, her senses on high alert.

Janet reached the edge of her block. Two-story townhomes lined the street. The siding for each house alternated in color, one beige, then the next one brown. The base of each place was trimmed in a mix of light-colored stone. Dim lighting showed in some of the upstairs windows. If she screamed someone might help her or call the cops, but she couldn't count on it. She walked faster and clutched the gun in her purse, the metal cool against her hand. The windows on the townhomes adjacent to hers were as dark as the brown paint surrounding them. A sneeze behind her sent her heartbeat into overdrive, obliterating any other sounds. As she closed in on her place, she grabbed the keys, then jabbed them into the lock and pushed open the door. The rush of cold AC greeted her like opening a freezer. She slammed the door shut and locked it, then peered through the blinds. Nothing moved.

She thought about calling the police, but no one had committed a crime. It was probably someone out for a walk. Those phone calls the other night had unnerved her. The voice whispering her name replayed in her mind. She poured a glass of wine, sank on her sofa, then turned on the TV. Her heartbeat slowed as her breathing returned to normal.

The grandfather clock chimed the hour. The clock didn't match the sleek line of the couch or the industrial coffee table, but she'd inherited it from her mom and couldn't part with the memories. During her childhood, the clanging tune signaled dinner, playtime, and bedtime. She missed those days of simplicity and freedom, even if it was punctuated every so often by her mother's latest male friend. Adult life was overrated.

Her phone rang, an unlisted number, she ignored it, but they left a message. Probably the anonymous ass, but she'd never forgive herself if a patient in need had called her. She played the message.

A voice whispered like the hiss of a snake, "Why did you run away from me?"

The doorbell rang. She crept toward the door and peered through the peephole, but no one stood on the doorstep. Her shoulders grew rigid, her jaw tensed. She picked up the TV remote and muted the sound. The hum of the refrigerator, the whir of the ceiling fan, and the tick-tock of the clock filled the void, then a tapping on a window.

Janet went for the gun in her purse but thought of a better option. She ran for her closet and pulled out her grandfather's old pump shotgun, then loaded three shells.

She stopped and listened. The rapping continued with no particular beat, just a constant knocking on a window coming from the back of the house.

She sucked in her breath, pulled the shotgun up, and moved toward the noise, following it into the kitchen. The sound came from a window next to the breakfast table. Blinds covered the window. The thought of raising the blinds and seeing a face sent her heart racing. She shook her head and the image vanished. Her jaw tightened as rage filled her mind, blocking reason. Tired of the harassment, the sleepless nights and fear, she slipped out the back door. Sliding along the siding, she crept to the corner and stopped, listening. Only frogs and crickets interrupted the night. She peered around the edge. A silhouette faced the window, a hand poised for rapping. Janet aimed the gun at the shape, then cocked it.

"I don't know who you are or what you think you're doing, but you'd better get the hell out of my yard."

The dark form raced toward the wood gate leading to the front yard, yanked open the gate, and fled.

Once inside she realized how foolish she had been. He could have carried a gun, shot her first. Another part of her felt satisfied that she had scared him.

Janet wondered who it was. The night hid anything other than a general shape. The form appeared similar to the convenience store druggie, but his frame seemed thicker, and he wore a baseball cap. Besides, Mr. Beer Belly would have joined him.

She thought on all her cases and one possibility came to mind, the erotic transference case. Mark Crawford struggled with female relationships. At first, he refused eye contact, then sought it. She considered this progress until he started flirting with her, said he had dreamed of her. He asked her to dinner. When she refused, he had gotten angry. Janet recommended another doctor for him, a male doctor. When she followed up with the doctor, Mark had never scheduled an appointment.

Like Mark, the person she had seen leaving her yard was several inches shorter than the six-foot fence, but thinner. Something about the way the intruder moved reminded her of someone else. The name teased her memory, but never caught.

Janet put the shotgun away, replacing the unfired shell, and setting the safety. She grabbed the Glock and laid it next to her bed, then selected a mystery on her tablet. At the end of the first page, she couldn't recall anything and re-read the page, but still couldn't focus on the character. She closed her eyes. Her mind revisited the night's events. She couldn't live like this, afraid of strangers, shooting at shadows, and deprived of sleep.

Stalking didn't constitute a 911 call, but she had to do something. Janet searched online for *who to call if someone is stalking you houston tx*. Skipping over the attorney sites and penal code articles, she selected an attorney general website. The information on the page recommended documenting and filing a police report on each incident. She called the police number for a non-emergency crime. A woman took her information and informed her someone would follow up with her but provided no time estimate. At least now, there was supporting documentation if she blew the stalker away tomorrow.

9

A motel door slammed somewhere in the building, jolting Harry awake. He crawled from underneath the covers like a snail emerging from its shell. Remnants of his fight with Drake and his consolation with Johnnie Walker last night lingered. The slivers of sunlight seeping around the curtain edges promised a bright day that didn't match his aching face and head. He checked the time on his cell phone: 11:00 AM.

Harry shook his head. Pain shot across his forehead. He closed his eyes and considered lying back down, then remembered he had to meet Buddy for lunch. Packing up would be a hassle, especially with the cat. He looked around the room but didn't see Van. He figured the cat would show up eventually.

Harry took a shower, but it didn't revive him. He fought the call of the bed and searched for his clothes from yesterday. Like Van, they seem to have disappeared. Instead, a different shirt and pants hung on the back of a chair. They looked like ones from his closet, but how the hell did they get there? The last time he had even come close to his place was yesterday when he saw Drake entering the lobby of his apartment complex.

Harry frowned as he sat on the bed and focused on last night's events. There wasn't much to remember. It had started with a nap and ended this morning. He did have a couple of drinks.

The scotch wasn't on the dresser where he left it. The bottle wasn't anywhere, not even in the trash. Either someone was playing tricks on him, or he'd lost his mind. Jokes at his expense were annoying, but insanity scared him.

No one could have entered his room without a key and without him hearing them.

He had stopped taking the anti-depressants, but perhaps the effect lingered in his system and mixed with the alcohol last night. The thought of driving to his apartment and not remembering it rolled around in his stomach like rotten food.

At least he had returned to the Star without any trouble, unless a dead body and his fingerprints turned up somewhere today.

He emptied the litter box, dumped out Van's bowls, and packed everything in the shopping bags, making enough noise to wake even the laziest of cats. Nothing moved in the room, not even a roach. No doubt, Van had killed them all. Based on the evidence, he had eaten them too. Harry shuddered.

As he left yesterday, he remembered seeing Van curled up on the bed. When Harry had returned last night, he hadn't seen the cat in the room. He searched again, opening cabinet doors and drawers, checking the closet's top shelf, and peering under the bed.

When he was a kid, their neighbor's cat always came running when she called. He couldn't imitate the pitch but could at least try the words.

"Here Kitty, Kitty," he called.

Except for dust floating through the air, the room remained still. Harry wasn't a big fan of cats, but he hadn't gone to all the trouble of picking it up from the pound just to leave it at the Star. Besides, what if the mystery woman from the other night returned for her cat? For all he knew, he'd agreed to keep the animal for her while she went out of town. Perhaps she had an emergency and left. Of course, if the woman was Lisa, it didn't matter anymore.

Harry noted the vacuum tracks along the carpet. They weren't there when he checked into his room yesterday. He was too tired to have noticed them last night. Van must have escaped when the maid came in and vacuumed. That explained the lack of dead roaches. The front desk manager might know something or have seen the cat wandering around. If nothing else, he could tell him who last cleaned his room.

Before entering the motel lobby, Harry pasted a smile on his face. With Lisa's dead body, the fight with Drake, and the loss of Van, he wasn't in the mood for smiling, but forced one because he wanted answers.

Behind the counter, Sam pecked out letters on a keyboard.

Harry stared at him and waited for some recognition of his presence. The clicking continued, Sam's eyes focused on the screen.

Harry cleared his throat.

Sam looked up, then his eyes widened. "What happened?"

Harry ran his fingers over his swollen cheek and busted lip, then winced.

"Ran into a tree. Texting. Didn't see it."

"Bummer." Sam returned to the monitor.

"Yeah. On top of that, my cat has disappeared."

Sam squinted. "Are you sure? Cats can be pretty tricky."

He hadn't pegged Sam as a cat man. "I've searched the entire room. He could have slipped out when the maid opened the door."

"What's your room number?"

"107."

Sam sucked on his lip as he checked through some papers, then said, "The maid last checked on your room yesterday afternoon."

"Is she here today?" Harry leaned against the counter.

"I saw her earlier."

"Could you call her?" Not that it mattered. It was doubtful she took Van home. Still, anything was possible, and what would he say if the mystery woman returned for the cat?

Sam frowned. "She's one of those private people." He leaned toward him, lowering his voice. "She's hot. Only the owner has her number." He winked. "Probably thinks she'll sleep with him, but ain't no way." Sam returned to his screen.

"She's cleaning rooms. You should be able to find her."

As Harry left the lobby, Sam shouted, "If I see the cat or anyone turns one in, I'll let you know."

When he walked toward his room, he halfway expected to see Van, but the sidewalk was empty except for a brunette pushing a laundry cart in his direction. Sam was right about one thing, she sizzled, filling out her maid uniform in all the right places.

"Could you help me?" Harry asked.

She stopped and stared. "Depends on what it is."

Harry glanced at the name tag high atop her assets, then focused on her face.

"Sophia, my cat has disappeared. Did you see him when you vacuumed my room yesterday?"

She shook her head. "I didn't see a cat."

"It's an orange tabby, part of one ear is missing." He gazed into her eyes, the color of whiskey and just as intoxicating.

"Do you think I took your cat?" She placed her hand on her chest.

Hoping to reassure her, Harry held out a hand and spread his fingers. "No, I didn't mean to imply that."

"Then what are you saying? Do you think I let the cat out?" She placed her hands on her hips.

"I'm not saying that either." He pulled a business card from his wallet. "It's possible someone let him into their room thinking he was lost. If you happen to see him, would you give me a call?"

She read the card. "Private Investigator." Her eyes traced the length of his frame, a slow assessing gaze. "Seems like you should be able to find him."

What a bitch. He faked a smile. "Even a PI needs help sometimes."

She frowned, then pocketed his card. "If I see him, I'll give you a call."

Harry figured she would trash the card as soon as he was out of sight.

Harry packed everything into his car. Before he checked out, he searched the parking lot for Van, but found only beer cans, cigarette butts, and fast-food containers.

Van could be anywhere by now. Harry checked his watch. He couldn't keep looking if he planned to meet Buddy on time. It was just a cat and based on the animal's appearance, a scrapper on the streets. Van could take care of himself, but Harry felt responsible for him. At least, the cat would have survived the night at the pound. He should have probably left him there.

What the hell. A pet meant work, and the last thing he needed was more work. If the woman returned to get Van and her clothes, he would just tell her the truth, the cat escaped. Harry had bigger problems than a lost animal. Besides, Van had probably found a better cat sitter, one not suspected of murder. Harry couldn't care for a pet from a jail cell anyway.

10

Janet threw aside the covers, picked up her Glock, and got out of bed. She shrugged into a robe and dropped the gun in the pocket. The weight and close proximity of it provided her a sense of security. She yawned as she wandered into the kitchen. The room brought memories of the guy tapping on the window and the haunting phone calls. Her chest tightened. She took a deep breath and exhaled, but it didn't release the tension.

By the time she had made the coffee and savored her first sip, her shoulders had relaxed. She grabbed a magazine, then settled on the couch with her mug. The doorbell rang. Her hand jerked, sloshing the liquid.

Maybe her stalker was going with a direct approach this time. She doubted it but pulled the Glock from her pocket just in case, then peered through the peephole. A man well over six-feet tall with shoulders the width of her doorway stood on the porch. Even though he was dressed in a suit, she didn't trust him.

"Who is it?"

"Detective Thibodeaux." He held up identification. "I'm here about the incident you reported."

Unless her harasser was a cop or had bugged her home, the guy was probably legit. She swapped the gun to her other hand, opened the door the width of the chain lock, then stared into his brown eyes as if she could detect crazy in their depths. He held her gaze and smiled. Lines spread from the corners of his eyes, marking a life of smiles and laughter. She read the information on his badge, then dropped the gun in her pocket, released the chain, and opened the door wide. With her five-foot-two frame, she felt short standing next to him.

"Come on inside." Janet motioned to a chair. "Have a seat."

He sat down and pulled a small notepad and pen from his jacket. She dropped onto the couch across from him.

"Tell me what happened." His voice carried a deep southern accent with husky undertones like a bullfrog.

As she described the incident, he took notes, asking questions every so often. At the completion of her story, she wondered if he believed her. Perhaps he thought her crazy or paranoid. In his shoes, she might think the same.

"So, these calls you've been getting, did you write down the phone number?"

She resisted rolling her eyes. An idiot would know to write the number down if there was one.

"The number was blocked."

He rubbed his chin. "What about the voice? Did it sound familiar? Man? Woman?"

"Whoever it was whispered." She had assumed it was a man,

but it could have been a woman.

"Do you have any enemies?"

She thought over everyone she'd known, but Mark was still the only name that seemed like a possibility. "Maybe Mark Crawford, but I can't be sure. He was a former patient." Even though he wasn't in her care anymore, she couldn't share any details.

Thibodeaux noted the name. "Anyone else?"

"Not that I can think of." She shook her head. "I might come up with someone else later."

He put away his notepad and pen, then stood. "Would you show me where you saw the intruder?"

She led him into the kitchen. Magazines cluttered the breakfast table. One day she'd get around to reading them all, maybe after they found her stalker. Until then, concentrating on anything might prove difficult.

He checked the lock on the back door. "Be sure and deadbolt this."

The word "Duh" came to mind, but she decided to keep her thoughts to herself. Janet wanted all the help she could get.

They stepped into her backyard, an eight by ten area she called her own. Not even a breeze broke the relentless heat thrown by the sun. White blossoms from a crepe myrtle littered the path leading to the side yard. The alley separating her house from the neighbors wasn't wide enough for them to walk side by side, so she watched from a distance as he inspected the space.

He pointed to the kitchen window. "He knocked on this?"

Janet nodded.

"Was he wearing gloves?"

She pictured the scene from last night, his hand at the window. The figure running to the gate, then his hand as he pushed it. "I think so."

Thibodeaux searched the ground, then walked toward her. "Doesn't look like he left anything behind." He stepped back and stared at the house. "You might want to look at installing some security cameras."

They returned to the kitchen. She shuddered as the cool air evaporated the sweat from her skin.

He turned toward her. "The shotgun probably scared him off. It would have me. But just in case…" He handed her a card. "Phone me if you have any more problems."

She read it. Besides the contact information, it included his first name, Buddy. Somehow the name matched him, probably the southern accent and the smile. He looked as if he'd welcome everyone as a friend. Well, everyone on the right side of the law.

11

The noise level in Willie's Grill required lip reading and hand gestures. People loitered around the bar and the entrance waiting for a table. August in Houston meant available outdoor seating, so Harry signaled to the hostess a request for an outside table. Within seconds, he sat sweating under the shade of an oak and watched for Buddy.

As the line grew, more people opted for outside. They sat at surrounding picnic tables with only a patio umbrella protecting them from the sun's rays.

Well over six feet, Buddy stood out in the clumps of customers approaching Willie's. Harry stood and waved to get his attention. Buddy smiled and headed in his direction.

Buddy moved slower than when they were on the force together. Even then, his time to react and his agility was half that of Harry's, kind of like the tortoise and the hare.

Buddy settled across from him. Years in the sun had carved lines down his cheeks while laughter etched smaller ones spreading from the corners of his brown eyes. Grey streaks shot through black hair as thick as his southern accent.

"Didn't they have anything inside?" Buddy asked.

"No, and based on the line, they won't have anything for a while."

Buddy handed over a folder. "Figured you'd wanna see the crime scene photos. If Drake knew I'd showed them to you…" He rubbed his forehead. "Well, I don't want to think about what he'd do."

"I owe you." Harry could say he owed him, but Buddy would never agree to it. He touched the scar on his shoulder and remembered the day he took a bullet for Buddy. The bullet ripped through flesh and muscle but paled in comparison to losing his partner and friend. Harry never regretted pushing Buddy out of the path of that slime-ball's gun. He would do it again.

Harry opened the file, examining the photos in detail. The king-sized bed was still made. Lisa had fallen forward on the burgundy carpet. A dark red stain soiled the back of the white lingerie clinging to her thin frame. Her blonde hair waved around her tan shoulders. The wood dresser held a bottle of champagne and two glasses.

The pictures didn't trigger any memories for Harry. Maybe visiting the hotel, getting the vibe of the place would help.

"What's the latest on the case?"

"Drake still sees you as the number one suspect. Problem is he can't find a motive."

Harry tapped the photos. "Where did they find my fingerprints?"

"I really shouldn't tell you." Buddy looked at him.

Harry shrugged. "It's not like I'm going to tell anyone."

Buddy rubbed the side of his face as if contemplating the truth of Harry's statement, then sighed.

"Yeah, why would you?" Sweat beaded on Buddy's forehead. Heat always bothered Buddy which surprised Harry since the man spent his childhood in the deep south.

Buddy pointed at the champagne in one of the pictures. "On the champagne bottle and both glasses."

"Did they find anyone else's fingerprints?" Harry asked.

"The only other prints on the bottle and glasses were Lisa's." Buddy checked out the menu. "What are you going to get?"

"I'll just get whatever you order." Harry didn't care what he ate. It wouldn't help him forget his problems. Only alcohol did that and it didn't last. He needed to know how his fingerprints ended up at a crime scene.

Harry flipped to the next picture. A hairbrush lay amongst the makeup bottles and skin lotions littering the bathroom counter. A woman's clothes hung on the towel bar. A white towel was slung across the top of the glass shower.

"Have they found the weapon?"

"Not yet." Buddy wiped his brow, then stared at him. "What were you doing in her room?"

Harry couldn't admit his lack of memory. Buddy might think he killed Lisa. For all Harry knew, he had. Client privacy always worked as an excuse for not revealing anything.

"I can't really say." Harry closed the folder as a waitress approached the table. They ordered, then he opened it again.

"You know, you're going to have to talk when Drake hauls

your ass in for questioning."

"Do you think he will?" Harry figured Drake wanted to stick it to him, but only if he had enough evidence to put him away for good.

"It's just a matter of time." Buddy sighed. "You might try playing nice with him."

He passed the file back to Buddy. "I've tried. He needs someone to blame for Beth's death and I'm it."

Even after twenty years, Harry could still hear Beth's voice asking what she should do. She was three months pregnant and couldn't tell her parents. They wouldn't understand or accept her situation. At least, that was what Beth believed.

Harry's crush on Beth started in elementary school. It took years for him to summon the courage to ask her for a date. They had only dated for a couple of months when she told him that she was expecting. He knew the child wasn't his and at twenty-three, marriage wasn't in his plans, much less fathering another man's child. The father's child didn't want Beth or the baby. She couldn't live with ending a life or putting the baby up for adoption or living with her parent's disappointment, so she took another option and ended both their lives.

Harry always thought her parents would have accepted the child, but he couldn't convince Beth. She never told Drake or Harry who the father was. Didn't really matter. Drake believed it was Harry's and blamed him for everything: the pregnancy and the death of Beth and her unborn baby.

"After you left the force, when Drake and I became partners, he told me some of what happened. Did you know he found her?" Buddy stared into Harry's eyes as if he searched for the truth in them.

Words failed Harry so he took the easy out and just shook his head.

The waitress set a mug of beer in front of each of them. Buddy drank some, wiped his mouth with the back of his hand, then continued. "He heard the car running and raised the garage door. He dragged her body outside, tried CPR, but it was too late."

The scene played before Harry's eyes. The food arrived, but the smell of the burger and onion rings along with the talk of Beth made him queasy. He shoved the food aside and looked around for distractions, anything to erase the memories from his mind. People around him chatted. The sun continued to shine. The birds hovered in the trees, waiting for scraps. A few hopped on the ground gathering crumbs from empty tables.

Buddy bit into his burger. "Aren't you going to eat?"

Before he could say anything, Harry's phone rang. He didn't recognize the number, but welcomed the interruption, so he answered.

Sophia's voice floated down the line. "I found where the cat went. A couple saw an orange cat with part of its ear missing in the parking lot. They heard a woman calling it. The cat ran towards whoever it was, then the person picked up the cat and left."

No one would want that varmint, would they? Maybe some cat lady felt sorry enough for the animal to take it home.

Without Van a lonely night waited for him, then he

remembered Sophia's assets. He had more questions and didn't want to keep her on the phone with Buddy watching him.

"Great detective work. I owe you. How about dinner tonight? I'll swing by the motel and get you."

What was he thinking? He needed to find Lisa's killer, not spend time with a woman. Although, if he ended up incarcerated, he would regret not grabbing the opportunity to have one last meal with a hot date.

"I don't know," Sophia said.

A five-star meal might entice her.

"How about Alessandra's?" He could conduct business while on a date, so technically he wasn't wasting time.

"Hmm, Alessandra's." She paused.

Harry held his breath.

"I can't go tonight. How about tomorrow night?" she asked.

He wanted to go to Alessandra's tonight, but a date gave him the perfect cover for being there.

"Tomorrow night, then. Six?"

"See you at six," she said. "I'll text you my address."

Harry hung up and added Sophia's number to his phone contact list.

Buddy eyed him. "A hot date?"

Harry smiled, then took a bite of his burger.

Buddy frowned. "Are you taking her to Alessandra's so you have an excuse for visiting the crime scene?"

"Maybe." Harry took a swig of beer. "Which room was she killed in?"

"You should know. Your fingerprints were found there."

He rolled his eyes. "Just tell me the room number."

"1705." He picked up an onion ring, pointing it in Harry's direction. "You know if Drake catches you there, you'll probably end up in jail."

"Let him try. Last time I checked, it wasn't against the law for a guy to take a girl on a date."

Buddy smirked. "Not if Drake has his way."

If Drake had his way, Harry would spend his life staring through iron bars or on a fast track to hell.

12

Harry scanned the parking lot of his apartment complex looking for any sign of Drake. The sun glinted on the empty cars. A man in swimming trunks and t-shirt dragged a cooler toward a car. A woman wearing shorts and a floppy hat followed him, her eyes covered in sunglasses. Harry imagined sitting on the beach listening to the water wash over the sand. He sighed. Unless he cleared his name soon, his beach days were over.

As he rounded the corner of his building, he spotted a car backed into a parking spot close to the fence in the far corner of the complex. A line of trees cast a shadow over the black mid-sized sedan. The car was too far away for him to see if someone sat in the front seat. Harry parked in his usual spot, then walked toward the stairway entrance, watching for any movement out of the corner of his eyes.

No one approached him as he opened the door to his place. Once inside, he grabbed a pair of binoculars, then headed straight for the one room whose window faced the area where the sedan sat. He opened the blinds, then peered through the binoculars, focusing them until he could clearly see the driver. Sunglasses hid the man's eyes. His mouth was set in a hard line as if a smile never crossed it. The thin long face with dark hair trimmed short on the sides and left thick on the top didn't remind Harry of anyone he knew on the force. He focused on the front bumper, but the car didn't have a tag. Still, it seemed too early in the investigation to waste resources surveilling his place, but with Drake, one never knew. He left the binoculars on the windowsill and turned toward his bed.

A cat jumped on the bed and stared at him. Harry eyed the scruffy orange tabby fur, the torn ear, and wide green eyes. Van had returned.

"How the hell did you get here?" Someone was playing tricks on him.

The cat ignored him, sat down, and licked a paw. Harry pulled a gun from his holster. If the prankster was still in Harry's apartment, the gun should scare whoever it was.

Harry returned to the living area. Streaks of sunlight bled through the blinds and reflected off the big screen TV on the wall. His mail lay undisturbed in a small stack next to the monitor on his desk.

In the far corner of the kitchen, a plate with breadcrumbs shared the counter space with a glass, dregs of milk coated the bottom. Someone had not only entered his home, but they had also taken time to eat. The person either wasn't worried about DNA evidence or was too stupid to care. He would bag the evidence later.

Scissors lay next to the sink. Harry wondered why the

intruder needed them.

Since his bed was still made and the pillows leaned against the headboard just as Harry had left them, she hadn't spent the night, or she'd made up the bed. He would wash the sheets anyway.

In his closet, some of the blue shirts intermingled with the white shirts. Harry would reorganize them by color after he'd dealt with the kitchen mess. At least, the person hadn't sliced up his clothes with the scissors.

Van rubbed around his legs. Harry put away the gun, then bent down and scratched the cat's neck.

"If only you could talk."

Van purred.

Harry sighed. "Purring doesn't count."

Harry returned to the kitchen. He doubted he would get much from the fingerprints or the DNA on the plate and glass. More than likely, neither were registered in any database. Besides, he'd have to ask Buddy to do it and what excuse would he give?

Someone was probably pranking him. Again, Candy came to mind. She enjoyed playing tricks, but this bordered on harassment. She wouldn't think it was funny if the cops showed up at her door and arrested her for breaking and entering. Candy probably still had a key to his place. So technically it wasn't breaking and entering. When he thought about it, no harm was done to the apartment. Nothing that couldn't be fixed. He'd talk with Candy again, give her another chance to admit to it.

As he wiped down the countertop, he noticed an object wedged between the coffeepot and the toaster. A black ribbon handle hung from a shiny-pink-striped gift bag edged in black. The words Victoria's Secret were emblazoned in black across the middle. Harry had never entered the hallowed walls of the lingerie store but allowed himself sidelong glances at the provocative displays as he passed. Nothing in the display case hinted at any gift appropriate for Harry unless a live model came with it.

He removed the pink tissue overflowing from the bag and extracted a slim vinyl pink and white credit card case with three exterior slots. Only one held a card. He freed it and read: Jack's Joint, Booze and Entertainment, 5757 Slaton St, Houston, Tx. Harry had passed by the place before, but never stopped. He had given up on bars years ago. Drinking at home was cheaper. Plus, no idle conversation or dress code was required.

Harry cast a glance at Van. "You're better company than anyone I've met in a bar." He looked around the room. "Although, you're not much of a guard cat."

He flipped the card over. The name Lisa flowed in blue ink, slanted forwards with a curl on either end of the L. Dead women didn't sign cards. Either someone already had this signed card, or the signature was added by someone other than David's wife. It could be a different Lisa, but he doubted it.

Harry held the card out to Van. "Are you Lisa's cat? Is this her signature?"

Van sniffed it, then walked away with his tail waving in the air as if he could care less about the problems of common humans like Harry.

Harry shook his head. Only crazy people asked a cat a question and expected an answer. It wasn't as if Van would sniff the card, then run find the person like dogs did in the movies.

He examined the case. Along the bottom of it and in the center, a tiny gold V was embossed on a small black metal emblem. A gold chain with an empty key ring hung off the zipper running along the top. He unzipped the case and peered inside: nothing.

Harry wondered who had returned the cat and left the card case.

Somehow someone got in his apartment. He didn't collect his keys from old girlfriends because they all parted on good terms. At least, he thought they did. The landlord had a key but wore cowboy boots and a big buckle belt. Not exactly the kind of guy to buy a pink card case. Charley had a key, but she wasn't the Victoria's Secret type.

The night Van escaped, Sophia said someone picked him up in the motel's parking lot. Maybe the same person conned the landlord into gaining access. He tucked the Jack's Joint card in his billfold, dropped the case in his pants pocket, then called the landlord. When the man answered, he denied letting anyone into Harry's apartment.

Harry might have missed something when examining the woman's items. He walked to his bedroom, then opened the bottom dresser drawer where he had left them.

A small cloth square rested in the drawer: a Victoria's Secret label, probably the one from the bra. That explained the need for scissors. He searched the house for the clothes or any other clues, but only found his shirt and pants from the previous day stuffed in the dirty clothes basket. Harry sank on the couch and looked around the room trying to remember last night.

He recalled returning to the motel, drinking some scotch, then waking up this morning.

Scenarios played in his mind, until he found an acceptable one: a woman followed him to the Star motel. When he left, she stayed in the parking lot, waiting for him to return. She watched as Van escaped from his room, picked him up, then took the cat to his apartment. The woman left the cat, gathered her clothes and some clothes for him. Returning to his motel, she waited until his lights went out, but what then? Had she knocked on his door and he, drunk out of his mind, let her in the room? Then she left the fresh clothes and took away the dirty ones to leave at his place? How did she get in his apartment without a key? He shook his head. None of it made sense.

Harry returned to the living room, pulled the card case from his pocket, and checked each slot again in hopes he'd missed something. Empty. He tossed the thing on the end table.

Charley might have seen or heard something. He grabbed his keys. No way was he leaving his place unlocked, not even if he was just going next door. Although, locks hadn't stopped whoever was playing jokes on him.

Harry glanced at Van immersed in a tongue bath. "I'll only be gone a few minutes. Stay here."

Van flicked his tail. Harry sighed. Expecting a cat to obey a human command, he had indeed lost his mind.

Harry locked the door, then looked up and down the hall. The sound of country western music came from the apartment across the hall, but no one lingered outside any of the doors. He knocked on Charley's door. Within a minute or two, she opened the door and motioned him inside.

"Back again already?" Harry only saw Charley about once every couple of weeks. He enjoyed her company, but he was always too busy to stop by and visit with her. For her part, if she wasn't working or hacking into systems, she was playing video games.

Charley's hair fell around her face in soft curls. Long lashes framed her eyes and her lips shone with a rosy shade against her pale skin. A loose-long-sleeved-buttoned-cream shirt hung below the top of her grey sweatpants.

"Come on in. I've got a video conference in an hour." She rolled her eyes. "At least, they aren't making me come into the office for the waste-of-time quarterly meeting." Somehow, Charley had negotiated a work-from-home job which required very few office visits.

Harry walked inside but remained standing. "I won't keep you long."

"It's ok. I'm already prepared for the meeting." She waved her hand over the upper part of her body.

"Did you see anybody go in or leave my place yesterday?"

Charley shook her head.

Harry squinted. "Hear anything unusual?"

"No." She raised her eyebrows. "Why? Somebody drop off another cat?" She smirked.

Harry gave her a shortened version of the latest events. Once again, he omitted mentioning the woman's clothes. No need for her to think less of him than she already did.

She looked as if she struggled believing him, then pointed a finger at him. "I think you should lay off the booze. You're getting older. Maybe your body can't handle it anymore."

His head jerked back as if she'd hit him. "What?" Charley enjoyed winding him up every now and then. He refused to take the age bait. "Forty's not that old."

Charley waved her hand at him. "I can't tell you what's going on over at your place, but I got something on Drake." She moved to her desk and pulled a yellow sticky note off the side of her monitor. "He's involved in something but the security surrounding it is tight." She pointed to the note. "It's something to do with that name."

Harry looked at the letters on the note and said, "Paul Ledger?" He tilted his head. The name meant nothing to him.

"I researched that name, but it's like he just disappeared." Her eyes widened and her words came out in a rush as if she could barely contain her excitement. "Do you think Drake killed him? Or this Ledger guy went into the Witness Protection Program?"

"If Drake killed someone, I would have heard about it. Buddy would have told me." At least, he thought Buddy would have. He looked around the room, then focused on Charley. "When you have time, would you get me all the info you can on this guy? A timeline of activities, an image, anything that might help nail him down."

"It will be a while. I'm working on a special project for work, and it's got a fairly tight deadline."

Harry wondered what it was but knew better than to ask. Charley never talked about her work or even who she worked for. The few times he brought up work, she had changed the subject.

Charley returned to her desk chair and focused on her screen.

"Thanks Charley. I owe you."

"One day I'll collect." She smiled up at him. "I'm thinking a Ferrari or a mansion."

He left to the sound of clicking as her fingers flew across the keyboard.

When Harry returned to his apartment, the last couple of days played through his mind. He had to focus on finding Lisa's killer. If Drake arrested him, any investigation into the other weird happenings in his life would end. In order to catch whoever murdered Lisa, he needed to know more about her. Harry grabbed his phone and called David.

"David, I need to go through Lisa's things and see if I can find any clues as to who might have killed her."

"I'm sure it was that guy she was seeing."

"Then we need evidence, or the cops are going to suspect you." No need for Harry to mention the cops were more likely to arrest him than David.

"Come on over. I'm not doing anything anyway." David

hung up.

Before he left for David's, Harry called his go-to man for quick installations. If Harry couldn't control or remember what happened at his place, he could at least record it.

"Joey, I need some video equipment installed."

"You got it man. When?"

"Tomorrow, if possible. I'll pay you double." Harry would pay any price to get answers.

"Where?"

"My place. If I'm not there, the landlord can let you in." Harry gave him all the details, then headed for David's.

13

Harry enjoyed seeing what people did with their money. Some spent their cash on entertainment, others on cars and houses. He wondered which one David was. Of course, some had enough to spend it on everything. Based on their previous meetings in restaurants and bars, David spent his on food and drink. Harry exited the freeway and drove to David's.

The white pillared mansion rested on an acre of Houston prime real estate in the heart of old money, River Oaks. Moss-ladened live oaks dotted the landscape and azalea bushes edged the house. As Harry walked along the front walk, he inhaled the fragrance of freshly mowed grass. He rang the doorbell and figured David had enough money to buy anything he wanted. An enviable position, but it hadn't saved his wife from murder. Unless David had wanted her dead. In which case, perhaps his money had paid for her death.

Just as Harry raised his hand to press the doorbell again, the door opened.

"Come on in." David motioned Harry forward.

He led Harry into a two-story entryway as large as Harry's

apartment, then past a curving staircase. If David wanted to kill his wife, a slight push down the marble stairs would have done it. All he had to do was wait for a good rainstorm, drop some rainwater on the steps, and the investigating officer would rule it as accidental, but maybe the idea had never occurred to him.

"Where did Lisa keep personal items? Photos, cards, notes."

"In her study. I doubt you'll find anything, but you can look."

Harry followed David down a hall and into Lisa's study. A large paned window overlooked a garden filled with red roses, yellow lantana, and dwarf gardenias. A flagged-stone path led to a concrete bench where someone could rest and enjoy the scent of the flowers.

David pointed to a cleared desk. A few wires lay piled on the floor. "The cops already took her computer."

Harry pulled out the drawers until he found a paper with writing on it. A list of locations ran down the side: bank, grocery store, cleaners. Harry tailed her the day before her murder, and she hadn't visited any of the places listed. He held up the piece of paper.

"Is this what Lisa was doing the day of her murder?"

David shrugged. "I don't know. I went to work. You're the one paid to follow her."

"I couldn't that day." Harry had to get his car inspected and an oil change, otherwise he would have tailed her. "This is her handwriting - right?"

David nodded.

Harry examined the note. The letters slanted toward the left as if each looked backward in time. The writing on the Jack's Joint's card left in his apartment slanted forward. Lisa hadn't signed the card.

Harry crossed over to the bookshelves lining one of the walls. Mysteries, romances, classics, and photo albums filled the shelves. Each album binder was labeled with a date. He selected the most recent and paged through it, searching for people who repeatedly showed up in the pictures. One woman appeared in a lot of the shots. Her brown owl-like glass frames highlighted green eyes and gave her a studious appearance. Clouds of wavy dark hair framed her pale face and jetted out in all directions like a female Einstein. Harry pointed to her.

"Who's this?'

David leaned in close. "That's Rachel Langston. Lisa's best friend from high school." He pulled out a photo album and opened it to a photo of a bridal party. David pointed to a younger version of Rachel. "She was the bridesmaid in our wedding."

David turned a page. A wedding picture of him and Lisa embracing smiled from the picture.

"Lisa was beautiful. If only I'd spent more time with her." Sadness crept across his face. He covered his eyes with his hand.

Harry wished for a watch with a teleport button. He looked everywhere but at David, then cleared his throat.

"I'd like to follow up with Rachel. Do you know where she lives?"

David lowered his hand, then blinked a couple of times. "No." His phone rang. He checked it, then looked at Harry. "I gotta take this."

Harry snapped a picture of Rachel with his phone, then checked the rest of the bookshelf. He shook the fiction books, but only bits of dust flew through the air. He put away the last book and left the study.

As he walked toward the front door, he found David leaning against a wall, his cheek pressed against his phone. Harry had questions for him. He wanted to know if Lisa had left Van at his place and if she owned the woman's clothes left in his bathroom. Even if she had, who stole them from the drawer? She was dead by then. He waited until David finished his conversation.

"Did Lisa have an orange cat with part of one ear missing?"

"Who the hell knows? She had all kinds of cats she picked up and fostered. Why?"

Harry searched his mind for an excuse. "I saw one when I drove up. Thought he might have gotten loose."

David frowned and waved his hand. "It can stay outside. Someone just adopted the last one yesterday. If there's another one, I don't want to know about it. I never liked cats." He opened the front door for Harry. "Call me as soon as you know something."

Harry nodded and left.

When he got in his car, he called Buddy.

"Hey, would you get me an address for a Rachel Langston?" Harry figured she and Lisa were the same age. "Probably 30 years old."

"What? You think I'm your personal assistant?" Buddy asked.

"Just add it to the list of favors I owe you."

Buddy sighed. "Hold on, let me write it down."

"Also check with DMV and get a description of her car. Thanks Man, I owe you."

When he returned to his apartment, Johnnie Walker, the source of his trouble, called him. Charley was right. Liquor had caused enough problems. It was time to take control, no more booze.

Harry gathered all the alcohol, then started pouring the contents down the kitchen sink. He stopped short of emptying the entire contents of the Johnnie Walker. His face and body ached. A shot of liquor was probably healthier than ibuprofen or aspirin. He poured the last bit of the golden liquid into a glass, then sat in his recliner and slowly sipped it, savoring every last drop as it spread through his body and eased his pain.

Van curled up in his lap. Harry scratched him under the chin. The last thing he remembered before drifting off to sleep was the soothing sound of Van's purr.

14

Charley sat in her desk chair and stretched her back. Sitting hunched over the keyboard and staring at her monitor all morning left her muscles stiff and aching. She got up and grabbed a soda from the kitchen refrigerator. As she popped the top off the can, her phone rang.

"Charley, what's the status on the message." Her boss's voice held a note of urgency.

"I haven't cracked it yet, but I've eliminated a lot of possible encryption keys."

Derek cleared his throat. "We received some additional intel. Looks like the FBI needs the information sooner," he said.

Charley gripped her phone. "How soon?" She looked at her to-do list. There was still a lot to check.

"Monday or sooner if possible."

Charley widened her eyes. It would take a miracle for her to get an answer that soon.

Derek continued on, "I have a resource that is freeing up. He's a Senior Cryptanalyst and an excellent mentor. Tom's going to call you on Thursday and discuss how he can help you."

Charley gripped the phone tighter. She didn't enjoy working with anyone else but turning down assistance would seem like she wasn't a team player, and she could use the help.

"Thanks. I appreciate it."

"I'll let you get back to work," Derek said as if he expected her to focus on the message twenty-four hours a day.

She sighed. The soda gurgled in her stomach. Even if she worked 24/7, it was doubtful she would come up with a solution in time. Hopefully, Tom was as good as Derek promised.

15

Janet reflected on her day as she sipped a glass of wine and steeped in a warm bath bubbling with the scent of gardenias. The water stroked her skin. The heat seeped deep into her muscles relaxing her. Her phone rang in the distance, but she ignored it. Nothing was worth getting out of the tub.

After her bath, she slipped into her bathrobe. The doorbell rang. Her shoulders tensed. Maybe the stalker had returned. She shook her head. It was probably someone selling something or delivering a package. She grabbed her Glock just in case.

When Janet reached the door, she hesitated. It was unlikely danger waited on the other side, but still... She flicked on the outside light, then looked through the peephole. No face appeared, but a package the size of one of her couch pillows sat on the porch. Eight at night seemed late for a delivery, but not unreasonable. The estimated arrival for the shampoo and conditioner she'd ordered wasn't for another day or two, but sometimes deliveries arrived early.

Janet cracked open the door and eyed the area. Bugs

whipped through the air and swarmed the porch light, but nothing else moved.

She dropped the gun in her robe pocket, then released the chain. Mosquitos buzzed around her as she scooped the box up and shoved it inside. After securing the lock, she checked the package for her name and address, then placed it on the kitchen table. She grabbed the scissors from a drawer, ran the shears up under the clear tape, and flipped open the cardboard flaps.

A snake lunged at her, hissing. She screamed and jumped back, avoiding the strike. The box tilted and fell to the floor. The reptile uncoiled onto the beige tile and raised its head. Its body was thick and dark, easily a couple of feet long. Her breathing stopped, then wheezed its way through her tightened chest. She eased backwards, watching the snake, its tongue flicking in and out as if tasting the air. She raised the Glock. The gun shook in her hand. What was she thinking? She couldn't shoot it in the house. It was unlikely she'd hit the snake. A bullet might ricochet off the tile floor and hit her. Someone else would have to get it out of the house. She was leaving, but not in her bathrobe.

Janet turned and ran. With every step, she visualized the reptile chasing her, then jabbing its fangs into her leg. In her bedroom, she tugged on a shirt, thick jeans, and cowboy boots. The more she covered her legs, the better.

If she could contain the snake to one area, then someone could find it and kill it for her. She crept toward the kitchen, then scoured the room from the doorway. The package along with the floor was empty. The room held a maze of hiding places: under the oven, behind the refrigerator, or in the pantry. The one thing she knew for sure was somewhere in there, it lurked, and she couldn't stay.

The recliner was wide enough for the doorway. Maybe she could push it and block the snake from leaving. Forget it. She'd seen one climb a brick wall. Janet shuddered. Nothing in her house could completely cover the opening.

Her eyes moved back and forth searching for any sign of the snake as she made her way to the front door, then she stopped before opening it. What if her stalker waited outside? This could be a ploy to get her out of the house so he could grab her. Janet turned from the door. The snake slithered out of the kitchen toward her. She'd take her chances with the human.

Janet gripped her gun as she ran to her car, moving her head side to side, looking for a possible stalker. The wind blew across her face. The streetlights bled through the trees casting moving shadows on the pavement as the branches swayed. A dog barked as if it sensed a stranger. She yanked open her car door, jumped in, slammed the door, then pressed the lock button. Inhaling deep breaths, she leaned back in the seat. Once she could speak coherently, she called Detective Thibodeaux and told him what happened.

"Are you in danger now?" he asked.

She checked her mirrors but saw no one. "I don't think so."

"I can't get there for a couple of hours, but I can send over a patrol unit now."

"Will they get the snake out of my house?"

"Depends on who they send. They might call animal control, but they probably won't show up until morning. I can handle the snake. Growing up in the swamps of Louisiana, we played with 'em." He paused. "The problem is finding 'em. Do you know where it is?"

"Last time I saw it, it was leaving the kitchen." She shuddered.

He sighed. "I'll bring something to help us locate it."

She didn't know what he was thinking, but she wasn't playing any part in that "us".

"I'll call you when I'm on my way over."

No way was she staying in the house until he got there, she cranked the car and left.

The Mexican restaurant hummed with conversation and the odor of sizzling onions. Janet gulped a margarita, then licked the salt from her lips. The chips and salsa looked inviting, but her appetite for food was gone. Whoever stalked her carried an intense hatred or had a sick sense of humor. Mark knew her fear of snakes, but he wasn't too fond of them either. It was one of the few things they had in common.

The second margarita worked its magic. At least enough for her to assess the situation. She hoped Thibodeaux kept his promise and dealt with the snake when they met up later. Either it left, or she stayed in a hotel. No way was she sleeping in the house with that thing slithering all over the place. The thought of it had her kicking her legs up into the chair across from her. Janet took another swig of her drink, then clunked it down on the table. She checked her watch. There was just enough time left for a coffee and tres leches.

16

Harry got up from his recliner and tossed the Johnnie Walker bottle in the trash. He still had that one flask of scotch in his bedroom drawer. Before he could grab it, his phone rang. He checked the number: Buddy.

"Hey Man, sorry for calling so late. Does Candy still have a cat?"

Harry wondered if he'd misheard him or if Buddy had chugged a few too many beers. "What did you say?"

"I need a cat. A lady's got a snake in her house. I need something to find it."

Harry knew cats captured snakes. When he was a kid, a neighbor always complained to his aunt about her cat bringing snakes into the house. He owed Buddy. Plus, he might need his help again. Van could probably handle a snake.

"I've got one you can borrow."

"You?" Buddy laughed.

"People change. Even me."

"Right. She must be hot if she convinced you to get any kind of pet."

"It's a loaner." Harry never knew when Van's owner might claim him. "When do you want to pick him up?"

"In about thirty minutes?"

Harry eyed the fading scratches on his arm. "That works, but you have to get him in the carrier."

"Sure, no problem."

See you then." He hung up and looked at Van. "Looks like you're going to have some fun tonight."

Harry opened the door for Buddy. "Van and the carrier are in the laundry room. Good luck getting him in there."

"Not a problem. I've dealt with difficult cats before." Buddy strode into the apartment, opened the laundry room door, then shut it.

"That's a good kitty," Buddy said over the sound of scuffling.

Within minutes, Buddy exited with Van in the carrier.

Harry examined Buddy's scratch-free arms. "How did you do it?"

"The trick is turning the kennel on its end, then grabbing the cat by the scruff of the neck." He held up his hand as if he had picked up a piece of paper. "Like his momma carried him when he was a kitten. Drop him in the kennel and close the lid, then set the kennel right way around. We could have used a pillowcase to get him in there too. Heck, we used to take one of our cats to the vet in a pillowcase."

Harry opened the door for him. "I'm calling you next time I have to take Van anywhere."

Buddy smiled. "Sure thing. I'll show you how to do it." He lifted the carrier and looked inside. "Let's see what kind of snake catcher you are."

As Harry closed the door behind them, he wondered if Van's owner would come and get the cat one day or if she was already dead.

17

Dr. Worth parked in her driveway and debated whether to go inside. Janet knew she should face her fears. That's what she advised her patients. The snake was probably scared of her. She gripped the car handle, then released it. Forget it. This particular fear had fangs. She'd wait for the detective. He should arrive soon. Meanwhile, she'd watch for strangers on the street. The stalker might be waiting in the shadows looking for a chance to frighten her or worse. She re-checked the door locks, then pulled the gun onto her lap.

A car pulled in behind her, the headlights sliced through the dark, then died. She gripped her gun. The driver emerged carrying a large carrier: maybe a container for the snake? This man had to be the detective. Her stalker wouldn't just walk up to her, would he? Her hand tightened on the gun. The man drew closer. The moon moved from behind a cloud and cast light on his face: Thibodeaux. Her shoulders sagged in relief. She popped the locks and got out.

"Thanks for coming, Detective Thibodeaux."

"That's my job." He held up the carrier. "I borrowed some

help from a friend. Meet Van."

The glow of the porch light revealed the contents of the cage: a green-eyed orange tabby with the top corner of one ear missing.

"Will the snake hurt the cat?" Janet wanted the snake gone, but not at the expense of another animal.

"Nah. Had a cat when I was a kid. He would leave dead snakes on the back porch - kind of like a present."

"Not my idea of a present." She shuddered.

"Momma didn't think so either."

Janet thought about letting him go inside without her, but the night held more possibility for danger than the reptile. Besides, Thibodeaux said he could handle the snake. She opened the door and followed Thibodeaux, expecting the snake to lunge out at any moment like a scary face popping up from the shadows in a Halloween haunted house.

"Where did you last see it?" Thibodeaux placed the carrier on the floor.

She pointed to the cardboard box lying in the kitchen. "It fell, then came toward me."

He opened the carrier and released Van. A blur of orange raced by, heading for the back of the house.

"Are you sure the cat will find it?"

"Yep." He scratched his head. "Too bad my dog died last year. Best snake catching dog ever."

Janet wondered if he had died from a snake bite.

"But just in case the cat's a dud." Thibodeaux pulled a flashlight from his jacket pocket, then flicked it on and bent down to search under appliances and furniture.

Standing in the middle of the room, Janet realized she should have stopped at the restroom before leaving the restaurant or at least resisted getting that last margarita. One sneeze and her bladder would burst. She eyed the distance to the bathroom, then remembered the reports of snakes in toilets. A vision of getting bit on the butt kept her rooted in place.

Thibodeaux's search yielded nothing. "I'll check the other rooms. If you want, you can stay here."

Janet recalled the beady eyes watching her and the forked tongue flicking the air. She didn't want to be alone.

"I'll follow you."

He went into her bedroom. She sat on her bed, swinging her feet up next to her.

Thibodeaux walked to the far wall, then flashed his light up under the bed.

A movement caught her eye. Van slipped into the closet, crouched, then pawed at her shoes. A shoe moved. The cat slapped at it. The snake's head popped up. Van dodged it, then knocked it with the other paw.

Janet pressed her hand against her mouth, stopping the scream pushing to escape. She scooted against the headboard, then drew her legs to her chest and clutched her arms around them. In a low voice, she said, "The cat found the snake."

"Way to go, Van." As Thibodeaux approached the snake, a smell like rotten eggs filled the room. A gooey white substance trailed from the snake and across the shoes.

"That's awful." Janet pinched her nose close.

"It's what rat snakes do when they're frightened." Thibodeaux grabbed Van. "I'm gonna kennel the cat. Stay here and watch the snake." The cat squirmed in his arms as he left.

Janet didn't want to stay, but the thought of leaving the safety of the bed frightened her more. She hugged her legs tighter to her chest, her back ramrod straight against the headboard, then watched as the snake slithered deeper into the closet.

Scuffling and swearing sounded from the other room, then the zip of the carrier.

Thibodeaux returned. "That cat really wanted that snake." A couple of scratches ran the length of his forearm. "Where'd it go?"

He followed the direction of her pointed finger, then eased shoes aside until he closed in on the creature. Janet watched, fascinated by his technique. Coming at it sideways, he laid a hand on its body. The snake jerked. Janet sucked in air. A shiver crawled up her back. Thibodeaux didn't move but waited a few seconds before closing his fingers around it. He placed his other hand on the snake, then picked it up. The snake writhed around his arms. Janet feared it would fall to the floor or worse, on her bed. As he swung around with it, she moved to the far edge, away from them. Thibodeaux left the room. Janet exhaled.

She heard the back door slam. Janet doubted she'd ever step in her backyard again.

Thibodeaux appeared in the doorway. "It's gone." He looked at the white liquid. "Sorry about the mess."

"That's okay. I'm throwing the shoes away. Gives me a good excuse to buy some new ones."

She slid off the bed and trailed him to the kitchen. Thibodeaux pulled vinyl gloves from his pocket, then tugged them on. He examined the snake's cardboard box.

"Air holes punctured on the side. No return address. There's a QR code and a barcode." He looked at Janet. "Doubt we get anything from those. Whoever did this probably pulled sample codes off the Internet. I'm guessing he wore gloves. I'll get it checked anyway."

He walked to the front door, grabbed the carrier, then turned toward her. "Phone me if you have any more problems." He smiled. "Try to get some rest."

Janet figured it would take a bottle of wine or a sleeping pill to knock her out enough to sleep.

After the detective left, she grabbed a trash bag, a can of disinfectant, and a broom, then walked into her bedroom. The sulfur smell permeated the room. Opening a window would help get rid of the odor, but the stalker might lurk in the dark. Black spots and pinpoints of light swam before her eyes, she dropped onto the bed. After a few minutes, she braced herself, popped the top off the disinfectant, and sprayed the shoes until the bleach scent covered the snake stench, then swept the shoes into the bag. She sniffed. The sulfur odor still lingered. The closet carpet would need cleaning or replacing. Maybe tossing the bag would help. She could throw the stuff in the back yard, but the thought of opening the door to a creature, walking or slithering, stopped her. The laundry room would have to hold it until morning.

Later, she soaked in a hot bath while she sipped a chilled glass of chardonnay. The ritual always relaxed her and took away the troubles of the day, but not tonight. Even the perfumed water couldn't eliminate the sulfur and bleach mixture emanating from her bedroom, nor could it wipe from her mind the night's events. The knots remained tight across her shoulders. Her teeth clamped together. One hand gripped the curve of the glass, while the other clutched the edge of the tub.

The nightmare would end if she could identify who hated her enough to do this. She summoned up the night she saw the stalker, focusing on the events as if she sat in an audience watching a movie. In her mind, his face remained shadowed, the hand on the gate gloved, his frame athletic, his movements fluid. All the details she had already shared with the detective. A description that applied to thousands of men in Houston.

Janet drained the glass of wine, then poured another. The wine wouldn't erase her fear, but perhaps it could numb it.

18

Harry opened his apartment door wide enough for Buddy and the carrier.

"You got a snake catcher here." Buddy set the carrier on the floor and unzipped it.

Van bolted.

"Probably hoping to find another snake." Buddy laughed. "You should have seen 'em."

Harry grabbed a couple of bottled waters from the refrigerator and handed one to Buddy. He looked at it as if Harry had offered him spoiled milk. "No beer?"

"I need to make a liquor run." Explaining to Buddy his reason for no liquor would take time and another lie. Anyway, he wasn't ready to tell Buddy the truth. He needed more information first, enough to catch the killer. If he said anything now, Buddy might think Harry had killed Lisa. At the very least, he would figure Harry was crazy.

Harry waved toward the living room. "Have a seat."

Buddy sank into the couch. Harry sat in the recliner across from him.

"So how big was the snake?"

"Couple of feet long, about as thick as a broom stick. Average size for a rat snake. Last week, I picked up one in the backyard. Six feet long and as thick as my fist." He balled up a fist the size of a baseball.

Buddy told stories as long as the snake he captured. "It's a little late for swapping snake stories," Harry said rubbing his eyes. Besides, Harry had other things to discuss.

"Has Drake got someone watching my place?"

Buddy frowned and shook his head. "Not that I know of."

He stared at Buddy, trying to determine if he told the truth. They'd been friends for a long time, but Buddy had a family to feed. He couldn't tell Harry everything without risking his job.

"Why do you ask?" Buddy said.

"Someone's sitting in a car outside. Last time I checked he was still there. I'd show you, but it's too dark to see him." Even during the daylight, the trees cast shadows on the parking spot. If Harry hadn't been looking for someone, he would probably never have noticed him.

"Did you get the plate number?"

"He didn't have a front plate. If he's not one of yours, then the back plate is probably a stolen one." In Harry's experience, if someone wanted anonymity, they found ways to get it.

"You got any updates on who killed Lisa?" Harry asked.

Buddy leaned forward, resting his elbows on his knees. "We found the knife that killed her."

"Where?" Harry held his breath.

Van strolled into the room and settled close to Harry. He

rubbed Van's head as if he were Aladdin's lantern and a genie would emerge granting wishes and erasing all of Harry's problems.

"In the hotel dumpster. Wrapped in a bloody hotel towel. Blood type matches the victim's. No fingerprints."

Harry exhaled. "At least they didn't find my fingerprints on that."

"Yeah. Although, as Drake points out, you're not stupid enough to leave fingerprints on the weapon." Buddy leaned back and took a swig of water.

"But I'm stupid enough to leave fingerprints at the crime scene?" Harry rolled his eyes.

Buddy shrugged. "Yeah. It doesn't make sense."

"Anything conclusive about the knife?" A unique knife might point to the killer or at least narrow down the list.

"Butcher knife. Almost an eight-inch blade. I have one just like it for hunting. Got it at Walmart." Buddy set his bottle on the coffee table, then stared at Harry. "Are you going to tell me what you did that night?"

Buddy had once been his partner. Harry trusted him with his life, but things were different now.

"I didn't kill her." At least Harry didn't think he did.

Buddy stood up, tossed the bottle in the trash, then stared at Harry, locking eyes with him.

"Until you're ready to talk, there's not much I can do to help."

"I can't tell you." Harry almost told him about the blackout. If Drake wasn't Buddy's partner, he might have. Maybe.

"That client confidentiality crap is going to land you in jail." Buddy strolled over to the end table, then picked up the Victoria's Secret card case. "Got a new girl?"

Shit. He shouldn't have left that lying around. It showed his state of mind that he left it out at all. All he could do was play along.

Harry raised his eyebrows. "We'll see. Think she'll like it?"

"How should I know?" Buddy's eyes widened.

Harry shrugged. "You're married."

"Doesn't mean I know what women like. Hell, they're all different anyway." Buddy looked at Harry. "You know, playing the field gets old. You should settle down with someone. Have some kids like the rest of us." He dropped the case on the table. "Drake might leave you alone."

The game plan might include a wife, but no kids. If they turned out anything like Harry, only nights of worry awaited him. He'd rather battle Drake the rest of his life.

After he closed the door behind Buddy, Harry picked up the card case and rubbed his finger across the embossed V. Did he know a Victoria? In his mind, he flipped through past girlfriends, co-workers, and classmates like an old Rolodex. If he had known a Victoria, he had forgotten her. Harry dropped the case in a drawer.

Everything started with Lisa's murder so if he found the killer then the pieces of the puzzle should join and eliminate him as the fall guy. Unless he murdered her. He shook his head. They said even in a smashed state of mind, people didn't go against their principles. No way would he kill anyone except in self-defense or to save someone else. It just couldn't happen. With any luck, the lover killed her. That would keep Harry out of jail but didn't account for his memory loss. Alcohol might explain it. Although, he doubted it. Drinking had caused no problems in the past. If the problem was the antidepressants, then he would steer clear of them for the rest of his life. No matter who died or how hard life got.

That left the question of the pranks: Van, the woman's clothes, the card case. Of all the women he'd dated, Candy seemed the most likely culprit. She was unpredictable. He remembered the time she'd insisted he pick her up at a bar as if he didn't know her. Or the time she kidnapped him for a spur of the moment weekend in Galveston. Still, she had Richie now. Maybe Richie hated surprises and Candy was using Harry as an outlet for her mischievous streak. At this point, Harry wasn't a big fan of surprises either. He could call her and ask about the pranks, but her voice wouldn't reveal if she told the truth or lied. Instead, Harry would meet her for lunch, watch her face, and read her body language, then he'd know if she was the one harassing him.

However, if it was Candy, then why the Victoria's Secret items? It didn't make sense, or did it? A picture of a gold locket she wore flashed in his mind. The initials CMV engraved in cursive across the front: C for Candace and a large M for her last name, Monet, but he'd never asked about the V.

19

Charley poured another cup of coffee. The aroma almost obscured the smell of bacon she had cooked for her birthday breakfast. She dumped in cream watching it swirl in the black caffeine that fueled her day, then returned to stare at the code on her screen. What a way to spend her thirty-ninth birthday. If only the encrypted words would magically morph into readable text.

As she took a sip of coffee, someone knocked on her door. The threatening note she'd found on her doorstep popped in her mind: "Stop what you're doing or we'll stop you permanently." Her hand trembled as if the coffee cup was too heavy to hold. Warm liquid dribbled down her chin and onto her grey sweatshirt.

Charley mumbled under her breath, "Pull yourself together. It's probably Harry."

She wiped her chin as she got up and walked toward the door. Charley picked up the bat leaning against the wall and with a tight grip on it, peered through the peephole. At the site of the highlighted hair and the straight narrow nose, her grip relaxed. She returned the bat to its position and opened the door.

"Mom, what are you doing here?"

Her mom hugged her. "I came to take you to lunch for your birthday." She released Charley, stepped away, and took in Charley's coffee-stained sweatshirt and baggy sweatpants. "You'll need to change."

Charley glanced at her computer. She had never confirmed a lunch date with her mom. Maybe she could convince her to postpone it to another day. "Work is really crazy. Could we go next week instead?"

Her mom frowned. "But we always go on your birthday." She raised her eyebrows and smiled. "I've got reservations for us at The Alessandra."

Charley didn't really have time for lunch, but her mom could be relentless. Besides, Charley deserved a break, and it was her birthday.

"Alright, give me a few minutes to change."

As she headed for her bedroom, her mom called out, "Put some concealer under your eyes. I don't want anyone mistaking you for a raccoon." Her mom's laughter followed Charley down the hall.

Charley squinted in the bright sunlight as she exited her apartment building.

Her mom dropped her own sunglasses from the top of her head onto the bridge of her nose, then turned to look at Charley.

"Stop squinting, it causes wrinkles," her mom said.

Her mom pulled her car keys from her purse, then walked toward her car. The silver Mercedes glimmered next to Charley's dusty white Honda Accord.

"I'll drive," her mom said.

"Mom, you know I get carsick if I don't drive. You don't want me barfing in your car. Do you?"

In the past, her mom had told her the sickness was psychological. Charley wished it was all in her mind, then she could do something about it. When she went on a date, the man always wanted to take the wheel. When she explained her problem, they seemed put off as if she had a communicable disease.

Her mom shook her head and sighed. "Fine. I hope you cleaned it. Last time, I had to clear the floorboard of water bottles."

"I could drive your car." Other than the occasional valet, her mother allowed no one else in the Mercedes' driver's seat, but Charley figured she could at least offer.

Her mother looked at Charley from the corner of her eyes. "That's okay. I've seen how you drive the Honda. Just let me get your present."

Charley wondered what she might have in the front seat of the Accord. Papers? Books? An empty fast-food bag? She smirked at the thought of what her mother might find. At least the trunk was empty. Charley had moved stuff from there to the backseat, thinking if it was in view, then she'd remember to drop it off at Goodwill. So far, the strategy hadn't worked.

Her mom popped the Mercedes' trunk, pulled out a Neiman Marcus shopping bag and handed it to Charley with a smile. "Happy birthday."

Charley took the bag and smiled. "Thanks, Mom. I'll open it at the restaurant."

Between the sun beating down on her and the heat rising from the pavement, Charley wanted some air conditioning as fast as possible. Charley's mom moved toward the passenger side of the Honda and reached for the door handle, standing far enough away to avoid getting any dust on her white blouse and turquoise skirt.

Charley popped the trunk and peered inside. A thick clear plastic covered a human shaped frame. She jerked back, gasped, and pressed her hand against her mouth. Her heart hammered against her chest, then everything blurred. Charley shook her head as if to reset her vision, then focused on the body or whatever it was. The plastic covering was so thick, she couldn't make out any features. Perhaps it was a mannequin. The person who left the threatening note may have dropped off a shrink-wrapped dummy in her trunk just to scare her.

Maybe touching it would tell her if it was fake or human. Charley didn't want to touch it. What if it was a person? She had to know. With her pointer finger extended, she moved to within inches of the shape. She closed her eyes and screwed up her face.

"Charley, do you ever clean out your car?"

Charley yanked back her hand and looked over the raised trunk lid.

Her mother stood at the open passenger door, frowning. "Look at all this stuff." She waved her hand at the seat. "Where am I supposed to sit?" She peered in the back seat and shook her head. "The back seat is full too. Maybe we can move some of this into the trunk."

20

"Charley, did you hear me?" Her mom pointed to the front seat of the Honda. "Is there room for all this stuff in the trunk?"

Charley stared at the plastic encased body. This morning's eggs, bacon, and coffee rose up in her throat. Her mom moved toward her, closing in on the trunk and its contents. "You've got that carsick look on your face. Are you okay?"

Charley slammed the trunk shut. "I don't feel so good. Must have been what I ate for breakfast."

"You do look pale." She wrinkled her nose. "I thought I smelled bacon in your place. All that grease settling in your stomach, clogging your arteries. Oatmeal is better. I eat it every morning with blueberries." She smiled.

Charley gagged. Any more mention of food and she'd lose it. Her mom stepped back, shut the Honda's door, and sighed. "Let's try for lunch another day."

Her mom had never been good with any type of illness or injury. At the age of ten, Charley barfed on the wood floor. Her mom insisted Charley clean it up. A couple of years later,

Charley broke her leg and her mom sent in someone else to hold Charley's hand while the doctor examined her.

"That's a good idea." Charley struggled to keep her voice from wavering. "I'll give you a call. Thanks, Mom."

"Your voice is shaky." Her mom frowned. "Do you need me to stay?"

Charley forced a smile. "I'll be fine in a couple of hours."

She had to get her mom to leave. Whether the body was real or not, Charley had to call the cops and she didn't want her mom involved in the fallout. If she thought the mess in her car was bad, then the trunk contents would send her mother over the edge. After one look, her mom would probably pass out, hit her head on the asphalt, and end up with a concussion.

Her mother smiled and squeezed Charley's shoulder. "Okay. Call me if you need anything." She pointed at the shopping bag at Charley's feet. "I hope you like the present. I'll text you about rescheduling lunch when you're feeling better." She got in her Mercedes and left.

Charley wondered if her situation warranted dialing 911. It wasn't an emergency. No amount of rushing to the scene would make a difference and she'd just tie up a line for someone who had a real emergency. Harry would know what to do. She called his number. The phone rang, then transferred to voicemail. She sighed and hung up.

Harry had a cop friend who told her if she ever needed help to give him a call.

"What was his name? Something Cajun." Charley scrolled through her phone contacts, then landed on his name: Buddy

Thibodeaux. She pressed the number.

"Detective Thibodeaux." Traffic noise sounded in the background.

"Buddy, this is Charley Hayes." She doubted he remembered her. "Harry's next-door neighbor."

"Oh yeah. What's up? Harry hasn't gotten himself in trouble again, has he?" He chuckled.

"It's not Harry." At least, she didn't think it was Harry in the trunk. What if it was Harry? Her stomach tightened.

"Someone put something in my car." Her voice shook.

She held the phone close to her mouth and whispered, "It has a human shape, but I'm not sure it's really a person."

"Can't you tell?" He sounded like he thought she was on crack.

"It's wrapped in lots of clear plastic. I can't see any features." She reached out to pop the trunk open just to make sure she hadn't imagined it but stopped. Her vision blurred. She couldn't look at that thing again and if it wasn't still in there, then she had lost her mind.

"Where are you?" Buddy's tone took on a note of urgency.

"In the parking lot of my apartment complex." Charley wiped the sweat from her brow.

"Get in the car and lock the doors. I'll be there in five minutes." She climbed into her car and hit the lock.

"Are you in the car?" Buddy asked.

"Yes." Her head ached from the heat. She cranked the car and put the A/C on high. Cool air hit her face and cleared her mind. Whoever left the thing in her Honda could be watching.

A prickling sensation ran across her skin. She glanced around the parking lot. The ten or so cars sat empty.

A squirrel ran across the top of the fence at the back edge of the lot. In the far corner, was a black sedan. It could have someone in there, but she couldn't tell from this distance. She looked at the two apartment buildings facing the parking lot. Like her window, blinds covered all the other windows as well and nothing twitched at them. A woman with a stroller entered the breezeway connecting the two buildings.

Charley had never had a run in with the law before other than the occasional speeding ticket. She'd watched a few mysteries on TV and had an idea of what would go down if the body was real. Based on what she'd seen, the cops would suspect her, even though she'd reported it. It was good she hadn't touched the plastic. At least, they wouldn't find her fingerprints on it.

Buddy's voice interrupted her thoughts. "I'm turning into your apartments. Which car is yours?"

"The white Honda Accord." Charley took a deep breath, turned off her car, and got out to face whatever happened next.

21

Filtered sunlight cast a glow on the people chatting and laughing in the restaurant. Silverware clinked against plates. Harry drummed his fingers on the white tablecloth as if the motion would make Candy appear. People arrived dressed in everything from suits to jeans. The fragrant odor of French bread triggered a grumbling in Harry's stomach.

When the waitress arrived, Harry ordered Candy's favorite red wine and a glass of scotch for himself.

Candy made her entrance, a vision no one could ignore. Her white shirt disappeared into a red leather skirt showing legs long enough to wrap around a man's waist. She swayed on black stiletto heels toward Harry's table, leaving a wake of men's eyes fixed on the provocative swing of her hips. Chatter diminished to a hum.

Once she took a seat, the noise level resumed, and an occasional outburst of amusement rippled through the room. Harry smiled. Since the day he met her, Candy had always been an attention-grabber.

Candy took a deep breath. The shirt stretched around the

buttons. Harry watched, anticipating a few to pop, but none did. Disappointed, his eyes moved upward. A fringe of blonde bangs hovered around eyes as soft as a deer's, but he knew a fox lurked underneath.

She smirked. "You miss me?"

Harry missed her. Visions of times they spent together ran through his mind: beach days in Galveston followed by candlelight dinners and drinks while soaking in the hot tub, followed by... Harry's phone rang. He glanced at the caller ID. It was Charley.

"Do you need to get that?" Candy asked.

Harry shook his head. "I'll call them later."

The waitress arrived with their drinks.

Candy picked up her glass and swirled the red liquid. "That's what I like about you, Harry. You always know just what I want." She leaned forward and lightly stroked his hand.

"So, what did you want to talk about?" she asked.

That's what he liked most about Candy, her ability to get straight to the point.

Harry could be just as direct. "Have you been pranking me?"

Her eyes widened. "No. Richard takes up all my free time. Unlike when you and I dated, he has time for me, so I'm never bored." She smiled and leaned back in her chair. "Why? Someone drop off another cat?"

If she thought another woman played tricks on him, Candy might get jealous. She might want him again. Not that he wanted her permanently in his life. He couldn't handle her mess. Last time he was in her car, cosmetics and coins filled every cup holder, receipts littered the carpet, shopping bags cluttered the back seat.

Harry told her everything except for his memory loss and Lisa's murder. He watched her face for any hints of guilt. Her eyes grew wider as he told her about the woman's clothes, Van's appearance, disappearance, then reappearance. At the mention of the plate of breadcrumbs, the glass with remnants of milk, and the credit card case, her mouth fell open. After watching each reaction throughout his tale, he knew she wasn't the culprit. Instead of looking guilty, she appeared intrigued as if watching a mystery unfold.

"Victoria's Secret? A woman with good taste, but it's a little tame for me." She laughed, a rumbling sound like a cat's purr. He shook his head, breaking her mental hold on him.

She smiled and leaned into his space. "Perhaps her name is Victoria."

He had thought the same but coming from a woman and a prankster it gave the theory more weight.

Her gold locket caught the light in the room.

Harry pointed to it. "What does the V stand for?"

Candy sipped her wine, put down the glass and stared into his eyes. "Vivienne."

She licked her lips as if savoring each drop of wine or perhaps savoring a lie, then raised her eyebrows. "Wait a minute."

She leaned back in her chair and pressed her hand against her chest. "You think I'm Victoria? I wouldn't go to that much trouble for a man. Not even you."

Unless her lying skills had improved in the past year, she told the truth. Harry's shoulders slumped. He'd counted on her being Victoria, resolving at least one of his problems. If he could just find this woman, Victoria or whoever, that owned the clothes and Van, then he would have his alibi for the night of Lisa's murder. Drake could find someone else to bully.

Later, he picked up the tab and watched the women frown and the men ogle her as she left. Next time, he'd bring Sophia and see what happened. Maybe Sophia could replace Candy in his life, but it was too early in their relationship to tell. Hell, they'd only had the one date.

On his way home, Harry's phone rang.

"Hey, this is Joey. Got the camera installed. I left the instructions on the table. If you have any questions give me a call."

Harry had dealt with video equipment in the past. "Thanks Joey. I doubt I'll have any problems."

As he hung up the phone, he took a deep breath, then exhaled. No more nights of wondering what he did or who entered his house. Digital media didn't lie or forget.

22

Harry turned into his apartment complex. A red Camaro that looked like Buddy's was parked next to a cop car. Two officers stood in the parking lot.

Harry's heart beat fast against his chest. They must have found enough evidence to arrest him for Lisa's murder. He thought about turning around, avoiding the situation, but knew they'd find him eventually. Still, if he could buy himself some time, he would have a better shot at clearing his name. As he turned the steering wheel, Buddy exited the apartment building and waved at Harry.

If he left now, he'd look guilty. Harry straightened the wheels and pulled forward. The cops held up their hands, indicating for Harry to stop where he was. Heat flamed Harry's cheeks. This was it. Next, they'd pull out the handcuffs. Harry exhaled in defeat. It wasn't as if he'd never spent a night in jail, but those were always the result of a bar fight. No one had died. Harry parked and got out of his car. Buddy walked toward him.

Harry forced himself to relax and pasted an innocent

expression on his face. "What's going on, Buddy?"

"Someone dumped a body in Charley's trunk." He squinted at Harry. "I don't suppose you know anything about it?"

"What? There's a body in Charley's car?" Harry's stomach tightened. "Is she okay?"

Buddy nodded. "She's shaken up. You might want to check on her." He looked up at the building. "She's upstairs. I'm done questioning her for now."

The CSI van pulled into the lot. As Buddy turned to leave, Harry grabbed Buddy's arm.

"Any ID found on the body?" Harry asked.

Buddy faced Harry. "No ID was found in the trunk. The body is wrapped in plastic." Buddy shrugged. "We won't know much else until the medical examiner gets a chance to look at it."

"Sounds like a professional hit." Harry watched a man snap pictures while someone else pulled a body bag out of the van.

Buddy nodded. "Looks like it." He frowned and motioned toward the crime scene. "I gotta go check on the guys."

"If you need me for anything, I'll be with Charley." As Harry walked toward the building, he hoped the victim wasn't anyone he knew.

23

Charley laid on the couch with a pillow supporting her head and a thick blue throw covering her body. She stared blankly at the TV as scenes from some comedy flashed across the screen. The jokes and resulting laughter from the audience fell flat. Her phone vibrated in her hand. Whoever it was, could leave a message.

She should call her manager, but what would she say? What would he think? She had only been working for Derek for a few weeks. Still, if this had something to do with the note and her work, then he should be notified. Even if it didn't, the CIA would probably want to investigate.

Someone knocked on her door. Charley widened her eyes. Cold seeped into her body. She shivered and curled into a ball.

"Charley, it's me, Harry."

Harry! The body in the trunk wasn't Harry's. His voice sent warmth through her. She smiled, muted the TV, threw off the blanket, and raced for the door. If anyone could help her, it was Harry. She flung open the door and wrapped her arms around him.

Harry cleared his throat. "Are you okay?" he asked.

Charley released him and nodded. "I thought it might be you in the trunk."

Harry touched her shoulder. A wave of electricity tingled across her skin. She looked at his face to see if he felt something too but saw only a slight smile and a crinkling at the edge of his eyes as he said, "Not today."

He led Charley to the couch and sat next to her.

"Is there anything I can do for you?" Harry asked.

Charley rubbed her forehead. "Just find the person who did this."

"Okay, let's start with who you think might have done it. Has anyone got a grudge against you?"

"Not that I know of. At least nothing that would warrant this." She waved her hand in the direction of the parking lot. Charley wanted to tell him about the note, but she couldn't reveal her work with the CIA.

Harry pointed to her face. "You're biting your lip. A sure sign you're not telling me something."

He knew her too well. She could mention the note without revealing she worked for the CIA. Charley released her lip and confessed. "I did get a threatening note left on my doorstep.

"What did it say?" Harry leaned closer, planting his elbows on his knees.

"Stop what you're doing before we stop you permanently." She looked up at him.

"What are you doing?" Harry frowned. "Does this have something to do with researching Drake's past?"

Charley raised her head and looked into his eyes. "I don't think so. Besides I haven't had enough time to dig very deep."

Harry stared at her for a few moments. "If it's not Drake, then what else could it be?"

She shrugged. "I don't know. I'm doing some translation work. Nothing earth shattering."

Charley held his gaze until his face relaxed.

"Show me the note," Harry held out his hand.

"I don't have it anymore." Charley focused on wrapping the throw's fringe around her finger. "I took a picture of the note though." She grabbed her phone, pulled up the image, then handed it to him.

"Did you show this to Buddy?" Harry stretched his fingers across the screen and zoomed in on the note.

Charley nodded. "He's following up on it." Buddy had asked for her boss's name and phone number.

Someone rapped on the door. Charley got up and checked the peephole. Buddy's face peered back at her. She let Buddy inside. A uniformed cop followed him. Buddy frowned. Charley held her breath. Pain shot through her chest. What did the cops want now?

24

Harry searched Buddy's face. The frown, the narrowed eyes, the tightened jaw all spoke of trouble.

Buddy motioned his hand at Harry. "Harry, I need you to come with me."

Harry's shoulder blades tightened, then relaxed. From what Buddy told him earlier, they hadn't found any ID in the trunk. They wouldn't unwrap the plastic in the parking lot for fear of contaminating the evidence. Nothing linked him to the crime scene, then again, he had forgotten a lot lately. His head throbbed as he followed Buddy and the cop out of Charley's apartment. He held any questions until they had exited the stairwell and passed through the breezeway into the sun-drenched parking lot.

"What's up, Buddy?" Harry squinted.

Buddy glanced sideways at Harry. "We found another body."

"In Charley's car?" One body was unbelievable, but two? Her Honda was always packed with books, papers, and fast-food bags. He didn't see how one body would fit in it, much less two. Harry couldn't think of anyone who hated Charley enough to do something like this. On the other hand, Harry attracted enemies like black pants attracted cat hair. So, if it had been his car, then it would make sense.

Buddy stopped walking and shaded his eyes with his hand. He turned toward the car pulling into the apartments.

"Shit! That's Drake's car," Buddy said. He looked at Harry. "Go to your place. I'll catch up with you later."

Harry nodded. If Drake caught Buddy showing him a crime scene, then Buddy would catch hell. It didn't help that Harry's last encounter with Drake had ended in a fist fight. Too bad the dead body wasn't Drake.

Harry headed quickly for the breezeway and didn't slow down until he reached the door of his apartment. As he inserted the key in his front door, Harry dreaded what he might find inside, another animal, more women's things, or total destruction.

When he walked inside, the living area looked just as he left it except for the camera hanging in a corner, facing the entrance to his place.

Harry's headache moved to the forefront of his head and threatened him with a full-blown migraine. He grabbed a glass of water from the kitchen and carried it to the bathroom. Evidence of Van littered the place. The toilet paper laid in a pile on the floor. Nail clippers, his reading glasses, and a bottle of vitamins cluttered the tile.

Harry grabbed a couple of aspirins and downed them. He

picked up Van's mess, then searched the apartment for him.

In the living room, he found the video equipment instructions on an end table. He looked around. No cat hovered under the coffee table, beneath his desk, or perched on the sofa. As much as Harry hated to admit it, he'd grown accustomed to his new roommate, not the litter, but the companionship. He shrugged.

In time, he would come out of hiding or… Harry grabbed a can of cat food and popped the top.

Van bounded into the room.

"At least I know what it takes to get your attention. If only women were that easy." Van purred as Harry dumped the food in a bowl, then set it on the floor.

With the snake hunter eating, Harry could focus on the activity outside. He peeked through the window blinds. A wrecker was hooked up to Charley's Honda. Two cop cars and a CSI van surrounded the dark sedan he'd noticed earlier in the week. He got out the binoculars and zoomed in on the area, but the van blocked his view of the driver's seat.

Harry picked up the video instructions, stuffed them in a drawer, and started playing with the equipment. He walked in front of the camera, then checked the recording. It had captured his movements. Going forward, he'd know who came into his apartment and when.

25

"Charley, I'm glad you called. How's that message coming along?" Her boss's voice sounded upbeat as if he had just received good news.

"I'm getting closer to solving it." Charley looked over at her computer and frowned. She hadn't made much progress today, but work wasn't a high priority at the moment.

"Remember, the FBI needs the information by Monday," he said.

Charley rolled her eyes. Leave it to Derek to add more stress to her day. What would he say when the cops showed up at his door? She had to warn him they were coming and why.

Dropping a bomb like a dead body in her trunk wouldn't be easy no matter who it was, but she'd worked for Derek less than a month. He'd think she was some kind of crackpot.

Derek continued on, "Tom's going to call you tomorrow and discuss how he can help you."

It was bad enough her manager thought she couldn't do her job, now she had to tell him about the contents of her trunk.

"Why did you call?" he asked.

"The cops will probably come by to talk to you about the note the guy picked up from me. You know, the one I found on my doorstep."

"Why are the cops calling me?" Derek sounded confused. "Did something else happen?"

The human wrapped in plastic flashed in her mind. Charley's breakfast threatened to make a quick exit. She swallowed hard. Her heart beat loud in her ears. There was no good way to tell him. She'd just have to blurt it out.

"Someone put a body in my trunk."

She stood up from the couch. Her blanket fell to the floor.

"The police think the note might have something to do with it."

Charley walked back and forth across the floor. She rushed on, the pace of her words competing with the warmth flooding her face.

"I showed them the note on my phone, but they want to see the original. So, I gave them your name." She paused. "I hope that's all right."

"What?" Her boss's normally calm voice shouted in her ear. "A dead body?"

"It was wrapped in plastic."

"Wrapped in plastic? What the hell is going on over there? Look, I don't think it's safe for you to stay. We can move you to a safe house until the CIA figures this out."

"I don't need to move. The message should be decoded in the next couple of days." She didn't sleep well away from home.

"I still don't get it. No one outside of the CIA knows what I'm doing so…" Her voice shook.

"I get what you're saying." He sighed. "Let me work this on my end."

Charley looked out her window. They had already taken her car. She wondered when they would return it. Did she really want it back? She had just paid it off and hated the thought of picking up car payments again. Her mom had an extra car. Maybe she'd let Charley borrow it for a while.

Her boss cleared his throat. "Are you okay?"

"Yeah." What a stupid question to ask. Of course, she wasn't okay, but who admits that to their boss?

"When did you discover the body?"

"Around lunch time."

"Next time, call me first. You work for the CIA, and this is CIA business," he said firmly.

Next time? She had worked for the CIA for several years and nothing like this had ever happened. It's not like she was a CIA Officer.

"Did the cops leave contact information?"

Charley rattled off Buddy's details.

"I'll give him a call. We don't know what else they might do to stop the translation of that message. We'll make sure someone watches your place." He paused. "If that message is the reason for this, the sooner it's cracked the better."

Her boss cleared his throat again. "I'll make sure we have someone watching you. Call me immediately if anything else happens." He hung up.

Only a few people knew Charley was decrypting the message. Did the CIA have a leak within their organization? If so, who could she trust?

26

Dr. Worth stood at her office windows and scanned the parking lot. The late afternoon sun beat on the ten or so cars, each cushioned by empty spaces, waiting for their owners. Her silver Lexus waited in the middle row, facing the building. A grey-haired woman leaning on a cane moved across the sidewalk toward a handicap spot. A couple lingered in the shade of a tree, smoking cigarettes. Janet observed the man's frame. He was taller and thinner than her intruder.

She doubted the stalker would risk attacking her during the day in front of witnesses, but she wasn't taking any chances. Janet slipped the strap of her purse over her shoulder, then tucked one hand in it and gripped her gun. She took a deep breath and exited the building. Forcing a confident stride, she focused on her car as her heart thumped against her chest.

Hurried footsteps sounded behind her. Janet resisted the urge to run but grasped her gun tighter. The steps grew closer. The clattering on the sidewalk drowned out every other sound. The noise grew louder. Any moment the person would reach out and grab her.

"Excuse me."

Janet froze, her muscles tensed, then relaxed as her mind interpreted the tone of voice, a woman's voice, soft and apologetic.

As the heavyset brunette passed Janet, she raised her hand. "I'm late picking up my kids from childcare." The powdery smell of baby lotion trailed after her. The woman jumped into a white Jeep and peeled out of the parking lot.

Janet slid into her coupe and hit the locks, a sound as reassuring as the tumblers on a safe. She checked her rearview mirror, looking for anyone who resembled her harasser, but only the empty cars and the smokers reflected in the glass.

She drove away from the building. Glancing in her side mirror, she noted a black Ford pickup hovering a block away. A mid-sized red Honda pulled in front of her.

Behind her, the pickup gained speed and hugged her bumper. She wanted to accelerate but couldn't without crashing into the Honda. The truck followed her, honking, and flashing his lights. Janet's throat closed.

At the upcoming traffic light, the two-lane traffic became four giving her an opportunity to pass the Honda. The light turned yellow before the single lane widened into two.

The red car hesitated as if the driver didn't know which lane to choose. It moved into the right-hand lane as the light turned red. Janet took the left lane. The pickup stopped behind her.

The Honda turned right. Janet watched in her rearview window as the pickup truck backed up, swerved, then pulled into the right lane, next to Janet. She gripped the steering wheel, gritted her teeth, and stared straight ahead.

In her peripheral vision, she saw the truck's window roll down and heard the man shouting but couldn't decipher what he said. She shivered. Her mind blanked, then anger raged through it. No one would force her to live in fear.

Janet pulled the gun from her purse, clutched it close to her, low and out of sight of the driver, then rolled down her passenger window. She turned toward the man.

Brown eyes focused on her. A smile stretched across a face that bristled with a five o'clock shadow.

"You left something on the back of your car."

No way had she left anything on her car. She had walked out with only her purse. Her grip tightened on the gun.

He raised his eyebrows. "Looks like a book."

The light turned green. The pickup took off. She exhaled and released her hold on the gun.

Janet looked in the rearview mirror and saw nothing on the trunk. The man had lied.

"But why would he lie?" She shook her head. "It doesn't make sense. Unless... He's the stalker and wants me to get out of my car. He could have circled around the block."

She checked her mirror again. A man cycled in her direction, but no black truck appeared.

The brake light box blocked part of her view of the trunk, enough to hide a book. Even so, she wasn't stopping to check. Her townhouse was only a block away. Nothing would fall off before she reached home.

As Janet approached her driveway, she scanned the area. A

woman pushed a baby stroller along the sidewalk. Further down the block, a man walked a dog, heading away from her house.

She parked and looked around her, checking the mirrors. Janet didn't want to leave the car, but she couldn't stay in it. She took a deep breath and popped the locks.

As she stepped from the car and closed the door, a pickup truck came down the street. Janet froze. She couldn't believe the guy would follow her home. The black truck sped down the street toward her. A blonde woman sat in the driver's seat. Janet sagged against the car.

A warm breeze brushed her face and rustled the leaves in the trees. The sun slid behind her house. She thought about sprinting to her front door, but curiosity changed her mind. As Janet moved toward the back of her car, the woman with the stroller walked by and waved.

"Nice afternoon." She pointed to Janet's trunk. "You left something on your car." The woman smiled. "I've done that too. Left his diaper bag on the trunk."

Janet nodded. "Guess everyone's done it at least once."

The woman nodded, then continued on her way.

She spotted the book behind her brake light, a hardback, bound in navy blue cloth with a square white piece of paper taped on the edges to the front cover. She reached to pick it up, then thought of fingerprints. Grabbing a tissue from her purse, Janet picked up the thick book, then ran to her house.

Once inside, Janet kicked off her shoes, slumped on the couch, then placed the book on the coffee table. The title was one she recognized, one she'd read, *Watch Jane Run*. In the story, a man stalked the main character, a female. In the end, the hero prevented the stalker from killing her. Janet shivered and wondered if a hero would save her or if she'd have to save herself.

Janet leaned closer to the book and examined the square of paper. In the center of the square, four words blurred in purplish-blue ink ran horizontal across the white paper. The drizzling rain had smeared all the letters, making them indecipherable. Whoever left the book hadn't accounted for the possibility of rain or maybe they hoped she would find the book sooner.

She wondered if the stalker had also written on the flyleaf but didn't want to look. An inscription would make it personal; the words would burn into her brain like a horse brand, the fear lasting a lifetime. No, she'd had enough for one day. For now, she would call Thibodeaux. Maybe by the time he arrived, she could handle whatever might wait inside the cover.

Janet pulled a bottle of wine out of the refrigerator, then exchanged it for a Coke. She opened a kitchen cabinet, grabbed the rum and a glass. Pressing the ice dispenser brought a clanging noise that intensified the tension across her shoulders. She poured a double shot of Bacardi over the ice, then watched the Coke fizz as it mixed with the rum. The liquid burned as it slid down her throat. Her shoulders relaxed and the pounding of her heart eased. By the time she was on her second drink, the doorbell rang.

She grabbed her Glock and checked the peephole: Detective Thibodeaux. She opened the door wide and waved him inside.

He pointed to the gun. "Is that thing loaded?"

"Of course. What would be the point otherwise?"

"You have a license for it. Right?"

She nodded, then sat on the couch, placing the gun on an end table. "Have a seat."

Thibodeaux eased into a recliner across from her. "You mentioned a book over the phone?"

"Here it is." She pointed to it on the coffee table. "I picked it up with a tissue in case it had fingerprints."

Plus, she hadn't really wanted to touch it. Silly, really. What could the cover possibly do to her?

Thibodeaux pulled latex gloves from his pocket, then tugged them on. He picked up the book and examined the front cover, then the sides.

"Must have rained around here today." He leaned in close to the white square of paper. "Whatever message they left is unreadable and the page edges are warped."

She looked up at the ceiling and replayed the day in her mind. "When I left this morning, it was drizzling. Not enough for an umbrella, but enough for me to run to the car and jump inside. I think it drizzled most of the day."

Thibodeaux nodded.

Janet held her breath and watched his face as he opened the book and turned a page. He brought the book closer to his face, then frowned. Janet sat still. The sound of the air conditioner kicking in filled the room.

She cleared her throat. "What is it?"

He turned the book toward her and pointed at the title. Janet leaned in close, her eyes drawn to the page like a scene in a horror movie. Someone had altered the title page by adding a t after Jane. A shiver rippled across her body as if the stalker had touched her. The words *Watch Janet Run* blurred as black spots appeared before her eyes. She took a deep breath, gripped the edge of the couch, and recited in her mind over and over again: they are just words.

Thibodeaux's voice floated above her mantra. "Are you ok?"

No, she wasn't, but she wasn't going to admit it. She swallowed hard and nodded.

Thibodeaux flipped through the rest of the book; his expression noncommittal. He shook the book. Nothing fell out of it. He sniffed it, then laid it back on the table.

"Anything interesting in it?" Janet asked.

"Looks and smells new. Doubt we'll find any fingerprints. Even if the owner didn't wear gloves, there's no guarantee we could match the fingerprints to anything in our database." He smiled. "Still, there's a chance."

Thibodeaux frowned. "Why tape the message to the front of the book? Why not write it on the flyleaf or put it inside the book?"

Janet shrugged. "Maybe they wanted to make sure I saw it."

"Could be." Thibodeaux nodded as if considering the validity of her explanation. "It would have been smarter to use wide clear tape and cover the message too. Then the rain wouldn't have ruined it."

Janet figured she might sleep better not knowing what the message said. Still, it might have given them a clue as to who left the book and why.

He pulled out a pen and a palm-sized black-spiral-bound notebook. "It would help if we had a place and time frame when he left it on your car."

"Let's see." Janet squinted. "This morning I drove from home to the office. It could have been on my car then. I wouldn't have noticed what with the rain." She shrugged. "I only got in and out of the car. There wasn't any reason to check the back of it."

"I doubt there are any surveillance cameras around here. There might be some around your office building. I'll check."

Thibodeaux made a note on his pad, then looked at her. "I followed up on Mark Crawford. He doesn't have an alibi for the night of your intruder incident. He denied he did it. Not that it means anything." He scratched his head. "Is there anyone else you can think of who would do this?"

She considered all her patients, ex-boyfriends, and peers, but no one came to mind. Janet shook her head. It was even hard to believe Mark would do it.

"This guy hasn't tried to harm you, but we don't want it to get to that." Thibodeaux put away his pen and pad of paper, then stood. "When I talked with Mark Crawford, he seemed nervous, like he was hiding something. Although, some people get that way around cops. We'll keep investigating him."

From what Janet recalled, Mark hid a number of things, some of them not very well, like his insecurity and lack of self-control. Mark thought his girlfriend was cheating on him, so he followed her until the girl spotted him, then she dumped him. He also lost a job when he called his boss an asshole. Mark probably had other issues too, but she never got a chance to uncover them.

"We'll assign a cop to watch you. I'll also see if we can find someone to tail Mark." Thibodeaux smiled. "Don't worry. We'll figure out who's doing this."

As Janet closed and bolted the door behind him, she wished she was as confident as the detective. Until they found the stalker, she would sleep with her Glock.

27

The sun hung low in the sky as Harry parked in front of the address Sophia had texted him. A waist-high-iron-grate fence stood in front of the row of brownstones, each with its own gate. The facade on each home was unique. On Sophia's house, a white framed bay window of clear glass protruded from the second floor creating space for an enclosed balcony on the top floor.

As he walked up the sidewalk and climbed the staircase to the front door, Harry questioned how she could afford the place on a maid's salary. Perhaps she had family money or a wealthy ex-husband.

Harry rang the doorbell and checked his image in the reflective glass inset into the wood door. He ran his fingers through his hair, smoothing a few stray strands. A sniff of his dress shirt brought a whiff of oranges and limes, verifying he'd applied cologne. He was ready for whatever the night held.

Sophia answered the door in one of those simple knee-length black dresses every woman had, but Sophia's figure made the dress anything but simple. Her eyes, the color of whiskey, met his. Harry wanted to skip dinner and go right for dessert at her place. She smiled as if she read his thoughts.

Harry raised his eyebrows. "Nice dress. You look great."

"Thanks. Come on in. I've just got to find my purse, then we can leave." She opened the door wide. Cool air washed over Harry. Not quite as good as a cold shower, but it would do for now.

As he walked inside, the scent of cinnamon welcomed him as if Christmas existed year-round in her home. The cool air and the color of the place continued the wintry-like theme. White walls enclosed the living room and flowed through a wide opening into the kitchen. Canned ceiling lights gleamed on the white cabinets and glistened on the white countertops. Only the dark wood floors provided any warmth to the room.

Sophia pointed to a white couch. "Have a seat. I'll just be a minute."

Harry followed her directions and sank into the couch. Investment magazines lay scattered across the coffee table. Investing might be how she paid for the place. If so, maybe she would share some tips with him.

She put her hands on her hips, then looked around the room. "Where did I put that purse?"

Harry picked up a framed picture off an end table. An older couple, a younger version of Sophia, and a boy stared out of the glass. "Is this your family?"

"What?" Sophia pulled her purse off a barstool tucked under the kitchen island. She walked over toward him. "Yes, that's my parents, me, and my brother." Her voice cracked when she said brother.

Sophia held up her purse. "We can go now."

Harry wanted to know more about her, about her family. He started to ask but changed his mind. Asking questions about her family might lead to questions about his. Questions he didn't want to answer, at least not yet.

Sophia headed for the door and jingled the keys in her hand as if in a rush to leave. He put the frame down and followed her.

Classical music filled the lobby of Alessandra's. The black veined white marble floor and light cream walls with large arched windows triggered no recent memories for Harry. As the hostess showed him and Sophia to their table, the men watched her cross the room. Harry figured if he wanted her to keep dating him, he'd have to up his game or someone else would take his place.

They ordered drinks, then looked over the menu. Sophia pushed hers aside and leaned in Harry's direction revealing a hint of cleavage.

She stared into his eyes. "I know you're worried about the cat. So, I asked the couple about the person who picked him up."

Here was his chance to tell her Van had returned home, but no plausible explanation popped in his mind.

"Did they give you any more information?" Harry leaned in closer.

She sighed. "They said it was too dark to see much, other

than a general shape: average height, not real thin, but not overweight either."

Most of the women Harry knew fell in that category.

Sophia frowned. "Not much of a description, but they thought it was the cat's owner, so they didn't pay much attention."

Harry figured it was the owner too but wondered why she left the cat at his place again. It didn't make any sense.

She leaned back in her chair. "If you want another cat, I can probably find one for you. People are always dropping off animals around my house."

"I don't really have time for pets." He rubbed his forehead. "The cat wandered into my place. I couldn't just throw him out."

"Why did you take him to a hotel? Cats usually do okay on their own for a night or two." She cut her eyes at him.

Harry ran through excuses in his mind until he found a plausible one that worked for him and Van.

"The power went out in my apartment. Only my unit." Harry rolled his eyes. "The landlord told me he couldn't get anyone to check on it until the next day." He pressed his hand to his chest. "I couldn't leave the cat alone in the dark without any AC."

Sophia's eyes softened as she looked at him. Harry hated lying to her, but he couldn't tell her the truth: his memory loss, the cat escapades, and the mysterious visitor. She'd think he was crazy. Hell, he thought he was crazy.

The waitress arrived with their drinks and took their order, giving Harry the opportunity to change the topic. "I noticed the magazines on your coffee table. Do you play the market?"

"Now and then. I find it interesting and fairly profitable."

Based on everything he'd seen so far; it was more than fairly profitable unless she had another source of funds.

"How long have you worked at the Star?" Sophia looked like she belonged in Alessandra's, not a sleazy motel like the Star. If Harry cleaned rooms, the Star would be the last spot he'd choose for employment.

"About a year. It's an interesting place. Unusual people." She gazed into his eyes. "I like the unusual."

If she liked unusual, then Harry was her man. Again, he contemplated telling her what had happened recently, but didn't want to risk scaring her off.

"Being a PI must be an exciting job." She sipped some wine, then licked her lips as if anticipating a good story.

Harry hated disappointing her, but this first year as a PI held nothing more adventurous than tailing people and taking pictures of errant partners.

"Some days are. Although, I saw more action when I was on the police force."

"Do you miss being a cop?"

Harry mentally compared his current life with his past, stakeouts with Buddy, talking about women, sports, and politics, then grabbing a beer afterwards.

"I miss the camaraderie." He missed everyone except Drake. Harry stabbed his steak and sliced off a piece.

"I'm getting bored with cleaning. So, let me know if you

decide to take on a partner." She smiled. Her eyes glimmered with mischief.

He grinned as he imagined stakeouts with Sophia. She would sure beat the hell out of any partner he'd had in the past.

"Can you start tonight?"

Sophia smiled and swirled the wine in her glass. "Maybe. Let's see how dinner goes."

After dinner, the waitress dropped dessert menus on their table.

"Would you excuse me for a few minutes?" Harry asked. He hated leaving her but viewing the crime scene might jolt his memory.

"Sure, take your time." She picked up the menu. "I'll check out the desserts."

Harry hustled into the lobby, entered an elevator, and selected seventeen. The door opened onto a foyer with a mirror hanging above a table with two lamps. No recognition flashed through his brain as he walked down the corridor. Yellow tape crossed the entrance to 1705. A woman and man were going over the room. He didn't recognize them from his time on the force, so he paused in the doorway.

"What happened here?"

The man narrowed his eyes, shook his head, and continued working. The woman frowned, crossed the room, and stood in front of Harry, blocking his view.

"As you can tell by the yellow tape, this is a crime scene." She placed her hands on her hips. "I hate vultures. No respect for the dead." She slammed the door in his face.

Damn woman. Harry didn't understand her anger. The body wasn't in the room anymore. He'd only gotten a glimpse of burgundy carpet and white tape outlining the body.

As he exited the elevator, Harry saw Drake walking in his direction. He considered ducking into a side hall or hiding behind a plant, but Drake quickened his pace and closed in on him. Purple bruises created half-moons under Drake's eyes. His long nose was swollen across the bridge.

Drake balled his hands into fists. "What are you doing here?" He narrowed his eyes.

Harry clenched his hands, then flexed them. "I'm having dinner. You should try the ribeye."

Drake leaned in close, then pushed against Harry's shoulder. "Don't be a smart ass with me."

Harry wanted to punch Drake's face in but resisted. He wouldn't strike the first blow, and technically, an open hand against his shoulder didn't count as a hit. Pushing Drake back might provoke him to throw a punch. If he did, Harry would beat the shit out of him this time. Still, shoving Drake seemed childish. He had better ways of spending his time tonight than fighting.

Drake glared at him. "Stay away from the crime scene."

The elevator dinged.

Drake looked beyond Harry. "I gotta go. This man may have the evidence I need to arrest you."

Harry turned to see the guy from the crime scene. Their eyes met and recognition crossed the man's face. Harry had to get out of there before the guy said anything. He moved past

Drake and into the restaurant.

Sophia sat at the table, focused on her phone. She looked up as he pulled out his chair.

"I was wondering if you'd left me with the tab." Her laughter erased the encounter with Drake from his mind.

"Me? Never. Did you choose a dessert?" Harry hoped she hadn't. If the forensics team had found any evidence implicating Harry, Drake would waste no time fastening cuffs on him. Not exactly the way he wanted to end the date.

"They didn't have any of my favorites."

Jack's Joint was a couple of blocks from Alessandra's. Maybe he could convince Sophia to go for a drink after supper tomorrow night. If Lisa frequented the bar, then so might her lover. Harry could shop the lover's picture around the place. Someone might recognize the face. It was a long shot, but Harry's life was a series of long shots and every once in while one paid off.

Harry checked his watch. "It's early. You want to try out being a partner tonight?"

She tilted her head and gave him a sly look. "What did you have in mind?"

Heat flooded Harry's body. He had a lot of things in mind but wasn't sure she was thinking along the same lines.

Harry cleared his throat. "I'm looking for a guy. He might hang out at Jack's Joint. It's just a couple of blocks over."

She shrugged. "Why not? I don't have to work tomorrow."

The atmosphere in Jack's Joint reminded Harry of a sports bar he and Buddy used to frequent, except back then the smoke-filled air added another layer of obscurity to the faces.

A football game played on several big screens. Harry spotted a couple of empty stools at the far end of the bar. The guys eyed Sophia and vocalized their approval as they walked across the room. Harry held her close, marking his territory.

They ordered drinks, scotch neat for Harry, red wine for Sophia.

After the bartender filled their glasses, Harry pulled out his phone and showed him a picture of Lisa's lover. "Ever seen this man?"

He leaned close to Harry's phone, touched it, and zoomed in on the photo. He pointed at the man's right eye. "Sure, he's got a scar at the corner of his eye. He's a regular. Comes in once a week. Always orders the same thing, Jack and Coke. Pays cash." He grinned. "Good tipper."

"Got a name?"

He frowned, then squinted. "Why all the questions?"

"You have a sister?"

"Yeah."

"What would you do if some guy was hitting her?"

He leaned in toward Harry. "I'd beat the shit out of him." The bartender shook his head. "He didn't seem like the type of guy to hit a girl. Guess you can never tell. I don't know his name. Sorry."

The bartender picked up a towel and wiped the bar, then stopped. "Wait a minute. Why not ask your sister for his name?"

Harry rolled his eyes. "She won't tell me. Afraid of what I'll do to the guy. Thinks I'll end up in jail." He stared at the bartender. "But some things are worth going to jail for."

The bartender nodded. "Yeah, you're right."

Harry ran his fingers up and down the side of his glass. "Did he drink with anyone else? Someone who might know his name?"

The bartender rubbed his chin and looked at the ceiling. After a few seconds, he said, "He talked with Jim a lot. He might know his name." He pointed toward the opposite end of the bar. "He's sitting down there."

Two guys sat at that end with a couple of empty stools separating them. One was a blond man dressed in a blue dress shirt who looked like he'd come from work or was waiting for a date. Harry glanced at the other guy. Tattoos crawled up his beefy arms, disappeared under his t-shirt, then wrapped around his thick neck.

"Jim's the one with the tats."

For once, Harry hoped he'd get the clean-cut guy instead of the one who looked like he'd done time.

The bartender raised his voice. "Hey, Jim. This guy wants to talk to you."

Jim looked up, then waved Harry over.

Harry and Sophia picked up their drinks, walked over, and introduced themselves. Sophia took the barstool next to the blond man and Harry grabbed the one next to Jim.

Harry pulled up a photo of Lisa's lover on his phone, then placed it on the bar. "Do you know this guy?"

Jim cut his eyes in Harry's direction. "Why do you want to know?"

The bartender placed a drink on the counter, then said, "The guy beat his sister. She won't give him a name." He glanced at Harry. "She's afraid he'll end up in jail."

"If there's anything I hate, it's a slime ball who beats a woman." Jim slammed his fist on the bar, the tattoos danced along his arm.

Harry choked on his drink. Sophia cleared her throat.

"His name is Chip. If he told me his last name, I don't remember it." Jim frowned.

"Know anything else about him?"

"He only talked to me when he was hammered, then all he did was complain about his job. He works at…" Jim stared into space, then turned to Harry. "Adrastos Oil and Gas, the downtown office. He hates the commute." Jim looked at his empty glass. Harry signaled the bartender for a refill.

After Jim's drink was poured, Harry asked, "Did he mention what kind of work he did?"

Jim swigged his beer, then wiped his mouth with the back of his hand. "His job had something to do with money. He griped because he had to work late at the end of every month, said it interfered with his bar time."

Harry picked up his phone and flipped to a picture of Lisa. "Ever seen her?"

Jim squinted at the image. "I've seen her in here with Chip." He looked at Harry and narrowed his eyes. "Is that your sister? She doesn't look much like you."

He shrugged. "She's a friend of my sister's. Her mother asked me to check up on her."

Jim's grip tightened on his beer as if it were Chip's neck.

Harry dismissed the twinge of guilt for lying about Chip. He needed to catch a killer.

"When did you last see them together?" Harry asked.

"Sunday night. They got into a fight. She stomped out of here."

"Could you hear what they said?" Harry wondered if the argument ended in murder.

"I wasn't close enough, but it must have been a doozie cause she slapped him." Jim smiled.

Harry raised an eyebrow. "What did Chip do?"

"He downed his drink, then went to the bathroom."

"What time did he leave?"

Jim shrugged. "I didn't see him after that, so I guess he left." He looked at the ceiling. "That was around ten."

The murderer stabbed Lisa sometime between ten and midnight. The walk to Alessandra's was ten minutes or less, plenty of time for Chip to kill her. Harry stood to leave. Jim grabbed his arm.

"Hey man, next time I see him I'll take care of him for you." He rolled his shoulders.

As much as Chip deserved a beating for adultery, Harry wanted him coherent enough to talk.

"If he shows up, call me first." He gave Jim his number. "I want the satisfaction of throwing the first punch."

A woman from the other end of the bar shouted for a

margarita. In the last few minutes, people had poured through the door. Harry wasn't claustrophobic but didn't like feeling bodies brush against his butt. Someone bumped Sophia, pushing her into him and spilling her red wine on the sleeve of his white shirt. Harry fought the urge to react as the liquid soaked into the material. He didn't want to ruin their evening.

Sophia grabbed her napkin and dabbed the stain. "I'm so sorry."

"Don't worry about it. It's not your fault."

Harry grabbed her arm. "Let's get out of here."

He flagged down the bartender, ordered another refill for Jim, and paid the tab, leaving a hefty tip.

Harry held out his hand to Jim. "Thanks for the information." They shook hands.

As Sophia and Harry passed a man seated at the bar, he leaned forward and shouted down the counter to another man, "Hey Matt, where's Victoria tonight?"

The name, Victoria, rippled through Harry's mind like currents after a rock was tossed into a pond. The bra, the card case, and the gift bag were all labeled Victoria. Were they left as clues pointing to the owner's name? He turned to get a glimpse of the man asking the question and the one answering, but the crowd closed in around them hiding both men and drowning the answer.

Sophia pulled him towards the exit. "Let's go before the stain sets."

The tension across Harry's shoulders eased as they left the bar and headed in the direction of his car. The night was quiet, and no bodies pressed against him, although he wouldn't complain if Sophia's did.

"What are you going to do when you find the guy who hit your sister?" asked Sophia.

Harry debated whether to tell the truth or not. If he wanted a long-term relationship with her, he couldn't continue to lie about his family. "I'm an only child."

She cut her eyes at him. "So, you lied?"

Harry raised an eyebrow. "I prevaricated."

"You lied," she said, snapping her mouth shut.

"I didn't say I had a sister. I said, what if some guy was hitting your sister. He assumed I had a sister who was being abused."

She put a hand on her hip and glared at him. "What do you think will happen when the bartender sees the guy in the picture?"

"Hopefully, I find him first." Harry's phone rang: Buddy. Sophia might get madder if he answered it or she might cool off while he talked. It was worth a shot.

He held up the phone. "Work. I've got to take this."

Sophia tapped her foot. Harry figured she didn't believe him.

"Hey Man, remember that favor you owe me. I'm collecting on it."

Buddy hadn't given him Rachel's information yet.

"How can you collect on a favor that you haven't done?" Harry asked.

"I promise I'll get it to you tomorrow."

Harry sighed. What do you want me to do?" He hoped it

was something quick and easy.

"I need you to tail someone for me."

Harry groaned. He didn't have that kind of time, but he needed Rachel's information. Plus, he would probably need Buddy's help in the future.

"I'm really busy, but I'll do what I can. Give me the details."

"I need you to follow a guy named Mark Crawford, a possible stalker. Write down where he goes and who he sees. Take pictures. If he does anything illegal, call me."

"Address? Car?"

"He's thirty-five, just under six feet tall, athletic build, brown hair, blue eyes. He lives with his mother at 603 Harwin. Drives a white Camry."

Harry looked over at Sophia while he memorized the details. "Who's he stalking?" Sophia's eyes widened.

"Aw, shit. Drake is calling. I gotta go." Buddy rang off.

Harry didn't need to know the woman's name. A guy watching and following the same woman too many times was easy to spot. Of course, Mark could be stalking a guy, but a woman was more likely.

Harry made notes on his phone, then looked at Sophia. With her crossed arms and frowning face, he wasn't getting anywhere with her tonight.

Sophia shook her head. "A fabricated sister, a lost cat, and now a stalker. What will it be next?"

Harry didn't want to know.

As Harry drove onto Sophia's street, she turned toward him

and said, "Do you always tell lies?"

Harry cleared his throat. "Only when needed for my job." He glanced at her and smiled. "I would never lie to you."

"Sounds like a lie to me." Sophia laughed.

Harry figured if she was joking and laughing, he might still have a shot at a kiss goodnight. He parked in front of her house and reached for his door handle.

"No need to walk me to the door." Sophia got out of the car, then leaned back inside. "Maybe next time." She smiled and shut the door.

Harry watched her until she walked inside her place and closed her door. As he drove home, the words "Maybe next time" lingered in his mind.

28

When Harry arrived home, he checked his watch. It wasn't too late to check on Charley. She was tough but finding a dead body would throw anyone off their game.

When they were kids, Charley hung out with the guys, catching snakes, frogs, and lizards. She even took on the neighborhood bully when he picked on a little kid. She grabbed the bully by his hair and dragged him around by it until he cried.

The phone continued ringing in his ear. Just as he was about to give up and walk over to Charley's, she answered, "What's up, Harry?" Her voice sounded weak as if she'd been ill.

"How are you doing?" Harry asked.

"I'm better now. Just about to take a hot bath." She paused. "What did Buddy want with you?"

Telling her they had discovered another body would only worry her.

"We didn't get a chance to really talk. Drake showed up so I left."

She laughed. "Probably a good idea."

"Yeah, I'm not his favorite person." He rolled his eyes.

Someone knocked on his door. A peek through the peephole showed Drake and Buddy standing in the hall. Harry knew not to ignore them; they'd keep trying until they got him.

He spoke into the phone, "Speak of the Devil, he just showed up at my door."

"Better let him inside before he decides to break in." She sounded amused.

"You never know with Drake. I'll call you later."

Harry hung up, pasted a smile on his face, and opened the door.

"Gentlemen, what can I do for you?"

Drake glared at Harry. The bruises under his eyes had faded but apparently not the anger.

"Seems we have a problem," Drake said.

Based on Drake's expression, Harry was the problem.

"Have a seat." With his middle finger Harry pointed toward the couch. He doubted Drake picked up on the gesture, but if he did all the better.

Buddy walked past Drake, sank into the couch, and pulled out a notebook and pen. Drake sat on the other end, but on the edge as if the back of the sofa might bite. Harry sank into the recliner. Van scooted out of the room. Harry wished he could leave too.

Drake rubbed his chin and looked around. "How's the PI business?"

Harry shrugged. "I like the boss."

Buddy laughed. Drake frowned.

Harry didn't have time for verbal games with Drake. "So, what's the problem?"

"Explain why your fingerprints were found in Lisa's hotel room," Drake said.

Harry suspected Drake planted the fingerprints to incriminate him, but he didn't have any evidence of such. Without any memory of that night, he couldn't accuse Drake. Besides, did Drake really hate him enough to risk his career in the police force? He doubted it.

Mixing truth with lies, Harry weaved a tale. "David Angel hired me to follow Lisa. He thought she was cheating on him."

Buddy nodded, indicating they already knew this.

Harry forced his body to remain relaxed as he danced around the information Buddy had given him; or perhaps he told the truth. With no memory of what happened, anything was possible.

"I followed Lisa and her lover to Alessandra's. I bought a bottle of champagne, borrowed two glasses and a corkscrew, then knocked on her door and offered it to her, compliments of the hotel."

Harry checked their expressions and body language. No pursed lips, no crossed arms. They seemed to buy his story so far.

"Her lover wasn't in the bedroom, but the bathroom door was closed. While opening the bottle, I looked around the room for any clue as to who he was but found nothing. I poured a glass for her, then asked if I needed to pour another. She nodded but didn't volunteer any information. I figured they were in for the night, so I went home."

Drake's eyes hardened. "We only found Lisa's and your fingerprints in the room."

"No way. Those hotel rooms are loaded with fingerprints from hotel staff and previous guests. Guests whose fingerprints probably aren't registered in your database." Harry clenched his hands.

Drake flushed. "All right, Smart Ass, then you should have a charge for the champagne."

"I paid cash." Harry looked around the room. "I'm sure I've got the receipt somewhere. Do you want me to look for it?" He hoped the answer was no.

Drake crossed his arms. "We don't have time for your bullshit. Bring it by the station later."

The receipt didn't matter. They'd check his story with the hotel staff. If nothing else, it bought Harry some time. Time to either find Lisa's killer or find an alibi.

"Did anyone see you enter her room?" Drake asked.

"Not that I remember." Harry had no clue as to what really happened.

"What's Lisa's lover's name?" Drake jangled the handcuffs on his belt as if he itched for a reason to drag Harry downtown.

Harry shook his head. "I don't know." Providing them just Chip's first name wouldn't help much. If he told them where Chip worked too, then they would have enough information to find him, but Harry wanted to talk with Chip before the cops did.

"Have you noticed anything unusual happening around

here?" Drake asked.

Buddy widened his eyes and shook his head slightly, indicating he hadn't told Drake that Harry knew about the bodies in the parking lot.

"I heard sirens just after lunch today." Harry pointed toward his window. "Saw cop cars in the parking lot. What's going on?"

"We found two bodies." Drake narrowed his eyes. "You'd better hope we don't find your fingerprints at those crime scenes." Drake stood and motioned to Buddy. "Let's go."

Van ran across Drake's path. He stumbled. "Damn cat."

Buddy snickered. Drake's head whipped in Buddy's direction. Buddy covered his mouth and cleared his throat.

After they left, Harry gave Van a rub and a treat.

"I should make you a partner. Bennett and Van Detective Agency."

Harry grabbed the flask from the drawer in his bedroom. One drink couldn't hurt. What was he thinking? One drink always led to more drinks. He carried the flask to the kitchen and poured the scotch down the sink.

He occupied himself checking email, then reading the latest news which made him wish he hadn't tossed the scotch. After about thirty minutes, Harry gave Buddy a call. If he was still with Drake, then he wouldn't answer the phone.

"What's up Harry?" Buddy asked.

"Got any updates on the body in Charley's trunk?"

"Yeah, but you can't share it with anyone else."

"Of course not." Harry decided Charley probably wasn't

included in the anyone else.

"Even Charley." Buddy's tone took on his cop no-nonsense formality.

Harry sighed. "You've got it." Besides, what could Charley do with the information?

"All right then. The body in her trunk was a thirty something Caucasian male. Shot in the head. Looks like a professional hit. We haven't got an ID on him yet."

"What about the other body? Where was it? Any ID?" Harry asked.

"The other body was found in a car in the far corner of the parking lot." Buddy sighed. "He had a CIA badge on him. We haven't notified his next of kin so I can't tell you his name."

"CIA?" Harry stared at his phone.

"Yep. Shot in the head too." Buddy paused. "Damn. Drake is calling me. I gotta go."

Harry hung up the phone. Why would the CIA be watching someone in the apartments? It didn't make sense. The building didn't seem like a hot bed of international crime, but that probably made it the perfect location for criminals.

Harry set the camera to record then went to bed where he stared at the ceiling. Possible suspects and explanations for his fingerprints ran through his mind followed by regrets and mistakes he had made. Unfortunately, there was no do-over button, he could press.

Harry picked up his cell phone and checked the time: 3:00 AM. He had to get some sleep, or he would never figure out who really killed Lisa. Visions of Drake arresting him, the satisfied smirk crossing his face as he threw Harry in jail, and the slamming off the cell door swam before his eyes. Harry got up and took a sleeping pill.

29

The next morning as Van scarfed down the cat pate, Harry wondered if the cat's owner would ever return to claim him. He kind of liked having a feline companion, less trouble than a dog and less stress than a woman. He looked askance at Van. Of course, a woman came with fringe benefits and no litter box.

Harry left Van to his breakfast and dressed in business casual for his trip to Adrastos, then headed for downtown.

Halfway to Chip's office, David called and demanded Harry drop by his place before doing anything else. He didn't want to go, but paying clients had first dibs on his time.

Harry pressed the doorbell. David answered the door. His eyelids had lost their puffiness, but his eyes looked haunted as if demons chased him.

"Come on in." David motioned Harry forward. "Let's go to my study."

Harry followed David through the entryway and into an adjoining room. Sunlight filtered through the trees and past three arched windows leaving trails of light on the oriental rug, wood desk, and the books sitting in shelves along the walls. David sat in the desk chair. While Harry took a seat on the other side as if he were a student waiting for a reprimand from the principal.

"The cops came by after you left yesterday. I told them about our arrangement," David said.

"What did you say our arrangement was?" Harry hoped it didn't conflict with what he'd told the cops.

"That I'd hired you to tail Lisa because I thought she was cheating on me."

David had given them the same answer as Harry which raised the believability factor of everything else Harry told the police. Although, that might not matter to Drake.

"Did you tell them I'm still working for you?"

David shook his head. "I didn't see any reason to tell them." He grabbed a pen and fiddled with it. "They said your fingerprints were found in the hotel room where Lisa was murdered." He looked at Harry. "You didn't kill Lisa. Did you?"

Harry frowned. "What reason would I have for killing her?"

"I don't know." He sighed. "The cops think I paid you to kill her."

"They're nuts." Drake would find any reason to implicate Harry.

David pursed his lips. "How did your fingerprints get in her room?"

Harry told him the same story he told the cops. Repeating it helped solidify it in his mind.

David stared and rubbed his lip as if weighing the likelihood of the explanation. "Like you say, you had no reason to kill her, but the cops think one of us did it."

Harry pegged David as the type to kill Lisa's lover. Maybe David saw Lisa as his possession and his alone. In which case, he might have murdered her to ensure no one else could ever have her.

"That's because they have no other suspects." Harry shrugged. "We're easy targets."

"Then we need to give them some. Better yet, find the sleazeball who killed her."

"I've got a lead on the guy Lisa saw every once in a while." Somehow, Harry thought it inappropriate to say Lisa's lover.

David clenched his jaw. "When are you seeing the bastard?" He scribbled lines back and forth across a pad of paper, pressing hard as if the anger could transfer from his body to the sheet.

"I was going to check out the lead when you called."

"Let me know what you find." David ripped off the paper, wadded it up, then tossed it aside.

Harry thought based on the fate of the paper, the police might find Chip's lifeless body next.

"Will do. Of course, he might not have killed her."

"I'm betting he did." David narrowed his eyes. "And I'm expecting you to prove it."

The closest available parking garage was several blocks from Adrastos's multi-story mirrored building. After circling the garage ten times, climbing ever higher, Harry finally found a parking spot. Opening his car door, brought a one-two punch: the stench of exhaust fumes and oppressive humidity.

By the time he got to Adrastos, sweat dripped off him like he'd walked through a steam room. When he walked in the lobby, he took a moment to enjoy the cool air greeting him.

Behind the counter, a twenty-something blonde receptionist smiled. Harry flashed his sexiest smile.

"Can I help you, Sir?" she asked.

Harry's eyes widened and his mouth fell open. No one had ever called him, Sir. Sir conjured up pictures of old farts.

"I'm here to see Chip…" He rubbed his chin and looked at the ceiling. "What is his last name?" Chip wasn't a common name. With any luck, only one worked for the company.

She rolled her eyes. "It's okay, Sir. Take your time."

She probably thought his memory was shot. He could play this to his advantage.

"It's something like…" He moved his eyes back and forth like he searched for an answer in the air.

A line started forming behind him.

"Do you know what department he works in?" She chewed on the tip of her fingernail.

Harry enjoyed this game. He scratched his head. "Something to do with money."

She looked at the ceiling. "Probably the Accounting Department." She clicked away on her keyboard. "Chip Barnes?"

He pointed a finger at her. "That's it."

"Let me call him. What's your name?"

"Harry Bennett."

She punched a few buttons on her phone, then spoke into her headset. "Mr. Barnes, a Mr. Bennett is here to see you."

"Just have a seat over there." She motioned to some chairs. "He should be down shortly, Sir."

Harry squinted in the direction she indicated as if he couldn't see them.

She sighed. "Walk right pass the fake tree, then the chairs are on your right."

Harry left the counter and grabbed a seat in the far corner, next to the windows.

Within minutes, a guy carrying a notepad exited the far bank of elevators. As he headed for the lobby, Harry recognized him. Chip walked with a swagger and a smile as if everyone liked him. His white polo stretched tightly across his broad shoulders. He pushed his blond hair back from his forehead on his way to the front desk. Chip exchanged a few words with the receptionist, then she pointed at Harry.

As they shook hands, Chip's eyes searched Harry's face as if trying to place him.

"Harry Bennett. I was a friend of Lisa's." He smiled.

Chip furrowed his brow. "Lisa?"

"Lisa Angel." Harry arched an eyebrow. "The two of you were having an affair."

Brown eyes the color of mud popped wide. "What?"

Harry had expected exaggerated denial. It's what the guilty did. "No use playing games. I have photos of the two of you together."

Chip's eyes narrowed. "What are you doing taking pictures?"

"It's my job. I'm a private investigator." Harry flashed his identification.

"Who hired you?" Chip leaned into Harry's space as if doing so would force him to answer.

Harry stared at Chip and kept his face impassive. "I don't reveal client information."

"Why are you bothering me with this?"

"I've been hired to find Lisa's killer."

Chip sucked in air and blinked. "Lisa's dead?"

Harry figured either Chip didn't follow the news, or he should take up acting.

Chip nervously turned toward the reception area as if to collect his thoughts. Harry followed his gaze. Drake stood in the waiting line at the front desk. He wondered if Drake had discovered Chip was Lisa's lover. It didn't matter. Harry needed to get out of there before Drake saw him.

"I don't want to keep you from work. Let's get together later," Harry said.

Chip's face hardened. "I don't have to talk to you."

"No, you don't." Harry leaned closer. "Although the police might find the pictures interesting." Chip's expression didn't change. Harry noticed the gold band circling the ring finger on Chip's left hand. "Or perhaps your wife?"

Chip eyes widened and he held up a hand. "All right. Not tonight. Come by my place around ten tomorrow morning. My wife will be out." He ripped a page out of his pad, wrote down his phone number and address, then handed it to him.

"By the way, you might want to stay away from Jack's Joint for a while," Harry said.

Chip squinted. "Why?"

"I heard a couple of guys are out to get you. Not sure why, but it's probably best to avoid the place." At least, Harry had warned him. If Chip went there later, he deserved whatever happened.

After Chip left, Harry walked along the wall toward the exit, watching as Drake moved past the fake tree. Just as Harry thought he was in the clear, Drake stopped. His head turned back as if he'd felt Harry's eyes on him.

Harry slid between two men talking to each other. They frowned as if annoyed by his interference. He searched for something to say that would excuse his behavior.

"Sorry for the interruption, but I'm running late. Do you know where I can grab a cab?"

Harry smiled but didn't listen to their answer. Instead, he watched as Drake's head slowly turned, searching the lobby. Harry held his breath as Drake's gaze swept past the two men hiding him and onto a man talking on a phone. Drake shrugged, then continued walking in the direction of the chairs.

Harry exhaled and returned to the cab discussion. The two men looked at Harry like they expected him to speak. Harry thanked them, then exited the building and headed for his car.

As Harry buckled his seat belt, Buddy's text came through.

I checked the silver Mustang at 5151 Kirby. The woman still had the car, but it wasn't worth buying.

Buddy's cryptic message showed his paranoia. With Drake as his partner, he might have good reason.

Harry keyed in 5151 Kirby into the GPS app and hoped Rachel's silver Mustang still sat in the driveway. He wanted names of people who hated Lisa enough to kill her and Rachel might be just the one to give them to him.

30

Charley picked up her pencil and checked another item on her list. It was mid-morning, and she was no closer to cracking the message. She walked into her kitchen and grabbed a Diet Coke.

Her phone rang. She checked the display. At the sight of the name, her shoulders tensed. She took a deep breath, exhaled, and answered. "Hi Derek."

"I called to check on you." He paused. "Look, I understand if you're not up to working. Tom has offered to take over decoding the message."

"Thanks for the offer but working helps. It distracts me from thinking about things." A snapshot of her trunk and the plastic-wrapped body popped inside her head. She focused on the script displayed on her computer screen.

"Tom can, at least, help you. He should call you sometime today so think of what he can do to speed things up." He paused and cleared his throat. "The police came by my office."

Charley chewed on her nail.

"I need to tell you some things before the cops show up again at your place." His voice sounded hesitant, almost apologetic. "We were concerned when we couldn't locate your predecessor, so we assigned someone from the CIA to locate him. It was unlike John to disappear, so we also had someone watch your place."

Charley dropped her pencil. "What? You knew I was in danger and didn't tell me?"

"We didn't want to worry you if it proved to be nothing."

She narrowed her eyes. "You didn't tell me because I might not have taken the job."

"I can assure you that wasn't the reason." His voice had a cutting edge to it.

She slammed her palm on the desk. "You suspected something had happened to the guy who was trying to crack the message. I was just bait."

"We don't use our office workers as bait." He cleared his throat again. "The guy we had watching you was found dead in his car. The police also identified the body in your trunk. It was John Howard."

Charley's mouth fell open. "What? John? The one who had this job before me?" She looked at her door and verified the deadbolt was locked. "This job is not worth me risking my life." Charley's thoughts raced. She could get another job. If money got tight, she could move in with her mother. Charley frowned. Sweat beaded on her forehead. She yanked off her pink sweatshirt.

He cleared his throat again. She had just about had it with all the throat clearing. "We need your help to catch the killer."

She stood and paced in front of her desk. "Are you kidding

me? I'm a cryptanalyst not a CIA Officer." Charley ran her fingers through her hair. "So, you just want me to sit here decoding this stupid message while some guy is out there waiting to kill me?" She shook her head. "I don't think so. Besides, you just said you don't use office workers as bait."

"We'll send someone else over to watch your place."

She laughed. "Like that worked so well last time."

Charley wondered why they hadn't killed her already. They might have figured she didn't have enough experience in decoding and wasn't a threat. Or they couldn't shoot her because she rarely left her apartment and kept all the blinds closed.

"The cops are going to question you. They may even look at you as a suspect. We need to catch who did this for your sake as well as ours. Just focus on work and we'll take care of the rest."

Charley gritted her teeth. She didn't want to go to jail for something she didn't do but she didn't want to die either. If she quit, how long would it take for the assassin to get the message she had quit? Probably not quick enough to stop the guy from killing her. The CIA might be her only hope.

Derek cleared his throat again. Charley rolled her eyes and waited for the next bomb to drop.

"Unfortunately, the CIA only intervenes with the police for our officers not for our general staff. So, you'll have to undergo whatever the cops feel is necessary for their investigation. However, don't worry I'm sure we'll catch whoever did this."

As she hung up, Charley realized he had stopped short of

saying "before they kill you."

Charley stared at her monitor. The cursor blinked, demanding her to do something. She sighed, then picked up her empty coffee mug and headed for the kitchen. A shot of caffeine might improve her productivity. She poured the liquid and gazed into its dark depths as if they held the answer to her problem. The ringing of her phone interrupted any wisdom the liquid might have imparted. She checked the caller ID. Tom's name flashed across the display with a request for a FaceTime session.

Charley looked down at her red and black plaid pajamas and wondered if they could pass for regular clothes. She snatched the pink sweatshirt off the sofa, pulled it over her head, looked in the mirror on the wall above the sofa, smoothed her hair, and checked her teeth for food particles, then answered the phone.

"Hi Tom." Charley had met him at the last team video conference. Even then, the resolution of her screen couldn't stop the sparkle in his blue eyes from reaching her. When he smiled, his white teeth flashed against his tan skin. No grey showed in his dark hair. Her intel put his age at forty-five, single, and a player.

"Hi Charley. I'm calling to help you in any way I can."

Charley had ideas of how he could help her, but none were work related. She sat at her desk and placed the phone so it leaned against her monitor.

"Maybe you'll have better luck with finding the encryption

key than I have so far," she said.

"Let's start with what you've tried and go over what you plan to try next," Tom said.

She opened her notebook and went through the list while Tom scribbled notes on a pad of paper.

Tom tapped a pen against his five o'clock shadowed face. "Let's split up what you have planned. I've researched the sender and receiver and have some other keys we could try too." He paused. "From what Derek told me, this is on a tight timeline."

"Yes, the sooner we solve it the better." Charley wasn't sure if he knew about her trunk incident but didn't want to discuss it anyway.

Tom's eyes softened and the sparkle disappeared. "Derek told me what happened." He shook his head. "It's hard to believe. Why would someone shoot John, wrap him in plastic, and leave him in your trunk?" He frowned. "I'm surprised you haven't quit."

Charley widened her eyes. "So, he was shot?"

Tom nodded. "The other guy was shot too." He squinted. "Didn't Derek tell you?"

She let out an exasperated sigh. "No, he didn't." Charley wondered what else her boss had neglected to say.

"He probably forgot. He's got a lot going on." Tom shook his head. "And now this."

"Maybe." Her boss seemed to have a habit of hiding things from her.

"Well, I'd better get started on my list." He winked. "I'll keep you posted on my progress."

"Thanks, Tom." Charley smiled and hung up. Players weren't her style, but maybe it was time to give it a try. She shook her head. What was she thinking? The message had to be cracked or she might not live to do any playing.

Charley showered, applied makeup, and dressed in her best jeans and a black shirt. She didn't want to greet the cops dressed in her plaid flannel pajamas.

It was another hour before Buddy and Drake knocked on her door. She took a deep breath, exhaled, then opened the door and let them inside.

Charley had known Drake since childhood when they both attended the same school. When they were children, Drake would sit at his desk and sulk. Based on the frown spread across his face, he hadn't changed much as an adult.

"We have some questions for you," Drake said.

Charley forced a smile and motioned them into her living area. "Have a seat."

Drake sat in one beanbag chair and Buddy took the other one. Both looked uncomfortable with their backs unsupported, and their legs sprawled out in front of them. One day she would get a sofa and a couple of recliners or maybe a loveseat. Although, it was kind of entertaining watching Drake struggle with the beanbag.

"Can I get you something to drink? Water, iced tea, a soda?" She wasn't sure if it was proper etiquette to offer cops anything, but southern hospitality required it. Plus, she wanted to get on their good side. If Drake even had one.

"No thanks." Buddy smiled.

Drake shook his head. They each brought out a pocket notebook and a pen.

Charley cleared away some papers from the remaining beanbag chair and sat across from them.

Drake leaned toward her and said, "The body in your trunk was John Howard. From what we understand, he was previously in your position." He stared at her without expression. "How well did you know him?"

"I didn't know him. He disappeared before I took this role." They couldn't think she had anything to do with his death. Why kill someone you never even met?

"Had you been wanting this position for a while?" Drake's face was a stern reflection reminiscent of her mother when Charley did a major faux pas.

"Not really. I thought the role would be a good fit for me and I was ready for something more challenging." She resisted rolling her eyes. Did they really think she would kill someone to get a job? Charley looked over at Buddy to see if he shared her opinion, but he was busy taking notes.

Drake rubbed his bottom lip as he consulted his notebook. "Do you know of anyone who he had problems with? Or who had problems with him?"

"Like I said, I didn't know him. His name never came up in conversation except when I discussed the position with my manager."

Drake checked his writing again. "Do you know a Vincent

Minnelli?"

Charley shook her head. She figured Vincent was the other dead body. His name sounded like someone from the mob.

"Besides the note you got, have you had any other threats?" Drake asked.

"Nothing else."

"Do you own a gun?" Drake looked around the room as if he expected to see one.

"No." She opened her mouth to say how ridiculous it was to suspect her, but decided the less said, the better. She put her hand over her mouth as if suppressing a yawn.

"Does anyone else have keys to your car? Or are you in the habit of leaving it unlocked?"

"I keep the spare key here. I usually lock my car." She paused. "The last time it was raining, and I had groceries, so I might have forgotten."

"Before yesterday, when was the last time you opened your trunk?" Drake asked.

She stared off into space and visualized the last few days. "Monday."

Drake referenced his notes. "Where were you between the hours of two and four yesterday morning?"

"Here. Asleep in bed. By myself." Her days of partying into the wee hours of the morning were long gone. Now, she struggled staying up past midnight.

Drake stood to leave, and Buddy followed his lead. "That's all the questions we have for now," Drake said.

After they left, Charley reflected on what they had asked.

The alibi question seemed strange. It must be the time of death for Vincent. It could be John, but he had been missing for close to two weeks. Had they held him captive and tortured him before killing him? A quick death was one thing, but torture? Charley shivered.

She grabbed the sharpest knife from the kitchen, placed it next to the bat by the front door, and double checked the lock.

31

When Harry's car turned the corner onto Rachel's street, the afternoon sun forced him to flip down the visor and crank up the AC. Once he located her address, he pulled close to park in front of the white framed cottage. Before he could get out of his car, a silver Mustang backed down the driveway with Rachel in the driver's seat. He followed the car and hoped she traveled to a spot conducive for asking questions. With his luck, she'd probably end up at a nail salon or a library.

She exited the freeway, drove a few blocks, then pulled into Jack's Joint. Harry blinked. With all the options in Houston, he was surprised she had chosen Jack's. Harry didn't think the price of the drinks, or the ambiance justified its apparent popularity. He glanced at the time, 4:14, a little early for hitting a bar. Maybe Rachel was as wild as her hair.

Harry parked in the far corner of the lot and watched as she got out of her car. The owlish glasses were still perched on her nose, but the errant hair was tamed into a bun. Her knee length black skirt revealed shapely calves struggling in high heels on the uneven pavement as she made her way to Jack's entrance.

He waited until the door closed behind her, then headed for the bar.

As Harry stepped into the place, cold air, and the smell of stale beer assaulted him. Without Sophia to distract him and with the sunlight from the open door, he had a better view of the interior. Dim lamps hung above wood tables, each surrounded by barstools. Booths lined the walls. Rachel sat in a back booth looking up at a waitress. Once the door closed behind him, the room darkened as if the night reigned twenty-four hours a day.

Harry chose a corner booth farthest from Rachel's, then slid into the shadows. After the waitress left Rachel, she dropped by his table and took his drink order. With only a few customers, she returned quickly and placed a beer on his table. As he took a swig of his beer, a shaft of light infiltrated the darkness, then vanished. Harry couldn't see who had entered but noticed Rachel smile and wave.

As the person passed near a hanging lamp, Harry recognized the swagger, the shoulders straining the seams of the white polo, and the blond hair, Chip.

Harry choked on his drink.

Chip must have met Rachel through Lisa. Maybe they were commiserating her death. It was the only thing that made any sense. Still, Harry didn't think Chip's wife would appreciate him meeting another woman in a bar.

Chip walked to the back booth and sat across from Rachel. She smiled but offered no physical contact. Harry watched them, looking for signs of intimacy. Rachel chatted but stayed in her own personal space. Chip's hands never strayed toward her.

Light spilled into the place. Rachel glanced up, then returned to talking with Chip. As the customer walked up to the bar, Harry recognized the muscular arms and the tattoos scrawled along them. If Jim saw Harry, he might ask about his sister or if he'd dealt with Chip. Harry hid behind his menu.

Jim pulled up a barstool and sat with his back to Harry's booth, then ordered a beer. Harry needed to sneak out of the place. He couldn't hide behind a menu forever.

Harry dropped cash on the table. As he slid to the edge of his booth, Jim looked around the bar. Harry ducked behind the menu and watched Jim out of the corner of his eye.

Jim looked at the bartender. "Business is slow."

The bartender nodded. "It's early yet."

Harry's peripheral vision caught movement in the far corner. Chip picked up Rachel's drink, walked to the bar, ordered a refill, and smiled at Jim.

"How's it going?" Chip asked.

Jim frowned and nodded toward Rachel. "She know you hit women."

Chip pushed back from the bar. "What are you talking about? I never hit a woman in my life."

"That's not what I heard." Jim narrowed his eyes. "Some guy said you hit his sister." He looked at Rachel.

"I told you. I don't hit women. You can ask her." He motioned toward her and raised his voice. "Rachel, would you come over here?"

Rachel eased out of her booth and walked toward them.

"Look Man, if you're hitting her, she's not going to say anything." Jim took a swig of his beer.

Harry would catch up with Rachel another time. He dropped the menu and slid out of the booth. Chip was on his own. Next time he might just follow Harry's advice.

Chip ran his fingers through his hair. "What guy said I hit his sister?"

Jim looked in the mirror behind the bar. His eyes met Harry's.

Harry had run out of time. He raced for the exit.

Jim turned and pointed at Harry, "That guy."

Harry pushed through the door and ran to his car. He opened the door, fell into the seat, and started the car as he yanked the door closed. The tires squealed as he floored the accelerator and sped out of the parking lot. In his rearview mirror, Harry saw Jim standing at the bar's door, shading his eyes with a hand, looking in his direction. Harry hoped Chip hadn't seen him. If he had, he'd either refuse to meet Harry again or take a swing at him when Harry showed up at Chip's house.

Harry figured he should stay away from Jack's Joint for a while, maybe forever. He didn't really have time to tail the stalker for Buddy, but a promise was a promise. He pulled into a gas station and plugged Mark Crawford's address into his GPS.

32

Harry brushed the crumbs from his lap, wadded up the burger wrapper, then shoved it in the takeout bag. He hated eating food in his car, the smell, and the mess, but it was part of his job when he worked as a cop and still held true as a PI. If anything, the work of a private investigator required even more hours of watching and waiting.

Mark's white Camry sat in the driveway, but no one had come in or out of the red-brick-ranch-style house. The place reminded him of the one he lived in as a kid. When he and Drake were friends, playing ball in the front yard or four-square on the sidewalk. Drake always complained about his younger sister. Beth pestered them or even worse, tattled on them. Harry smiled. Good times.

Then came the teenage years when testosterone ran hot, and Billy moved into the neighborhood. From the day Billy arrived, he caused trouble with the teachers and picked fights with the other kids. A vision of Billy on top of Drake slugging his face flashed in Harry's mind. As Drake struggled to get free, Harry had grabbed Billy by the hair and yanked him off Drake, then

Harry punched Billy in the face. Billy jabbed Harry in the gut. Harry returned a right hook and knocked him out.

From then on, Harry and Drake went everywhere together, until college separated them: Drake to the University of Texas, Harry to Texas A&M. Beth followed Harry to A&M. Unfortunately, so did Billy.

Harry checked his rearview mirror. In the distance, the sky turned black, and lightening flashed. Harry hated following someone in the rain. The residential streets didn't pose a problem, but on the freeways, the cars turned into a blur of taillights. He drummed the steering wheel with his thumbs and focused on Mark's front door as if willing it to open.

The sky darkened, wind blew through the trees, and rain began drizzling, then turned into a downpour. Water streamed down his windows dimming his view of the house.

Through the haze, a light poured from the front door, then stopped. A guy with an athletic build ran through the storm toward the Camry. Red taillights backed down the driveway. Harry followed him, driving close. In this weather, no one would suspect or even see a tail.

Harry trailed the Camry onto the freeway ramp. A few minutes later, the Camry exited and pulled into the Star Motel. For such a sleazy place, it sure was popular. Harry frowned. If Mark was meeting a woman, he wouldn't impress her with his choice of motels. No woman would appreciate the decor or filthiness of the establishment.

The rain slowed to a drizzle. Harry debated whether to wait in the car or go inside. He needed to verify that Mark drove the car and not someone else.

Harry followed the Camry driver into the lobby, then picked up some brochures for local sights. In between flipping pages, he peeked at the guy and verified Buddy's description of him: brown wet strips of hair plastered his forehead forming bangs that hung just above blue eyes. Foggy glasses crowned the top of his head.

Sam stood behind the counter. "What can I do for you?"

"Mark Crawford. I have a reservation." Mark handed cash to Sam.

Sam counted the money and stuffed it in a drawer. He checked his monitor, then handed him a key. "Just leave the key in the room when you're done."

Harry doubted Mark planned to stalk anyone at the motel. Otherwise, why bother checking into the place when Mark could just watch them from the parking lot?

"Sure. Thanks." Mark nodded in Sam's direction and left.

Harry placed the brochure back in the stand, then headed for the exit, hoping to leave unnoticed.

"Can I help you?" Sam said.

Harry considered ignoring him but didn't want to arouse Sam's suspicions. Harry turned toward him.

Sam's eyes widened. "Did you find the cat?"

Getting into a discussion of how he found the cat would only prolong the conversation. Plus, Sophia didn't know Van had returned. With Harry's luck Sam would probably tell Sophia the cat had been found, then she would think Harry did nothing but lie.

"No, I just stopped by to see if someone had."

"Afraid not. Did you ask the maid?"

Harry moved closer toward the exit. Time was running out. He needed to follow Mark and document what he did.

"Yes, but she hadn't seen him." Harry reached the door and gripped the handle.

Sam wiggled his eyebrows. "She's hot - right?"

Harry nodded and opened the door.

Sam shouted after him, "Hey Man, the cat might turn up yet. Check back again or give us a call."

Harry waved as he walked out the door.

Harry drove around until he found Mark's car parked in front of a room between a truck and a SUV. The Camry was empty. A rusty room number, 118, hung at a slant on the black door closest to his car.

Besides a few crows picking through scraps left on the pavement, nothing moved. Harry backed into a spot in the far corner of the lot and watched 118 and the surrounding rooms. If Sam hadn't held him up, he'd know exactly which one Mark had entered.

Harry checked his watch; twenty minutes had passed. This was his first stalker case. Most people hired him for cheating partners.

Harry despised cheating. Once he committed himself in a relationship, Harry stayed faithful until it ended. Unfortunately, that wasn't always true of the women he dated. Well, at least, one woman. A vision of Beth flashed in his mind, brown eyes glistening with tears, a finger twisting a strand of blonde hair, as she asked his forgiveness. It was bad enough she two-timed Harry, but with Billy? When she turned up pregnant, he suspected the baby was Billy's, but he had no way of knowing. Since she cheated on Harry, she might have done the same to Billy. One thing Harry knew for sure; the baby wasn't his. Harry had never gotten past the kissing stage, but he couldn't convince Drake of that.

The door marked 120 opened. Mark got in his car and left. If that was a booty call, it was a quick one. Harry couldn't wait to see if anyone else exited the room. Tailing Mark was his job.

Harry followed Mark to his house and watched until the lights went out, then decided Mark was exhausted from his motel escapade. Harry headed home.

As he drove, he reflected on his situation. The last few days hadn't brought him any closer to discovering Lisa's killer or the mystery woman who'd left stuff in his apartment. Finding the owner of the clothes, the card case, and the cat would have to wait. His top priority was figuring out who killed Lisa and if it turned out to be the mystery woman, then all the better.

Harry needed insight into who murdered Lisa or at least a lead. Chip might have some answers. If Harry was lucky, Chip would prove to be the killer. He just hoped Chip had not seen him at Jack's Joint otherwise he might refuse to say anything, and Harry needed all the help he could get.

The lights and the flashing open sign of a liquor store called him. The anti-depressants would have washed out of his system by now. A glass of scotch and a good book would help him sleep. He had the book. All he needed was the Johnnie Walker. Like metal to a magnet, his car pulled into the parking lot.

33

Before leaving the parking lot the next morning, Harry called Chip, but he didn't answer. So, Harry left a voice message, "This is Harry Bennett. I should be at your place by ten."

As Harry pulled into Chip's neighborhood, he noted the expansive brick, stone, and stucco homes, the golf course, tennis courts, and community pool - every suburban couple's dream. Harry had never aspired to suburbia, but admitted it had its perks.

Chip's Mediterranean style house sat on an oversized lot between a sprawling-cream-modern home and a red-brick-traditional-two-story. Harry parked in the circular driveway behind a sporty red BMW. Opening his car door brought a whiff of recently mowed grass, reminding him of the summers he sweated cutting lawns as a kid for extra cash.

Birds squawked in the trees surrounding the place. A couple of squirrels darted across the yard as he walked on the sidewalk leading to an arched front door. Curved metal designs overlaid the glass door, adding an artistic touch. Harry pressed the doorbell and peered in between the patterns to the entryway.

Chip's body lay sprawled across the travertine floor; a thick gold braided curtain cord wrapped around his neck. Harry sucked in air and his heart went into overdrive.

The ex-cop in him said - call the police.

The murder suspect in him said - leave now.

The murder suspect won.

Harry looked around and seeing only squirrels, wiped the doorbell with the tail of his shirt, then sprinted for his car. He backed out of the driveway, then eased down the street. Sirens sounded as he drove out of the neighborhood. His hands gripped the steering wheel. There was no way the cops knew about Chip yet, unless his wife had discovered the body. Chip had said his wife wouldn't be at home. Harry took a couple of deep breaths, eased his grip on the wheel and wiped the sweat from his brow.

When the cops investigated Chip, they might discover Harry had asked about him at Jack's Joint. If they checked Chip's voicemail, Harry was doomed. Drake would pin Chip's and Lisa's murder on him. His dream of owning a successful PI business with an office and a secretary would vaporize. His name would be stamped on an arrest warrant rather than an office door.

He had to find Lisa's killer. Unless Harry's investigations proved he did kill her. His stomach churned. If only he could remember that night.

Harry didn't know Chip well enough to come up with a list of suspects, but he knew at least one person with a reason to kill him. He turned his car around.

Harry followed the sidewalk to David's house. He wondered if his sorrow for Lisa's death was all an act. Maybe David didn't miss his wife at all, but if that were the case, why would he hire Harry to find her killer and why bother killing Chip?

The sun pierced through the trees and beat on Harry's back. The crows taunted him with their cackles. With the way things were going, one would probably shit on him. Harry reached the entrance without incident and pressed the doorbell.

Sirens sounded in the distance. He wondered if they were coming for him, then muttered under his breath, "No way is that possible. Get a grip."

He inhaled the cloying scent of the thorny roses growing on either side of the front porch, then exhaled.

David opened the door and smiled. "Come on in. You got some answers for me?"

Harry shook his head. All he had were questions. Well, he had one answer for David, the name of Lisa's lover, Chip, but it was a dead end. Harry almost smiled at the pun, but he wasn't in the mood.

"Man, you look like shit. Let me fix you a drink." David grabbed Harry's arm and pulled him into the living room, past the couch, and up to the bar.

"Have a seat." David pointed to a barstool, then walked behind the counter. Harry sat and leaned his head into his hands, rubbing his temples.

"Scotch and water - right?"

Harry nodded.

David poured the scotch into a glass and passed it to Harry. He splashed rum into another glass and added Coke, then took a sip. Harry took a swig of his drink. The liquor burned down his throat, shocking his brain into clarity.

"Lisa's Memorial Service is here on Monday. The cops asked to attend." David shrugged. "Maybe they're looking for other suspects. I want you to come too."

"Sure. I'll be there." Harry stared at David. "Maybe they'll find the person who killed Lisa's lover too."

David's eyes widened. "What? Someone killed him?" He shook his head. "They're going to think I did it."

"Did you?" Harry hoped the shock of the question would root out the truth.

David stared, open mouthed. "How could I? I didn't even know his name."

"Chip Barnes." Harry watched David's face, gauging his reaction.

David frowned. "Wait a minute. That name sounds familiar. Let me think." He drummed his fingers on the granite, then stopped. "It must have been at least a couple of years ago. He and his wife sat at our table during a charity event. Something to do with the zoo. She's a VP at some company. I can't remember the name of the business. I think he was an accountant. Her name is Emma, fairly attractive, but not my type." He shook his head. "When you showed me the photos of him and Lisa together, I thought I'd seen him before but couldn't place his face." He shrugged. "From what I remember, Emma dominated the conversation."

"Anything else?"

"He drank a lot. She didn't. They seemed to get along." He added some rum to his drink, then held up the scotch bottle.

Harry shook his head. He wanted it, but another one would dull his mind. The bodies were piling up and he needed a clear head to catch the killer.

"With Chip dead, we need to find someone else who might have killed Lisa. Do you know if she had any enemies?" Harry asked.

"Not that I know of. Maybe someone from her dancer days. She worked at Barracudas. That's where we met." His eyes got a faraway look as if he could still see her dancing.

Harry stared at his drink and gave David some time to return to the present. He still wasn't convinced David hadn't killed Chip. He had a motive and admitted to knowing the guy. After a few minutes, David downed the rum and coke, then refilled his glass.

"When did she end her dancing career?"

"Before we got married. About three years ago."

"You remember Rachel, the one from the photo albums, Lisa's bridesmaid?" David looked at Harry.

Harry nodded. How could he forget that wild Einstein hair of hers?

"Anyway, Rachel worked there as a bartender but left last year." David shrugged. "She might know something."

Dancing wasn't the only thing happening at Barracudas. On a job a year ago, Harry followed a husband to the place. The guy left with one of the dancers and they'd done more than eat dinner at that fancy hotel. He needed to catch up with Rachel.

"Do you know where Rachel works now?"

"Some upscale restaurant in the Katy area." David rubbed his lips and looked in the distance, then shook his head. "I can't remember the name."

Perhaps someone had made a pass at Lisa when she worked as a dancer, and she shunned the guy. Someone who couldn't take no for an answer. Three years was a long time to wait to get revenge. Unless he'd only recently got up the nerve to approach her and she rejected him. Maybe he stalked her and found her cheating with Chip. If she'd cheat with Chip, then he might have figured he had a chance with her. Killing Lisa in anger would make sense, but strangling Chip seemed like a stretch of logic. However, insanity and logic rarely followed the same path.

A lot of dancers used cocaine. If Lisa acquired a drug habit, the list of suspects widened: junkies, loan sharks, drug dealers. She may have secured a pimp to pay for her addiction, a pimp angry he had lost an employee. Still, why kill her now?

He squinted at David. "Did she mention anyone she'd seen or met lately?"

"Not really. In the last few weeks, she mentioned inviting a friend over to meet me."

"What was her friend's name?"

"Victoria. Lisa didn't tell me her last name."

Harry ground his teeth. He was sick of hearing and seeing the name, Victoria, but maybe she could lead him to the killer. If nothing else, maybe she could provide him an alibi for the night of Lisa's murder.

As Harry drove away from David's, Victoria haunted him. Her name popped up everywhere: the bra left in his bathroom, the card case, Jack's Joint, and Lisa's friend. Hell, he didn't seem to be able to have a conversation without her name coming up. If everything tied to Victoria, then finding her was key.

A Victoria frequented Jack's Joint. It was possible Lisa met her there. Harry couldn't show up at Jack's asking questions again. Harry needed to stay away from the bar, but Sophia could go.

Who was he kidding? They barely knew each other, but she did say she enjoyed the unusual. She wasn't happy he lied about Chip abusing a sister Harry didn't have, but it couldn't hurt to ask for her help. Maybe they could go to dinner again and see where things went.

Harry headed for the Star motel. The motel parking lot held a variety of vehicles, ranging from pickup trucks to sports cars. It was hard to understand the popularity of the place. Either there were a lot of cheating spouses, or the Star served as a hot spot for cheap hookers, but if that were true, why was Sophia working there?

He parked, grabbed his phone and wallet, then checked the surroundings. Sophia walked out of a room. She stopped, looked around, then approached a dark blue sedan. The driver's side window rolled down. Sophia hesitated, looked around again, pulled something from her pocket, and slipped it into the outstretched hand of the driver. The hand size and chunky watch indicated a man. Sophia headed for a motel door as the guy drove away. Harry was curious as hell but had his own problems to deal with.

Sophia grabbed a cart loaded with cleaning supplies and pulled it along the walkway. Harry got out of his car and walked toward her.

"Need any help?" Harry asked.

She frowned. "I'm not sure you're up for the job."

He smirked. "I'm always up for the job."

She looked skyward as if she'd heard the line too many times. "Why are you here?"

"To ask a favor."

Sophia walked toward a door, opened it, pushed the cart onto the door jamb, then stopped. "The answer is no."

Not the response he'd hoped for. His lying shouldn't bother her. Based on the exchange Harry had witnessed, Sophia had secrets of her own. Of course, he couldn't mention that, or she'd accuse him of spying on her.

Harry raised an eyebrow. "It's easy."

"Well, I'm not." She picked up some cleaning products and walked into the room.

Harry leaned against the building, checked the news on his phone, read his email, and waited. Sophia reappeared and grabbed the cart.

"Why are you still here?" Sophia pushed the buggy along to the next room.

"You said you liked the unusual."

Sophia stopped, looked at Harry, paused, then rubbed a

finger across her plump lips.

She sighed. "What's the favor?"

Harry cleared his throat. "Go to Jack's Joint tonight. Ask for Victoria. If she's there, talk to her. If not, talk to the regulars. Get a description, last name, where she lives, anything you can get on her."

"Wait a minute. The other night you were asking about a guy."

Harry shrugged. "Asking questions is my job."

Sophia parked a hand on each hip, then jutted her chin forward. "Then, why don't you ask about her yourself?"

"I have an appointment tonight." He eyed her. "What about it?"

"Why don't you just do it another night?"

"A client wants the information by tomorrow." Technically, he wasn't lying. In this case, Harry was the client and wanted the details as soon as possible.

"I don't know." She shook her head.

"You said you might like PI work. Here's your chance."

She bit her lip.

"Of course, I'll pay for your expenses. Gas, drinks, whatever."

Another meal might sweeten the deal. Plus, it would give him the opportunity to spend more time with her.

"I'll take you to dinner at Vic and Anthony's one night too," he said.

She returned her gaze to him. "You drive a hard bargain." She smiled. "I'm always up for a walk on the wild side and

Jack's Joint is definitely the place for it."

"Stop by my apartment anytime afterwards. I'll be up late." Just the thought of Sophia coming to his place brought a smile to Harry's face.

She parked the cart on the door jamb of the next room, grabbed some cleaning items, turned her back on him, and walked in the room.

At least she'd agreed to do it. Harry would text her his address. Maybe Sophia liked him after all.

34

Harry drove to Rachel's. The silver Mustang sat in the driveway of the white framed house. He pulled in behind the car. He wasn't risking her leaving before he got a chance to talk with her.

As he got out of his car, he noted the security system sign prominently displayed in the yard. Burglar bars covered the shuttered windows. The vertical rods had a curved design in the center, giving the barricade an artistic flare. Either she walked in a lot of fear or someone she knew worked in security.

He rang the doorbell. A dog barked, not the yapping of a small one, but the heavy tones of something big.

Someone shouted through the door, "Who is it?"

"Harry Bennett, Private Investigator." He held up his card to the peephole.

The door opened a crack, a chain lock prevented it from opening further. A Rottweiler's muzzle pressed against the open space; a low growl rumbled in his throat. Only one of Rachel's green eyes peered at him.

"What do you want?"

"I'm investigating Lisa's murder. I need to ask you some questions."

Her eye narrowed. "Why me?"

Harry smiled, hoping it might bring him favor. "Her husband told me the two of you were good friends."

Rachel's eye softened. "We were." She blinked. "There's nothing I can do for her now."

The door started closing.

Harry put up his hand. "Wait a minute." The door stopped moving. "Don't you want her killer caught? It might be someone you both knew." His tone held concern as if she might be the next victim.

The door opened to the length of the chain. She stared at him. "Meet me at the Starbuck's on Westheimer Parkway. It's the one closest to here. I'll be there in about fifteen minutes."

"Can I get you anything? A coffee, tea, pastry?" Harry figured he could buy her cooperation or at least try.

"Tall Triple Mocha Frappuccino with whip." She closed the door.

Harry muttered the drink order to himself until he got to the car, then he spoke it into his phone and checked to make sure autocorrect hadn't screwed it up.

The Starbucks occupied a spot in a shopping center where a Kroger's grocery store took up most of the space. Harry went inside and joined the line at the counter. The smell of coffee and the customers' chatter brought an energy to the place, a vibe that transferred to Harry.

By the time Rachel arrived, he was seated in a back corner table with his Pike's and her Frappuccino. The light blue sweats she wore hung on her. Strands of wavy hair escaped from the bun on top of her head. Men sitting at various tables glanced as she walked past, but quickly returned to their conversations, phones, or books.

Rachel plopped into the chair across from him and grabbed her drink. "Thanks for getting me this." She reached inside the pocket of her sweatpants. "How much do I owe you?"

He waved her off. "It's on me."

"What do you want to know about Lisa?" She stared at him through wide round glasses that magnified her green eyes.

"Do you know of anyone who might have wanted to kill her? Someone who hassled her or frightened her?"

She sucked on her straw, then swallowed. "Not really. When we both worked at Barracudas, there was one guy, a regular. He was interested in her, but she kept putting him off. He quit coming not long after Lisa left." She shrugged. "Someone said he got married."

"Do you remember his name?"

She shook her head. "He didn't come across as a killer, but who can tell?"

"Did Lisa do drugs?" He sipped his coffee. The warmth spread through his mouth and down his throat.

"Not Lisa. Some of the other girls did, but she wouldn't touch the stuff." She wiped the condensation off her cup.

"When did you last talk with her?"

She looked past him as if visualizing the event. "A couple of days before she died. I met up with her and Chip."

He didn't think she'd seen him at Jack's Joint, so he feigned ignorance. "Who's Chip?"

"Lisa and Chip had a thing going on." Rachel leaned toward him. "I used to hang out with them at Jack's Joint every once in a while. We always had fun except for that one time when Emma showed up."

"Emma?"

"Chip's wife." Rachel smirked.

Harry smiled. "That must have been entertaining."

"You bet. Emma looked like she could spit nails." Rachel laughed.

"What did Chip do?"

"He asked her if she'd like to join us. Told her we were discussing some improvements for some software Adrastos had purchased."

Harry wondered if Chip had missed his calling. He sounded like PI material to him. Too bad he was dead.

"Did she join you?"

Rachel smiled. "Sure did. Talk about uncomfortable." She shook her head. "Anyway, Chip started talking numbers and throwing software jargon around. I took a computer class last year, so I knew enough to play along. Lisa said she'd have to discuss the enhancements with her manager."

"You think Emma believed it?"

She shrugged. "Seemed to. After a while she left. Made some excuse about needing to get home."

"That man has some balls." Harry downed the rest of his

coffee, then shook his head. "What happened after that?"

Rachel licked some whip cream off her lips. "We laughed about the whole thing, but I think Chip was spooked cause he left not long after that."

"I don't blame him." Harry set his cup aside.

"Did Lisa mention anyone named Victoria?"

She pulled at her lips and looked at the ceiling. "She did mention someone she wanted me to meet. Said she was a lot of fun. I think her name was Victoria." She fiddled with her straw. "Why? Do you think she killed Lisa?"

Harry shrugged. "I don't know. Someone mentioned her name in passing."

She sucked the last drop out of her drink. "Anything else?

"Did Lisa seem frightened or worried about anything recently?"

Rachel shook her head.

"I noticed you have a lot of security at your place." He tilted his head. "Any particular reason?"

"One of the guys at Barracuda's wouldn't take no for an answer." She frowned. "It's one of the downsides of working at a strip club. The money is great, but the clientele is sometimes less than desirable. That's why I left."

"Was he interested in Lisa?" Harry figured if the guy was persistent enough to scare Rachel into a security system, burglar bars, and a Rottweiler, then he could do most anything.

"No, she'd already left by the time he had started coming."

He handed her his business card. "If that guy gives you anymore trouble or you think of anything else, give me a call."

By the time Harry got home, his shoulders and back ached from the stress of the day's events. Each step took an effort like traipsing in a mud sucking swamp. Not even the June bugs buzzing around his porch light fazed him. As Harry unlocked his apartment, a shadow covered the keyhole.

"We need to talk."

Adrenaline pumped through Harry's body, infusing him with energy. He grabbed his gun from the holster and turned, then seeing a friendly face, the tension left his body and he put away the gun.

"You're going to get killed one day." He opened the door wide for Buddy. "Where's your partner?"

"He's out with his wife. It's her birthday."

Harry flicked on the living room lights, then motioned Buddy to take a seat.

Buddy settled on the couch while Harry sat in the recliner. "I guess you're here for a report on that stalker guy you had me tail, Mark Crawford." Van jumped in Harry's lap.

"We can start with that." Buddy pulled out his palm-sized notebook and a pen.

"He went to the Star Motel. Didn't stay very long." Harry raised his eyebrows. "I'm guessing it was a booty call. After that, he went home."

Buddy made a few notes, then looked up at Harry. "Do you know Chip Barnes?"

The tension in Harry's shoulders returned. He rubbed the back of his neck in an effort to ease the pain and feign nonchalance. "I'm acquainted with him. Why?"

"Barnes is dead, strangled." Buddy tugged on his ear. "We found your fingerprints on a glass at the crime scene."

No way. Shit. Harry sat up straight, gripping the arm rests. "What?"

"Look Man, this isn't looking good for you. Your fingerprints at two crime scenes?" He shook his head. "Do you have an alibi between the hours of ten and midnight last night?"

Harry remembered pouring a drink, then waking up this morning. "I was asleep in bed."

Buddy frowned. "Can anyone vouch for you?"

"I was asleep, by myself except for Van."

They both looked at the cat. Van yawned as if bored by the conversation.

The video would prove what Harry did last night, but he didn't want the cops knowing he recorded his movements. They might use it against him in the future. Not that he did anything illegal. He had nothing to hide from the IRS either, but he wouldn't give them his records without an official request. Like everyone else, Harry made mistakes.

"Their maid said she'd washed all the dishes before she left at three yesterday. So, when did you go to Chip's house?"

"I've never been in Chip's home. Drake must have framed me."

Buddy squinted. "How would he do that?"

Harry stared at Buddy while his mind sought a solution. His chest tightened. Every breath took effort. "Maybe Drake stole a glass I used."

Buddy rolled his eyes. "And he carried it around hoping he'd run across a crime where he could leave it?" He shook his head. "Think about it. He'd have to wear gloves, or his fingerprints would show up on the glass too."

Ideas raced through Harry's head. He discarded each until one possible solution rose to the top. "Drake killed Chip, then planted the glass at the scene."

"Drake hates you, but I can't see him killing someone just to put you in the slammer."

"I could see him doing it." Drake wanted revenge for his sister's death and would do anything to get it.

Buddy shrugged. "Why not just kill you?"

He had Harry there. Drake could kill him and make it look like an accident or self-defense. Perhaps he liked toying with Harry like a cat playing with a lizard until it stopped moving.

"Killing me would be too easy."

Buddy shook his head. "I don't believe you did it, but all the evidence points to you." He stood. "You'd better figure out how your fingerprints got on that glass before Drake comes for you."

Harry needed the crime scene photos. His glimpse through Chip's front door hadn't provided enough information. Besides, if he didn't ask for them, Buddy would wonder why he didn't.

"If I could get the photos of the crime scene and the report, then I might figure out how my fingerprints ended up there and who killed him."

Buddy's eyes widened. "I'll get sacked if Drake finds out."

"If I don't figure out who killed Chip and Lisa, I'll end up in prison." Harry rubbed his forehead. "Convicted of a crime I didn't do." He stared at Buddy. "It doesn't get much worse than that."

Buddy exhaled. "I'll bring them by tomorrow."

After Buddy left, Harry reviewed the video from the previous night, fast-forwarding until the screen showed him pouring Johnnie Walker into a glass. He watched as he downed the drink.

Dark shadows and bags under his eyes testified of sleepless nights. Yet, he didn't recall any restless sleep.

After another drink, the monitor showed him carrying the bottle and a glass, then turning off the lights and heading for bed. Streetlights seeped through the blind slits and around the edges, providing dim lighting into the living area. The camera picked up Van clawing the rug, jumping on the counter, and knocking mail on the floor.

Harry cut a glance at the cat and frowned.

At 8:45, the video showed Harry emerging from the bedroom dressed in jeans, a polo, and tennis shoes.

Harry froze the scene. "What the hell!"

He hit play and chewed on a cuticle as the screen showed the front door closing behind him. Openmouthed, Harry fast forwarded through scenes of Van wandering in and out of the camera's view until 1:34 when Harry reappeared.

"Shit! What did I do last night?"

He pressed pause and examined his appearance for clues.

The front of his shirt was wrinkled as if someone had grabbed and twisted it. Had Chip grasped his shirt as Harry strangled him?

Harry shook his head. Unintelligible thoughts swirled through his mind as if his brain reflected the chaos in his life. He wasn't sure of who he was anymore. What was wrong with him?

Even drunk, he wouldn't kill a man with his bare hands, but then again, he would swear he had slept through the night. He pressed play, looking for signs of intoxication, but he walked straight and with a confidence that conveyed a sense of purpose.

Harry reversed the video and checked the liquor level on the bottle, then walked to his bedroom and compared the fluid level with the bottle sitting on his end table. The difference between the two was one drink at the most. He wasn't drunk when he left.

If the cops saw the video, they'd arrest him. Harry wouldn't blame them. He deleted the file and all traces of it.

The clothes from last night might give him a clue as to where he went. Van followed him into the laundry room where the clothes lay tossed on the floor. Harry sniffed the shirt and inhaled mint and cedar, remnants of his body wash. He pulled a small box of peppermints from his pants pockets and a gas receipt from two days ago. Maybe he'd have better luck with his shoes.

The shoes lay in their assigned cubby in the closet. Harry examined them for mud, anything, but found nothing. *Shit.* He wanted a drink but settled for an over the counter sleeping aid. The thought of taking the whole bottle crossed his mind. Nobody would miss him.

Van rubbed around his legs. He picked him up and scratched behind his torn ear. The cat bumped his head against Harry's chin and purred.

"Who would take care of you? Nobody wants a scruffy cat with a ripped ear." Harry returned the bottle to the shelf. "I've got to find the murderer. If I'm the killer…" He touched his forehead against Van's. "We'll both end up in a cage. You in the shelter and me in prison."

Someone knocked on Harry's door. He shuffled to the entryway and checked the peephole. Sophia stood on his doorstep.

Van rubbed around his legs.

"Shit!" Harry said under his breath.

Sophia didn't know the cat had returned and now wasn't the time to mention it. She'd think he'd made up a story about Van's disappearance. He grabbed the cat and some treats, dumped him in the laundry room, and dropped the tidbits on the floor. A stuffed mouse lay on the tile. Harry picked it up, tossed it in the room, and looked at Van.

"You've got everything you need, litter, toys, water, and food."

He closed the laundry door, raced across the floor, then ran his fingers through his hair before letting Sophia in the apartment.

Sophia sauntered inside, plopped in the recliner, kicked off her red heels, and rubbed her feet. The black dress hiked up her thighs highlighting the length of her legs. Heat rushed through his body.

She looked up at him. "Victoria wasn't there tonight, but the bartender and some of the regulars gave me some information on her."

Harry sat on the sofa across from her. He wondered what was wrong with him or maybe the fault lay with Sophia, a woman so potent she distracted him even from the fear of a murder conviction.

"Did you get her last name?"

Sophia shook her head. "I got a description. She's a tall blonde with brown eyes and medium length hair. Great personality, but based on the men's comments, not much sex appeal." She arched an eyebrow. "Or she just wasn't their type."

The description didn't make sense. The provocative clothes left in his bedroom indicated a sexy woman. Maybe some other woman was the culprit. "Where does she work?"

"I asked, but no one knew."

"Anything else?"

She looked at the ceiling and bit her lip. "She smokes cigarettes outside the bar, but she's not a drinker. Only orders orange juice."

Harry wondered if Victoria was a recovering alcoholic.

Sophia looked around. "Speaking of which, have you got anything to drink?"

"Bottled water, soda, scotch?" Harry asked.

"Water."

When Harry walked in the kitchen, a bumping sound came from the laundry room.

Sophia turned around. "What's that noise?"

Harry raised his eyebrows and looked at the wall. "My neighbors."

She nodded and returned to rubbing her feet. Harry threw a handful of treats into the laundry room while using his foot to keep Van at bay. He shut the door as the cat ran to the goodies.

Harry grabbed a bottled water from the refrigerator and handed it to her.

She twisted off the top, took a sip, then leaned toward him. "The bartender remembered me from the other night when you and I went there. He said he was worried about Victoria. The last time he'd seen her, she was with Chip. Before he could warn her about Chip's abusive behavior, she'd already left with Chip." She did air quotes around abusive behavior.

"Did he say when he'd last seen her with Chip?" he asked.

"She left with him last night."

Either she murdered Chip or might have information to help him find the killer. Harry didn't believe he had done it no matter what his video showed.

Her eyes widened. "So, am I detective material?"

From Harry's perspective, the view alone earned her the honor. "If I hire a partner, I'll call you first."

Harry wanted a partner and Sophia had the woman's touch and perspective his agency of one needed, but he didn't know her well enough yet. The exchange between her and the man in Star's parking lot flashed through his mind. Harry contemplated asking her about it but figured he would wait until they knew each other better.

Sophia grabbed her shoes.

Harry didn't want to stay alone, anything could happen. If someone spent the night with him, he couldn't get into trouble. Harry looked at his phone. "It's one o'clock. Stay here. Driving this time of night isn't safe."

If Sophia stayed with him, there was an added bonus, he might get lucky. Van could spend the night in the laundry room. With enough cat food and treats, he wouldn't mind.

She tugged on a shoe, then looked at him. "That's one of the more creative lines I've heard."

"I can sleep on the couch." Not that he wanted to. "I have an extra toothbrush and a selection of t-shirts for pajamas."

Sophia slipped on the other shoe, then got up from the recliner.

Harry stood between her and the door. His mind raced with excuses to make her stay.

"I'll worry about you," he said.

"It's not a problem." She reached into the depths of her purse and pulled out a gun. "Smith and Wesson ride with me."

Sophia walked close to him, then leaned in as if waiting for a kiss. The scent of gardenias mixed with her minty breath created an intoxicating effect on Harry more potent than any liquor. Harry went in for the kiss. A bumping sound came from the laundry room. Sophia turned her head.

"What was that?" she asked.

Harry sighed. "Stupid neighbors. I wonder if they ever sleep." He reached to turn her face toward him.

Sophia looked at her watch. "It's late and I've got a morning shift." She walked past him to the door, then turned and smiled. "I'm looking forward to dinner." She raised her eyebrows and her eyes lingered on him for a moment, then she left.

Harry let Van out of the laundry room. The cat rubbed around his legs as if expecting more tidbits.

"Forget it. No more treats for either of us tonight."

Harry struggled keeping his eyes open. Tonight, even he sleepwalked, no way would he kill anyone, they would kill him first. If his unconscious-self ventured out tonight, odds were it would target Barracuda's strip club. He stripped to his boxers and crashed.

35

The crackle of lightning followed by the boom of thunder woke Harry. Rain beat hard against his bedroom window. Getting out of bed or doing anything today seemed like a bad idea. Harry wondered if he'd gone out last night. Part of him wanted to know, while another part wanted to lie in bed and pretend he'd dreamed the last couple of weeks.

Van jumped on the bed and kneaded the covers, then bumped his head against Harry's chin.

"I know you just want food." Harry tossed aside the covers and headed for the kitchen.

While Van consumed his breakfast, Harry reviewed the video from last night. He smiled as Sophia swayed across the screen. If only she'd stayed the night. Harry leaned closer to the screen. Van's nighttime activities flashed on the display, then nothing moved. Harry held his breath. When the image of him exiting the bedroom and entering the kitchen, then grabbing the cat food appeared on the screen, he stopped watching.

He exhaled and the tightness in his chest eased. He'd stayed home all night, but who knew what would happen tonight. Harry rolled his shoulders as if preparing for a fight.

He checked his phone: ten o'clock on a Saturday morning. Dr. Worth's office wouldn't open until Monday. He couldn't wait that long without some kind of resolution. Harry had handled problems and challenges in his life. but he was awake for those, aware of them. He had no control over this. Seeing Dr. Worth wouldn't guarantee a solution to his problem, but at this point, he'd try anything. He picked up the phone and called her. When voicemail answered, he left a message.

"This is Harry Bennett. I'm having blackouts again." Harry added a note of panic in his voice to entice her to meet. "Video showed me leaving my apartment, but I don't remember going anywhere. I need some answers. Could we meet today?" He added his phone number and hung up.

Until Dr. Worth called, Harry could research blackouts and sleepwalking on the Internet. He pulled out his laptop and started typing.

The phone rang. He checked his phone's display: Candy. No point in ignoring her, he knew she'd continue calling until he answered.

"What's up?"

"Richard is cheating on me." She clipped her words as if each were a punch.

Harry didn't believe it. Her sexual appetite was enough for any man.

"Why do you think that?"

"I caught the bastard pulling out of some sleazy motel

parking lot. The Star Motel."

What the hell was the fascination with the Star Motel? Harry didn't get it. Although it made for a perfect hideout. No one would expect anyone but lowlifes to stay there.

"Did you confront him?" Harry knew Candy wasn't the type to hold back.

"Of course, I did. The dick said he'd pulled over for a phone call."

With the name of Richard, he figured dick wasn't such an insult, but this wasn't the time to point out the obvious.

"Maybe he did." No way was Harry fueling her rage. Although she might get mad enough to leave Richie. Doubtful. For her, loads of cash could cover a mountain of sin. She would stick it to him by indulging in new cars, spa days, and shopping.

"I want to hire you to follow him."

Harry didn't need any more work. "I'd like to, but I'm really busy."

"I'll pay double your rate and recommend you to all my friends." Harry didn't have enough time to tail Mark Crawford and Richie.

Harry sighed. Candy was well connected. Her referrals would bring in customers with plenty of cash. He would have to let Buddy know he would need to find someone else to follow Mark.

"I can only do it in my spare time." Like Harry had any of that. Still, he'd like to catch Richie with his pants down.

"That's good enough for me." Her voice slowed, dripping

with a southern accent as sultry as a saxophone. "I look forward to seeing you again."

Harry gave up on the Internet search. He paced the floor, wiped down the kitchen counters, scooped the litter, then watched TV with the volume on low. The phone remained silent. Perhaps Dr. Worth didn't check messages on the weekend. She must have patients with emergencies, thoughts of suicide, anger issues, or breakdowns. He checked his phone. A couple of hours had passed since he'd made the call. If he was suicidal, he would have already topped himself. The phone rang. Dr. Worth's number flashed on the display.

"Dr. Worth, thanks for returning my call." He hoped she would see him today.

"I usually don't see patients on the weekend, but next week is booked. It doesn't sound like waiting a week is an option. Can you meet me at my office at 1:00 today?"

Harry released his breath as the tension in his neck and shoulders vanished. "I'll be there."

"With these blackouts, I'm not sure it's safe for you to drive. Can someone bring you?"

Harry didn't want to bother anyone. The blackouts only occurred at night. At least as far as he knew. Besides, his unconscious-self seemed to get around without any problems. He made it home safely the other night.

"I'll see what I can do," Harry said.

As he hung up, Harry wondered how he'd get everything done. The list grew longer and more complicated every day. Tracking down Lisa's and Chip's killer, tailing Richie, figuring how his fingerprints showed up at two crime scenes, and why he roamed at night without any memory of it was more than he could handle, but he didn't have much choice. Hopefully, Dr. Worth could answer the last one. If not, Harry would have to hire someone to keep him under lock and key or better yet, tail him.

Someone knocked on Harry's door. He checked the peephole, then opened the door.

"I brought the crime scene photos from Chip's murder." Buddy handed over a 9x12 envelope, then went to the refrigerator, grabbed a beer, and held it up. "I see you've restocked."

Harry nodded. Beer didn't tempt him as much as Johnnie Walker.

Harry spilled the contents of the packet on the kitchen bar, then examined each photo. The gold braided curtain cord lay wrapped around Chip's neck and trailed across the travertine floor, ending in a thick fringe. Chip still wore the white polo Harry had seen him in earlier at Jack's Joint. From the position of the cord, someone had strangled Chip from behind. The next picture showed a close up of the head and neck. Red raised scratch marks on his neck showed around the gold fibers where Chip had struggled to free himself.

"Skin tissue was found under Chip's nails, but it was all his." Buddy sighed. "The cord came off the curtains. We checked it for fingerprints but couldn't get anything identifiable."

At least his fingerprints hadn't shown up on the murder

weapon.

"Have they got any suspects other than me?"

Buddy popped off the beer top. "You're at the top of the list, but they're looking at others too. Seems Chip had a mistress. Don't suppose you know anything about that?" He stared at Harry; his mouth set in a line.

Buddy probably knew Lisa was the mistress, but Harry couldn't tell by his expression. He decided to play it safe.

"You mean Lisa?" Harry asked.

Buddy nodded.

Harry didn't want Buddy to think he'd withheld information. "I only found out a couple of days ago."

"Lisa's husband might have killed her and Chip, but his fingerprints weren't at either crime scene." Buddy shrugged. "Of course, he could have worn gloves."

At least the suspect list included more than Harry's name.

"You guys got any more leads?"

Harry could add a couple of names. Perhaps Rachel wanted Chip for herself. Although, he hadn't seen any evidence of intimacy between the two, a chance existed that the relationship was one-sided. Maybe Chip turned her down, and she went ballistic. It happened. If David was in the running, then Chip's wife should get equal suspect time. Victoria was another possibility, but Harry struggled to identify a motive for her. What the hell. He couldn't even find her.

"What about Chip's wife?" Harry asked.

Buddy took a swig of his beer, then wiped his mouth. "Emma? If Chip were drugged or drunk, she might be able to strangle him. We haven't got the toxicology results yet." He shrugged. "We're checking everyone's alibis."

Harry didn't put any physical limitations on women. With an adrenaline rush a woman could overcome most any man, especially if the man was surprised.

Buddy frowned. "Look, I'm sharing the photos because I believe you're innocent, but that's not how Drake sees it. So you'd better figure out who killed Lisa and Chip before he decides to arrest you."

Harry sighed. "It's not like I'm not trying."

Buddy nodded. "I know."

"Are you finished with the crime scene?" Harry wanted to ask Emma some questions.

"Yeah." Buddy raised his eyebrows. "You're not thinking of going over there, are you? If Drake catches you, there will be hell to pay."

Van jumped on Harry's lap. He scratched the cat under the neck.

"I know how to take care of Drake," Harry said.

"You're the only one then." Buddy raised his beer can as if toasting Harry. "Drake and I visited a bar called Jack's Joint. Seems Chip and Lisa went there a lot."

Harry wondered if they knew he'd talked with the bartender. An ache settled across his shoulders as if a vise gripped him.

"Bartender told us some guy was looking for Chip. Said Chip hit the guy's sister." Buddy stared at him. "The bartender described the man. The description sounded a lot like you."

"Really?" The vise tightened. Harry longed to roll his

shoulders, but kept still, feigning a relaxed position.

"Yep." Buddy downed the rest of the beer, then tossed the can in the trash. "I told Drake you didn't have a sister, but he's taking a picture of you by there tomorrow."

Shit. Harry clenched his teeth. No point in admitting it was him. Drake would find out soon enough. If he came to arrest him tomorrow night, he'd find the place empty anyway. On the positive side, if Drake threw him in jail, Harry wouldn't have to worry about sleepwalking. Still, there was tonight.

Harry tilted his head. "You have any plans this evening?"

"The wife is dragging me to dinner and a play." Buddy frowned. "At least it's not another ballet." He grabbed the envelope. "By the way, any more updates on Mark?"

Harry shook his head. "I could only do the one night of surveillance. I need to get Drake off my back."

Buddy nodded. "I get it. Nobody wants Drake gunning for them, and he's got a lot of reasons to come after you." He sighed. "I've got someone watching the woman too. Whoever is stalking her, he should nail him." He headed for the door. "I'll catch you later."

As Harry closed the door behind Buddy, he thought of another possibility. He could ask Sophia to dinner and possibly charm her into spending the night. He dialed her number.

"Sophia, this is Harry."

"Harry?" Her voice held a note of confusion.

How many Harrys could she know? "You know, the detective." In the past, women always remembered him. Maybe she was playing hard to get. Although, she had seemed interested enough the other night. Why were women so confusing?

"Oh, that Harry."

Harry frowned. "Are you available for dinner tonight?" Before she could say no, he added, "I owe you one for the PI work. Vic and Anthony's?"

He got another call. Candy's name displayed. He would phone her later.

"I guess so." Sophia's tone suggested she had nothing better to do or perhaps she was distracted.

They discussed logistics, then ended the call.

Based on Sophia's lack of enthusiasm, Harry figured he'd sleep alone tonight. He looked around the room. If he made it difficult to leave, his sleepwalking-self might give up and stay inside.

36

Dr. Janet Worth closed Harry's folder and moved from her desk to the seating area designed for the comfort of her patients. She wondered if Harry had continued taking the antidepressants and drinking. Her phone rang interrupting her speculation of the source of Harry's blackouts. She checked the display: Thibodeaux. Harry wouldn't arrive for another ten minutes, and the detective kept conversations short. Perhaps they'd caught her stalker.

"Hi Detective Thibodeaux, any news on the stalker?"

"We had someone tail Mark, but they haven't found any evidence of stalking."

"Maybe whoever it is decided to stop or for some reason can't do it anymore." She hoped he was in jail or in the hospital, or dead, then chided herself on wishing evil on the individual. Obviously, he had some mental issues.

"Possibly. Until we capture this guy or confirm he's stopped, we'll have someone follow you. At least, for the next few days. Give me a call if you have any problems."

The tension across her shoulders eased. So far, the stalker

had played mental games, but she feared they'd escalate into physical attacks. As long as a cop watched her, she felt safe.

As Dr. Worth hung up the phone, she gazed out the window at a grey day that matched her mood. A movement in the parking lot caught her eyes. She watched as Harry walked from his car toward the building with a confident stride. Unlike her other patients, life hadn't beaten the spirit out of Harry, at least not yet.

Janet exchanged greetings with Harry. She noted the dark circles under his eyes had deepened as if sleep eluded him.

"How are you doing?" She motioned him to a chair.

"Fine, except for the blackouts." He eased into a seat but gripped the armrests as if they were a lifeline.

At first, she thought Harry might have early dementia, but he showed no trouble finding words and didn't repeat himself during their sessions. She opened his folder and read the top sheet.

"In the voicemail, you mentioned a video?"

"I installed a camera in my place to record who entered my apartment." He leaned toward her. "I was trying to figure out who kept leaving stuff at my place. Instead, it recorded me leaving, but I don't remember going anywhere."

She picked up her pen and made some notes. "How long were you gone?"

"Almost five hours." He slouched in his chair.

That was a long time for a black out. "As a child, did you have any instances of sleepwalking?"

He squinted as if recalling his childhood. "My aunt never mentioned it. She would have teased me if I had."

"Sleepwalking can occur in adults." She figured he had mixed alcohol with the antidepressant again and triggered an episode. "Did you have any drinks or take an antidepressant that night?"

He tugged on the collar of his polo. "I didn't take an antidepressant, but I had a couple of drinks." He held up his hand. "Not enough to get drunk though."

"Antidepressants can linger in your system and increase the potency of the alcohol. You really should steer clear of the stuff." Unless she stayed with him 24/7, she couldn't control his drinking.

"Did you take any other medications? A sleeping prescription provided by another doctor?"

He shook his head.

"Let's start with a sleep study."

Harry widened his eyes. "A sleep study?"

She nodded. "You spend the night in a sleep lab. They attach electrodes to your body and take measurements while you sleep."

He folded his arms. "I have enough trouble sleeping without being hooked up to wires."

She'd found with patients it was best to ignore their protests rather than argue with them.

"You can take a favorite pillow, blanket, and a book. Whatever will help you sleep." She leaned toward him. "I've had other patients who felt the same way you do but were able to do it."

"What if I sleepwalk?" He frowned.

She never had a patient leave during a sleep study, but Harry was her first potential sleepwalker. "They check your activity throughout the night. Don't worry. Someone will stop you from leaving."

Harry rubbed his chin. "Do you think the alcohol is causing the problem?"

"Could be any number of things waking you: trouble breathing while sleeping, alcohol, restless leg syndrome. Based on what you've told me, it's probably the alcohol, but we need to rule out everything else."

Harry crossed his ankle on top of his knee, then ran his finger along an old wound seared into his skin just above his ankle. She'd never noticed it in previous sessions.

"How did you get that scar?"

He lifted his hand from the raised and knotted line of skin, then uncrossed his legs. "I was in a car accident."

"The same accident that killed your parents?" Harry had mentioned his parents' accident, but never said anything about being in the vehicle. Perhaps it was why he avoided the topic.

Harry nodded.

"Tell me about it." With the lack of sleep and all the stress, she hoped Harry was worried enough to relinquish control over his memories.

Harry took a deep breath, then released it. His shoulders slumped as if an anchor weighed on them.

"My father ran into a telephone pole, killing himself and my mother. I was knocked unconscious. When I woke up, I was in the hospital with my aunt sitting beside me."

"What caused him to run off the road?" She locked in on his eyes, watching for any sign of evasiveness. Harry might have survivor's guilt or perhaps felt he caused the crash.

Harry shifted in his seat. "Does it really matter?"

"It might." His reluctance to answer indicated it probably still bothered him.

Harry arched an eyebrow. "You know it would help if you served liquor." He looked around the room and smiled. "Even better turn this place into a bar. You could stand behind the counter and serve your clients drinks. You wouldn't have to ask questions. After a few drinks, they'd just tell you everything bothering them. You'd have clients lining up to see you."

She smiled. "I should just rent office space in a bar." Most patients avoided answering when the topic cut too close to the bone. "Harry, why did your father run off the road?" She dropped her smile.

His eyes widened. "To get to the other side?"

She looked at the ceiling and frowned.

"All right." He sighed. "He was arguing with me. I smarted off and he took a hand off the steering wheel, then looked back to slap me. The car went off the road. My mother screamed and that's all I remember." Harry picked at a hangnail until it bled.

She grabbed a tissue and handed it to him, then waited until he had wrapped it around his finger.

"The accident wasn't your fault. Your dad should have

stayed focused on driving until he found a safe spot to pull over and discuss your behavior."

Based on Janet's experience, she doubted the hit was a one off. "How was your relationship with your dad?"

Harry looked out the window. "It was okay."

She raised her eyebrows and let his answer hang in the air.

He shook his head. "When my aunt told me he died, I didn't cry. When she told me that my mom was dead, I wished I'd died in the accident."

"So, you didn't like your dad?" She wanted to dig as deep as she could. He might not ever open up about his parents again.

Harry turned to her. "Would you like someone who hit your mother?" His chest rose and fell. "He was a mean son of a bitch."

She wondered about the interaction between Harry and his dad.

"Did he hit you often?" She leaned closer to him.

"Usually just when he drank." Harry frowned. "What does this have to do with my problem?"

"Unresolved issues can cause all kinds of problems."

He shrugged. "It's resolved. The man is dead. Let's get back to the sleepwalking."

She noted his clenched jaw. No sense in pushing him any further. It wouldn't do any good.

"Once we get the sleep study results, we can narrow in on the trigger." Janet pulled a card from a pocket of her notebook and handed it to him. "That's the contact information for the sleep study. I'll call in the order. You schedule a night that works for you. Meanwhile, skip the alcohol."

She worried about him sleeping alone. If something happened to him, she'd never forgive herself.

"Is there someone who can stay with you at night? Or could you stay with someone?"

Harry stood up to leave, avoiding eye contact. "I'm sure I can find someone."

She doubted he would even try, but she couldn't control her patients. If only she could...

After Harry left, Janet pulled a psychiatric volume off her shelf. If it wasn't sleepwalking, there were other options, but she didn't want to scare the shit out of Harry.

37

As soon as Harry got in the car, he called the sleep lab. Music played over the phone while he waited for the woman to find an available time slot.

He wondered who could stay with him tonight. Buddy often worked evenings, so he wasn't an option. If he asked Charley, she'd want to know why. Lying to her wasn't an option. She could read him too well. If he told her the truth, she'd think he'd lost his mind. Maybe he could ask Sophia. The thought of her spending the night brought a smile to his face, then he frowned at the idea of telling her something was wrong with him. He'd have to find another way to convince her, or perhaps he could pay someone to stay the night. Harry shook his head. He would stay away from the alcohol and this time he meant it.

The music continued sounding in his ear, a soft soothing sound. His eyes closed and his head fell forward, then he jerked his head up.

"If they don't answer soon, I'll fall asleep waiting on the phone." Harry shook his head and opened his eyes wide.

Maybe he could install an alarm that went off when he opened his apartment door. The shock of the noise should wake him before he stepped out into the night unconscious.

The woman's voice returned to the phone. "We had someone cancel so tomorrow night is available. Otherwise, I have an opening late next week."

Harry thought his luck might have changed. "Tomorrow night works."

They settled on time, location, and what to bring. Harry hung up the phone. He hoped the sleep study discovered the reason for his lost memories. If not… Well, he didn't want to think about that.

Harry parked in front of Chip's house. A black Mercedes sat in the driveway. Either Emma had a visitor, or it was her car.

Harry inhaled, got out of his car and walked toward the house. He hated interviewing a spouse after their partner died, but he had no choice. Drake was compiling the evidence to convict Harry and he needed something to combat him. He rang the doorbell and mentally rehearsed what he'd say.

The door opened. Harry offered a smile.

A woman stood in the doorway. Pale blue eyes and a blinding smile of white teeth stood out against her tanned face. The sun highlighted the blonde strands in her shoulder-length brown hair. The black dress she wore failed to conceal the few extra pounds gathering around her waist.

"I'm Harry Bennett. Chip asked me to stop by if I was ever in the area."

"I'm Emma, his wife." Her smile slipped. "Chip passed away recently."

Harry widened his eyes as if Chip's death was news to him.

"What?" He leaned toward her. "I'm so sorry." He looked beyond her into the house. "I just saw him at his office the other day. He seemed fine. What happened?"

Emma opened her mouth to answer, but the beeping and grinding of a garbage truck overrode her. She motioned him inside, past the entryway, through the house, and into a combination sitting area and kitchen. A black leather couch, grey fabric side chairs, glass-topped coffee table, and some abstract art on the walls lent a modern touch to the room. Swirls of black ran through the white marble kitchen countertop.

"Have a seat. Would you like something to drink? Coffee, soda, water?"

Harry found individuals often found comfort in mundane tasks during times of grief, anything to distract them from the pain.

"A water would be great."

He sat at the kitchen bar and watched her. She stood just a few inches shy of Chip's height. Her arms were toned as if she lifted weights. He agreed with Buddy. If Chip had enough alcohol or drugs in his system and she caught him by surprise, she could have killed him, but why? Because of the affair? It ended with Lisa's death so killing Chip seemed pointless. Did Emma even know about the affair anyway?

Emma pulled a bottled water out of the beverage center and

handed it to him. She looked around the kitchen until she found a mug on the counter, then wrapped her hands around it as if seeking warmth.

"Chip was murdered." Her hands shook, the brown liquid sloshed over the side of the white cup.

Harry faked surprise. "Murdered? Why would anyone kill Chip?"

She looked at the counter. "I don't know." Her head lifted, and she met his eyes. "I think the cops believe I might have done it."

"Why?" Harry squinted.

She shrugged. "Don't they always suspect the spouse?"

Harry nodded. "Usually." He leaned across the bar toward her. "Look, I'm a private investigator. Used to be a cop. Maybe I can help."

Emma sighed. "That would be great."

"First thing they'll ask is where you were the night Chip was killed." Harry twisted off the bottle cap and took a sip.

"I already told the cops I left that afternoon for a two-day meeting. It was a couple of hours from here, so I stayed the night at the Marriott. The one closest to the conference center."

"Did Chip have any enemies?"

"Not that I know of." She bit her lip. "How well did you know Chip?"

Harry shrugged. "We kept in touch."

"Then you know he liked to party, liked liquor, and flirting with women. He might have gotten in with the wrong crowd or some jealous husband might have thought Chip took the flirting too far." She grabbed a dishcloth and swiped it across the counter.

"I'll check it out for you." Harry pulled a business card from his wallet. "Call me if you think of anything."

"Thanks. How much do I owe you?"

"This is on me. After all, Chip and I were friends." Harry smiled.

The low-level lighting in Vic and Anthony's, the soft chatter, the tinkling of silverware, and a belly full of steak relaxed Harry. He had joined Sophia in a glass of wine over dinner. After all, no one likes to drink alone. Besides, one glass of wine couldn't hurt. Scotch was preferable but might lead to a night of unconscious activity.

Sophia had to stay the night. Another night of unmonitored sleep might result in his fingerprints showing up at another crime scene. He figured Drake had planted the prints in Lisa's hotel room and Chip's house, but he wasn't sure anymore. If he could sleepwalk, then anything was possible.

What if he had killed Lisa and Chip while in an unconscious state? How would the courts rule on that? Would they put him away in some state hospital?

Drake would enjoy any type of incarceration for him. Harry had to stop thinking like this and focus on finding the killer. Even if it proved to be him. The not knowing was driving him crazy anyway.

First, he had to deal with today. Someone needed to spend

the night with him and his preferred someone was Sophia.

He watched as she sipped her wine. She didn't know Van had returned. Time to break the news.

"I forgot to tell you. Van came home." He smiled.

Cats did this kind of thing, ran off then mysteriously returned so he didn't need to elaborate.

Sophia eyes widened. "He found his way home? That's amazing."

Harry nodded. "Yep, just showed up outside. Accosted me on the way to my car."

She touched his arm. "I know you're glad he's home. It can be lonely living alone."

Here was the perfect lead in for asking her to spend the night, but first he had to eliminate any excuses.

"Do you have a pet?"

Sophia shook her head. "I want to get one eventually."

The waiter brought the bill, interrupting Harry's chance at a smooth line, not that he could think of one. Harry paid, then turned toward Sophia.

"Let's go to my place." Harry raised his eyebrows and the stakes. "You can meet Van."

Sophia smiled. "How could I pass up such an opportunity?"

If that's all it took to get a woman in his apartment, Harry would have gotten a cat sooner.

Van weaved around Sophia's bare legs, purring. She bent down and stroked his head. Harry wished he was Van.

"What a sweet cat."

Van's eyes slitted at Harry as if mocking him. Harry considered playing the video of the cat jumping on the kitchen counter, clawing the rug, and knocking items off tables, but decided cat jealousy was beneath him. Besides, Van was doing him a favor. Sophia might like Van enough to stay the night.

"How about a drink?" Harry asked.

"I really need to go."

Van stared at her wide-eyed and meowed, then jumped on the couch.

"I'll pet you one more time." Sophia sat next to the little charmer. Van bumped his head against her chin, his body rumbling.

"I'd like to take you home." Sophia scratched Van's neck.

"Let me grab my toothbrush." Harry motioned toward the bathroom.

Sophia cut her eyes at him. "I wasn't talking to you."

Harry held his hand to his chest as if crushed by her words. She laughed. Van settled in her lap.

"I think he wants you to stay."

Sophia caressed his fur. "Unfortunately, I've got an early shift tomorrow." She checked her phone. "It's late. I've got to go." Van placed a paw on her arm.

No doubt about it, Van made a great wingman. Wingcat?

Harry frowned. "But I picked you up from the motel. Don't they ever give you a break?"

"One of the girls quit. So, I'm covering for her until they find someone else."

She picked up Van, then placed him back on the couch. He

jumped down and stalked off with his tail in the air. Harry wasn't happy about her leaving either, but at least for him, there was still a chance for a goodnight kiss. She might even let him stay at her place. Harry didn't care where he slept. He just didn't want to sleep by himself and Wingcat didn't count.

As Harry pulled into the Star's parking lot, Sophia grabbed the door handle.

"Thanks for dinner," she said.

Harry thought about ways of extending the evening, but only one line came to mind: *We don't have to stop with dinner*, but he didn't want to scare her off. He wanted to tell her about all his troubles and beg her to spend the night, but she would think he was crazy or even worse, a possible killer.

The best he could hope for was another date. "Maybe we can do it again some time."

Sophia turned and smiled. "I would like that. Give me a call."

She got out of the car and walked toward the motel.

At least she hadn't shut him down completely.

Harry picked up his phone and pulled up the voice message Candy had left earlier. Maybe she had ditched Richie.

Candy's sultry voice purred in his ear, "Richard's going out tonight. He says it's some meeting at his office. I don't believe it. He's leaving the house around eight. Follow him."

Harry checked his phone: 9:15. Richie was probably home by now.

He texted Candy. *Sorry, I just finished with a client. Is Richie home yet?*

No. Candy added a frowning red-faced emoji.

Harry texted: *I'll check his office.*

He hoped he didn't find Richie's car at the office, but at some hotel. With any luck, Candy would leave him and spend the night with Harry. While he was at the motel, Harry might as well check Star's parking lot. Candy had already caught Richie leaving the place, so he doubted he'd visit it again, but some people believed in taking risks, even got a high off them.

The front parking lot held very few cars, none of them Richie's. The back lot held twenty plus cars. Harry scanned the cars. Parked in the farthest row from the motel, covered in the shadows of a thick stand of trees, sat a silver Mercedes coupe. The license tag matched Richie's. Either the man enjoyed living on the edge or a pull stronger than Candy had him.

Harry parked several spots over from the Mercedes. He watched for any movement at the motel. A blonde exited a room, hooker heels, a tight skirt, and even tighter shirt showcased her curves, definitely competition for Candy, at least in looks. A man followed her with an athletic build that matched Richie's.

Harry took pictures of the couple. The man got in a pickup. Harry sighed and returned to watching the rooms.

Light spilled from a door, highlighting another man with Richie's frame. Harry snapped shots of the man. The guy got in the silver Mercedes and left. Richie was probably going home, so Harry stuck around to see who else came out of the room. Candy would want a picture of her competitor. Besides, if Harry got enough evidence for Candy, she might come over to Harry's place and stay the night with him.

The door opened. Harry took a picture, then his mouth fell open. A slim man stood in the door frame, then walked toward a sporty black BMW. It must be the wrong room. He zoomed in on the previous photo, same room number. Harry captured the man, the car, and the license plate on his camera.

Richie never came across as anything but heterosexual. He was surprised Candy hadn't picked up on it.

Harry put his car in gear, ready to follow the man, when a light caught his eye. The same door opened again, and two more men exited. Harry threw the car into park and snapped some more shots. Either Richie liked a walk on the wild side, or his office had changed location. Some companies had offsite meetings, but at the Star? Talk about cost cutting measures.

Harry didn't have the patience or the time to fool with texting Candy, so he phoned her. She didn't answer. He left the details in a voice message and sent the relevant photos. She could figure out what to do with them, but Harry doubted she'd knock on his door tonight. Richie had some explaining to do and Harry figured it would take all night.

When Harry arrived home, Van greeted him. At least, the cat hadn't disappeared again, but Van couldn't stop Harry from leaving the apartment, doing hell knows what.

Harry looked around the room in search of something to block the door. Anything to slow his sleepwalking-self down enough to wake up or return to bed. He shoved the recliner against the door, then added several dishes in front of the recliner. The noise of knocking against the dishes might startle him awake. He doubted it, but it couldn't hurt.

If he drank enough caffeine, he might be able to stay up all night. Who was he kidding? He couldn't function on no sleep. Harry took an over-the-counter sleeping pill and hoped it knocked out even the sleepwalker in him.

38

Dr. Janet Worth watched the ice cream commercial. Her mouth watered. Maybe she hadn't eaten all the chocolate ice cream. She checked the freezer. Nothing but frozen vegetables and entrees stared at her. The craving for the smooth chocolate sweetness taunted her taste buds. The grocery store closed in thirty minutes, but it was only five minutes away. No stalker would attack her if she parked close enough to the grocery store. Besides, Thibodeaux told her an undercover cop shadowed her.

She snatched her purse and headed for the door. The stalker wasn't going to rule her life, maybe chocolate, but not this creep. Janet walked quickly to her car, watching for any movement. Once inside the car, she hit the lock. As she drove away, she glanced in her rearview mirror. Headlights followed a couple of car lengths behind her.

At the grocery store, she parked under a light, close to the entrance and waited until the headlights tailing her parked. A mid-sized black car pulled into the back row of the parking lot. Janet stepped out of her car and followed a couple inside.

Only one other customer eyed the ice cream flavors. Janet knew the spot where they shelved her favorite. She grabbed it, then noticed they had a buy one gallon get one free. Ice cream didn't go bad. She couldn't remember the last time the power went out long enough to ruin her frozen food. No hurricanes loomed on the horizon. If one blew in, she could ride out the storm in style sucking down the chocolate goodness.

Janet smiled while scanning and bagging her items, nothing better than getting a deal. When she exited the store, she glanced at the black car. From this distance, it was difficult to make out the driver, or even if there was one. She placed her bags in the back seat, then slid in the front and drove away as the headlights of the black car came to life. This cop wasn't sleeping on the job.

Janet checked her surroundings as she pulled into her driveway. A woman walked on the sidewalk. The townhomes on either side of hers were dark. Her front door and tastebuds beckoned her to go inside.

Down the street, headlights approached. The cop had her in sight. She slipped from the car, grabbed the bags, and scurried toward her house.

Gripping the bags with one hand, she inserted the key in the lock. As she opened the door, footsteps sounded behind her. A push sent her stumbling inside. The bags of ice cream fell from her grasp as she struggled to stay standing.

The door slammed shut. An arm locked around her neck. Janet kicked and opened her mouth to scream, but only screeched out a gasp.

The intruder dragged her to the couch and pressed her face into the cushion. His weight pinned her in place. She couldn't breathe.

She kicked her legs but made no contact. Her heart beat against her chest as if it wanted to escape.

She tried turning her head to get some air, but the person held her firm. The fabric would suffocate her soon.

A hand grabbed her hair and jerked back her head. She sucked in air. The smell of cigarette smoke mixed with the scent of gardenias filled her nose. Fingers stuffed something in her mouth. It felt rough and dry against her tongue. He tied a cloth around her eyes. Her hands were bound behind her back. Her feet tied.

She felt hot breath on her ear, then a voice in her ear, "Stay away from Harry."

The weight lifted off her back. Footsteps ran through the house. The back door creaked open, then shut.

Janet jerked her hands apart, stretching the rope, and loosening the cords until she worked her hands free.

She yanked out the gag and took deep breaths, grateful for fresh air. She untied her feet.

No way was she going outside to get the undercover cop. She stepped around the ice cream cartons. The contents of her purse lay sprawled across the floor. She grabbed her Glock and bolted the front door, then picked up her phone and dialed Thibodeaux.

"It's Dr. Worth. Someone attacked me."

"Where are you? Are you hurt?"

She walked toward the rear of the house. "I'm home. I've probably got a few bruises, but nothing requiring medical attention." Her hands shook as she locked the back door.

"Let me get in touch with my man. Last update shows him parked outside your home. You're there, right?"

"Yes." She wasn't sure she'd ever go out again.

"I'm on my way."

The attacker's words ran in an endless loop in her mind, "Stay away from Harry." The voice. A throaty voice. A southern accent. A woman's voice.

An ice cream carton had slipped the confines of the bag when she dropped it. Janet bent down and picked up the cold container, the sweaty sides wet her fingers. She tossed it in the bag, then picked up the rest.

The chocolate ice cream no longer held its allure. Instead, it represented violation, vulnerability, and fear. The thought of eating it made her nauseous. She threw it all in the trash.

Grabbing paper towels, she wiped the drops of moisture from the floor. She wished the memory of this night would wipe away as easily.

The doorbell rang. She jerked, tossed the paper towels aside, and grabbed her gun. She checked the peephole. Thibodeaux stood on the porch. She unlocked the door and let him inside.

He sat on the couch, then pulled out a pad and pen. "Tell me exactly what happened."

Step by step, she walked him through the night. Thibodeaux took notes.

When she finished, he frowned. "Do you know a Harry?"

Janet knew only one Harry. She nodded. "Harry Bennett."

Thibodeaux dropped his pen. "Harry Bennett?"

She nodded.

He picked up his pen. "And you're sure it was a woman's voice?"

"Yes." The thought of the voice sent a chill through her body. She grabbed a throw off the couch and threw it over her lap.

"So, Mark Crawford isn't the stalker." He leaned toward her. "Do you remember anything else?"

She replayed the events in her mind. "I smelled cigarette smoke and gardenias."

He made a note on his pad. "Do you know why she'd tell you to stay away from Harry?"

"I don't know." Janet rubbed her forehead. "Maybe she's jealous?"

Thibodeaux raised his eyebrows. "Are you seeing Harry?"

She shook her head. "Only professionally, but the woman might have thought something else was going on."

Thibodeaux snapped on some latex gloves, then examined the scarf used to gag her. The gauzy white material flowed over his fingers. "Is this yours or did she bring it with her?"

"It's not mine."

He held it closer to her. "Have you ever seen one like it?"

She resisted pulling away from it. Instead, she drew closer to it. Nothing about the material or the color stood out and it had no pattern. Even if someone she knew had worn it, it wouldn't have made an impression on her.

"If I have, I don't remember it."

"What about this?" He held up the strip of white cloth used to cover her eyes.

She shook her head.

"Maybe we can find something on one of these that will lead us to the stalker." He bagged both of them along with the twine used to tie her hands and feet, then closed his notepad. "Until we find the stalker, stay away from Harry."

"But he needs my help." Harry's case was the first interesting one she had come across in a while.

A look of confusion crossed Thibodeaux's face. "Why does Harry need your help?"

"You'll have to ask Harry."

Thibodeaux nodded. "Harry wouldn't want to compromise your safety. I'll have a chat with him." Thibodeaux stood and walked to the door. As he opened it, he looked across the street. "I'll also find someone better at watching over you."

As Janet closed the door behind Thibodeaux, she devised a plan on how to meet with Harry. She wouldn't let some disturbed woman stop her from helping a patient. Besides, it would give the cops a chance to catch the bitch and end the nightmare.

39

Charley checked off the last key on her list. She stared at the encrypted message. Her shoulders slumped as if an invisible force pressed on them. She had to have the message cracked by tomorrow. Perhaps, Tom had some better ideas. After all, he was the expert.

She picked up her phone and touched Tom's phone number. When he answered, his voice sounded deep and husky. For a moment, all thoughts vanished from her mind. She shook her head.

Charley swallowed the lump in her throat. "Hi Tom. I finished my list and have had no luck. How are you doing on yours?"

"I've finished mine too, but I'm working on a couple of other ideas."

Charley rubbed her forehead. "I'm worried I might have missed something. Would you mind checking my work? Also, I would probably learn a lot by reviewing what you've done." She paused. "Could we do a virtual meeting in an hour or so?" An hour would give her time to shower and dress in something other than her grey sweats.

"It would be easier if we did it in person. Why don't you come over to my place?"

Her skin tingled as if someone had plugged her into an outlet. "I don't have a car right now."

"No problem. I can come over to your place. Just text me the address."

Charley looked around at the papers stacked on her coffee table, the dirty dishes on the counter, and the overflowing trash can. "That works. How about two hours from now?"

"See you then." He hung up.

She texted her address to him, checked the time, then ran around the house cleaning.

Charley smoothed her hair, then stepped back from her bathroom mirror for a full body check. Her tight jeans sucked in whatever extra pounds the silky black shirt didn't hide. She unsnapped the top three metal white buttons, then leaned into the mirror. Just enough cleavage showed without shouting slut. The gloss on her lips might be too much for a business meeting. She ran her tongue over her mouth leaving only a pink tinge. She sighed.

During her teenage years, she'd asked her mother if she was pretty. Her mom had stared at her as if assessing the possibility. Finally, her mom had rubbed her chin, frowned, and responded, "Well, you're attractive."

Charley shrugged. Maybe Tom went for personality instead of looks.

A knock on the door interrupted her self-assessment. Charley turned her back on the mirror and flicked off the lights. She followed the vacuum tracks across the carpet toward the sugar-cookie-scented candle burning on the kitchen counter and blew it out. The counter and bar were crumb and clutter free.

On her desk, papers were stacked in a neat pile next to her notebook and pencil. Only the sun's rays spoiled the perfection as they spilled through the window and hit her monitor, highlighting dust and fingerprint smudges. She ran to the window and closed the blinds, then hurried to the door.

She checked the peephole. A sports coat accentuated Tom's broad shoulders. No doubt his white polo shirt covered washboard abs. The hall light gleamed on his blond hair as if he had a halo. Her heart fluttered. The flesh and blood Tom was even hotter than the virtual version. Perhaps she should have left on the lip gloss. She licked her lips and opened the door.

"Hi Tom." She waved him inside.

"It's great to finally meet you in person." Tom flashed a seductive grin. Her toes curled.

"Thanks. I'm glad we could get together too."

As he walked past her with his laptop case, she noticed his jeans had a well-worn look and hugged him as if they didn't want to let go. He placed his laptop on the kitchen counter then turned toward her.

Charley cleared her throat. "Would you like something to drink? Soda, water, juice?" She raised her eyebrows. "Or something stronger?"

He laughed. A spark ignited his eyes, but his face remained smooth as if no wrinkle would dare to make an appearance. "I'd better stick with water."

As she handed him a water bottle, his eyes met hers. A tingle ran across her skin. Player or not, Charley wanted him. She quickly glanced away in case he had magical powers and could read her thoughts.

Charley picked up her notebook, the stack of papers, and a pencil from her desk and carried them to the kitchen bar.

"Should we get started?" she asked.

He unzipped his case, pulled out his laptop, and some papers. "Sure. What do you want to do first?"

She visualized stripping him of his shirt and flushed. Charley pulled out a barstool then passed over her notes.

"How about we go over each other's work?" She reached for his papers.

"Sure." He raised an eyebrow and smirked. "I'll show you mine if you show me yours."

Heat rushed through her body. She resisted fanning herself as he sat on the stool next to her. The smell of a pine forest mixed with an orange grove washed over her. She inhaled the intoxicating fumes and resisted scooting closer to him. Tom picked up the top sheet of her papers and focused on it.

Charley forced herself to look at the work Tom had done. She scribbled comments in her notebook as she reviewed it. One key on his list intrigued her. She had wanted to try it, but when they split tasks, he took that one. In looking at the process he used, it seemed he had skipped one of the algorithms.

She pushed the paper close to him and tapped it with her pencil. "On this one, why did you skip this step?"

Tom leaned over the paper and frowned.

"Of course, you're the expert, but I'd like to try it myself." Charley shrugged. "Maybe the message will magically decode." She smiled.

He shook his head. "It's just a waste of time." Tom twisted off the cap of his water and took a sip.

"That's okay. I need the practice anyway." She stood and picked up the paper.

"Wait a minute." Tom snapped his fingers. "I just had an idea of something that might work." His fingers ran across his keyboard.

She leaned over his shoulder. He looked up at her, his mouth within inches of hers. Her mind blanked as if he had cast a spell over her. She had to put some space between them, or the message would never get cracked.

"You try that, and I'll work on this." Charley walked over to her monitor.

40

Before leaving for Lisa's Memorial Service, Harry sat on the edge of the couch and watched the video from last night. Van performed his usual nightly tricks. No wonder the cat slept all day. Nothing else entered the camera frame. Harry's shoulders relaxed. He'd stayed out of trouble last night.

Harry grabbed his keys and wallet, then left for David's house.

As he drove, Harry wondered what they did at a memorial service. He hated funerals. Those close to the departed, walked in a daze, tissue in hand, ready for any fresh onslaught of tears.

The reception afterwards always proved beneficial, at least for Harry. People spent time renewing old relationships and catching up on gossip. It was a great time for gathering intel on the victim and adding to the list of suspects.

By the time Harry arrived, cars lined the driveway and one side of the street. He parked his car, then hurried down the block and up the sidewalk. A butler opened the door and pointed him to the living room. Someone had cleared the furniture and filled the area with rows of about fifty chairs.

Only a few empty seats remained, two toward the front and one in the back corner. Harry took the one in the last row. It was the perfect place to observe guests without being noticed. He recognized Buddy in the row in front of him, but Drake wasn't with him.

A prayer was said, then family and close friends of Lisa's stood and talked about her, some complimented her, others shared fond memories. Rachel spoke of their years of friendship and how much she would miss her.

After the service, David invited the guests to the dining room for refreshments. Harry stayed in his seat and scanned the crowd, then he stopped and stared. His mouth fell open. What was Candy doing there? He watched while Candy hooked her hand around Richie's arm and they maneuvered past the chairs.

Someone tapped him on the shoulder.

Harry looked up into Buddy's face. He leaned over, enveloping Harry in coffee breath.

"We need to talk, but let's get some food first," Buddy said.

Harry followed Buddy to the dining area. A buffet lined one side of the room, a bartender stood behind a bar in the corner, four stools circled each of the dozen or so circular tables occupying the center of the room. The smell of bread, bacon, and fried chicken triggered a rumbling in Harry's stomach. The clinking of silverware and people chatting filled the room. Buddy and Harry grabbed a plate, then joined the line for food.

Once they settled at a table with food and drink, Harry pointed a fork at Buddy.

"What did you want to talk about?"

Buddy finished chewing and wiped his mouth. "Remember Mark Crawford?"

"Yeah, he's the stalker you hired me to follow." Harry picked up a fried chicken leg and bit into it.

"We thought he was stalking Dr. Janet Worth."

Harry lost the grip on his chicken. "Dr. Worth?"

Buddy nodded. "Turns out a woman is stalking her."

"Do you know who it is?"

Buddy finished off a bacon wrapped stuffed jalapeño. "Not yet. But get this, last night the woman attacked Dr. Worth. Didn't hurt her but told her to stay away from Harry." He raised his eyebrows. "You're the only Harry she knows."

Harry rubbed his chin. No one would care whether he spent time with Dr. Worth. Nothing was going on between the two of them. Besides, Harry had no commitment with anyone. It made no sense. He downed his scotch and considered asking the bartender for a double.

"Did she give you a description of the woman?"

Buddy shook his head. "The woman blindfolded her and bound her hands and feet." Buddy picked at a roll on his plate. "She did say the woman had a throaty sounding voice with a southern accent. Know anyone like that?"

Harry only knew one woman with that kind of voice, Candy. He glanced over at the table where she sat with Richie. She caught his look and smiled. Why would she stalk Dr. Worth? Candy did some wild stuff, but stalking his psychiatrist fell in the crazy category.

Harry turned toward Buddy. "I can't think of anyone. Did Dr. Worth say anything else?"

"The woman smelled of cigarette smoke and gardenias."

Candy didn't smoke and Harry knew her perfume, an intoxicating smell of roses and oranges. The clothes left on the floor of his bedroom smelled of cigarettes and gardenias. Victoria smoked. He had to find that woman.

Buddy cleared his throat. "Until we find the stalker, it's probably a good idea if you stay away from Dr. Worth."

Harry gripped his glass. He needed Dr. Worth to fix his sleep walking problems, but he didn't want to put her in any kind of danger. He'd just call her and get the results from the sleep study.

"I'll steer clear of her."

Buddy nodded. "Good." He squinted. "Why are you seeing her anyway?"

He had never taken Buddy for the nosey type, but then again, they had talked a lot on stakeouts.

Harry shrugged. "I'm having some trouble sleeping."

"You and me both." Buddy stood. "I'm going to mingle. See you later."

Harry noticed Candy by herself at the dessert table. He sidled up next to her.

"Which one do you suggest?" he asked.

She eyed him up and down. "Me, of course."

He laughed and glanced across the room at Richie. "Looks like you're taken. I'll have to settle for another sweet." He picked up a brownie. "How do you know Lisa?"

"I went to school with her. We kept meaning to get together." Tears formed in her eyes. "Now, it's too late."

Richie moved toward them, then slipped his arm around Candy. "Which one should I pick?"

Candy picked up a plate with a slice of pie on it and shoved it toward him. "Apple pie has always been your favorite."

Harry guessed Candy wasn't on the list of desserts for Richie after the Star debacle. He wanted to know how Richie explained the situation, but he'd have to wait until later to find out.

Candy grabbed Harry by the arm and looked at Richie. "You remember Harry."

Richie frowned. "Who could forget Harry?"

Candy waved across the room. "Harry, let me introduce you to Rachel." She turned to Richie. "I'll be back." She tugged on Harry's arm.

As they closed in on Rachel, she leaned closer to Harry. "I wanted to get away so we could talk."

Candy hugged Rachel, then touched Harry on the shoulder. "This is Harry."

"We've already met." Rachel tilted her head.

Harry smiled. "Tall Triple Mocha Frappuccino with whip, right?"

Rachel laughed. "You've got a good memory."

"Is there anybody you don't know, Harry?" Candy rolled her eyes.

Rachel checked her watch. "I've got to go." She touched Candy's arm. "Let's get together next week. Give me a call."

After she left, Candy pulled Harry toward a corner table. "I want you to keep investigating Richie. He gave me some bullshit story about having a meeting at the Star."

"They might be on a tight budget."

"Bullshit." She shook her head. "He's up to something. Find out and let me know." She looked across the room. "Here he comes. I'd better go." She smiled and left.

The crowd had thinned to less than a dozen, including the waitstaff. Time for Harry to leave too. He needed to buy some pajamas for tonight.

41

"I did it!" Charley grinned at the decoded message on her screen. She turned and did a high five sign in Tom's direction.

He squinted. "What?"

"Come see!" She motioned him over, then stared at her monitor with a smile. Maybe they would celebrate with supper at an elegant restaurant with white tablecloths and candles. She and Tom would gaze at each other through a candle lit glow while the waiter poured wine, and soft music played in the background. After the meal...

The zip of Tom's laptop case and the sound of approaching footsteps broke through her thoughts. Seconds later, he leaned over her shoulder. She inhaled the scent of his cologne. Electricity shot through her. He turned toward her; his breath warm on her cheek. Charley wanted to look at him, to kiss him, but resisted making the first move. Tom seemed interested in her, but he might just be a flirt. She stared at the monitor. Perhaps he would gently turn her face to him, touch his lips to hers. Charley swallowed the lump in her throat.

Tom whispered in her ear. "I wish you hadn't done that."

Her skin prickled. "What do you mean?"

"Decoded the message," he said, in a low monotone voice.

She didn't get it. Was he one of those guys who had to get the answer first? She frowned.

"It was a team effort. Now, we just have to pass it along to Derek." She picked up her phone and brought up Derek's phone number.

He reached across her, touched the keyboard, and cleared the screen.

"Put the phone down. You're not telling anyone." He pressed his hand down on her shoulder.

Charley turned and looked at him. The sparkle in his eye had turned cold. He wasn't hot enough for her to deal with this kind of ego.

She shrugged. "Okay, you can tell him." She handed him the phone.

There was a gun in his hand, pointed at her.

"You don't get it. We're not telling anybody. Put the phone down." The calculating tone in his voice sent shivers down her spine.

She placed the phone on her desk.

Charley glanced at the baseball bat and knife next to the front door. There was only about five feet between her and the weapons. A kick in the groin might buy her enough time to grab the bat and run for help. Bending down and picking up the knife would take too long.

He stepped several feet away from her and slung his laptop case across his shoulder.

"Get up," he said, waving the gun at her.

She stood. Her legs quivered. She leaned against her desk and inched toward the phone.

"Turn around and face the door."

Her stomach churned. "I need to go to the bathroom." She could slip the phone under her shirt, lock the bathroom door, and call 911. What was she thinking? He would bust down the door, shoot her, and leave before anyone arrived.

"Forget it. Just do what I said." He motioned toward the door.

As she walked forward, he followed, pressing the gun against her back. "We're going to leave here and take a trip in my car. Don't try anything." His voice deepened. "Or I'll have to shoot you."

What difference did it make? He was probably going to kill her anyway. Although, the longer she lived, the more opportunities she had for an escape. They could have an accident in his car. The cops could pull him over for speeding. Anything could happen.

She glanced at the bat and the knife as they passed by them. If only she had kept them close to her. Still, what chance would she have had against a gun?

When he shut the door, the sound echoed down the empty hallway. "Take the stairs. My car is parked near the exit."

The outside heat and dampness permeated the open-air stairwell, pressing heavily on her body. A moldy smell overwhelmed her. Breathing hard, she clutched at the handrail as Tom followed closely behind her.

Derek had assigned a CIA guy to watch her apartment. She could signal she was in trouble. He might tail them when they left.

When her foot hit the last step, Tom holstered the gun and gripped her arm. "Act normal. My car is the black Ford truck to your left in the second row."

As they exited the stairwell, Tom kept a tight hold on her arm. Charley looked around for a savior. The clouds hung low. Crows pecked at trash on the pavement and cawed at each other. A black sedan was parked in the far corner of the lot next to the fence. Tom waved and smiled. The window of the car slid down and the driver returned the wave.

"I'll have to send someone over to take care of him." Tom said, as he continued to smile at the driver. "Why didn't you just quit?"

Charley stumbled over the sidewalk curb. Tom's fingers pressed tighter and stopped her from falling onto the pavement. When they reached his truck, he released her, opened the passenger door, and helped Charley onto the running board. Her knees buckled.

Tom pushed her onto the seat. His jaw tightened. "Get the seat belt on, now."

Charley snapped the belt in place. Tom shut and locked the doors. He kept his eyes focused on her. His hand rested on the holster underneath his sports jacket as he walked around the hood and slipped into the driver's seat.

When they pulled out of the parking lot, Charley looked in the side mirror, but the black sedan didn't follow them. She balled up her hands. No one suspected Tom of being anything other than trustworthy. Her fingers tightened, the nails biting into her flesh.

She wished she'd never decoded the message. It was only a date, time, and place, all of which had vanished from her mind. Still, if she could remember the information and pass it along to the CIA, then knowing the sender and the receiver, they would have all the necessary information to stop whatever was happening. None of that helped her at the moment.

Tom took off his jacket and cranked up the AC. Cool air pushed through the vents and onto her face. He pulled out his phone and tapped the display. She slid her hand over to the door handle.

He reached for his gun. "Don't even think about it."

Charley pulled her hands onto her lap.

The phone rang. A cheerful voice answered. "What's up?"

Tom watched her as he responded, "We had some unexpected trouble." He frowned at her. "Take out the guy watching the apartment. Use someone on the inside. Someone the guy will trust." He sighed. "And this time ditch the car and the body where no one will find it."

"You got it, boss." The cheery voice hung up.

Charley wrung her hands. What did he mean by "on the inside"? Who else in the CIA was involved?

Tom drove out of the parking lot with one hand on the wheel and the other resting on the gun sitting next to him. His cologne strengthened in the confines of the truck. The once pleasant smell now reminded Charley of products used to mop floors and eliminate the smell of vomit. She gripped the edges of the grey leather seat.

"Where are we going?"

His eyes traveled the length of her frame. "Does it really matter?" He smirked.

A cold sweat broke out over her skin. The road ahead blurred as houses and trees flashed by. She focused on the inside of the truck. The leather seats were soft and supple as if on a strict diet of saddle soap. The black carpet looked showroom ready. The dashboard gleamed. Not even a fingerprint smudged the controls or the trim.

Charley wrapped her arms around her stomach and bent forward.

"I think I'm going to throw up." As nauseous as she was, it wouldn't take much.

His head jerked toward her, and his eyes widened. "What?"

He shook his head and his body relaxed. "You're just trying to get out of the car." He narrowed his eyes. "Any gagging and I'll throw you out of the car and leave you dead on the side of the road."

Maybe she could pop the lock on her seatbelt and the door fast enough to roll out when the car stopped, then she could run for it.

The houses grew farther apart as the woods thickened into a forest. Tom signaled and pulled onto a dirt driveway. Overhanging branches blocked out the sun. Trees pressed in on both sides. Charley glanced at him. He leaned forward in his seat as he focused on the driveway. Would he kill her and dump her in the woods? Or would he have his way with her first? She reached for the door handle.

He grabbed the gun from his holster and pointed it at her.

Her skin prickled as if thousands of spiders crawled across it. She returned her hands to her lap.

The car, the trees, the cologne all closed in on her. Charley's head pounded.

The road ended in a stand of trees. Tom got out of the car and locked the doors. She had to escape before her dead body ended up in the woods. Her fingers fumbled at the seat belt lock. It clicked. She hit the door lock and grabbed the handle. Tom's face appeared at her window. A slow smile spread across his face as if he were possessed.

Her stomach ached. The pepperoni pizza and salad from lunch rose up in her throat. She gagged. Tom opened her door. Charley slid out and stood on the running board. She placed her hands on his shoulders, leaned over him as if going in for a kiss, and threw up.

Tom shouted, "Shit!" He wiped his eyes. Charley jumped off the running board and kneed him in the groin. Tom doubled over, still gripping the gun, and fell on his knees to the ground.

Charley raced into the forest.

Charley ran, zigzagging between the trees. She listened for sounds of Tom following but only heard the beating of her heart and her ragged breath. Sweat plastered her shirt to her skin. A pain shot up her side. No time to stop.

She raced for a clump of trees and the rushing sound of

water. Footsteps sounded right behind her. She pumped her legs and arms harder. Why didn't he just shoot her?

A tug on her shirt pulled her backwards.

"Gotcha!" He shouted.

Charley screamed. Adrenaline surged through her body. She flailed forward, digging in her heels. Tom laughed. She wouldn't let him get her. With both hands, Charley popped open her shirt snaps. The shirt pulled free. Tom cursed. She ran.

Branches clawed at her bare skin as she raced through the trees and underbrush. The dirt gave way. For a moment she was free falling. She looked down, tucked into a cannon ball shape, shut her eyes, and held her breath just as cool water closed over her head. Bullets pinged the water around her.

Charley swam underwater with the flow of the river and angled for the far side. In her brief glimpse of the river, it was at least four car lengths wide. If she could get across it, Tom would have a harder time shooting her. Her lungs ached from holding her breath. She had to breath. Her head felt as if it would explode. She bobbed to the surface, gulped in air, and searched the area, but didn't see Tom.

The bank was only a few yards away but rose in a steep cliff to the woods. She touched the river bottom with her feet. It was shallow enough for her to stand and leave her head just above the water. Staying in the river wasn't an option. Tom would find her.

Farther down, the bank was low enough for her to climb up it. She ducked down in the water and swam, wondering if alligators were in the area. Being shot would be better than a gator eating her. When she resurfaced, the low bank was within a few feet. Charley checked her surroundings, but there was no sign of Tom, so she walked the rest of the way with the mud sucking at her shoes.

Just as Charley approached the bank, a snake slid into the water. She gasped and jerked backwards. Her foot pulled free of her shoe. The river could keep it. No way was she staying in the water any longer. She scrambled up the bank and into the woods. Her other shoe sloshed, and her jeans weighed down her every step. Rocks poked at the bottom of her sock encased foot. She stared at the endless stretch of trees. Was Tom out there waiting for her? Which direction should she go for help? She looked down at her black bra and wondered what kind of help she would get?

Charley glanced into the forest. If she went into the woods, her sense of direction, already stretched, would only get worse. She turned and ran along the riverbank.

Downriver, a truck crossed a bridge. She dropped to the ground. Her heart raced as she focused on the vehicle. Its color looked more silver or grey than black, but next time it could be Tom's truck. She stood, then darted amongst the trees growing close to the river.

Up ahead, deeper in the woods, voices sounded. Charley crept toward the noise.

A grey-haired woman stood on the porch of a white clapboard bungalow which was only slightly larger than

Charley's apartment. The sun glinted on the two windows on either side of the screened back door.

"Don't forget the milk," the woman said.

A wiry man in well-worn jeans and a t-shirt stood between a faded blue Chevy truck and a red Ford minivan. He ran his fingers through the few wisps of hair still attached to his scalp.

"If you think of anything else, call me." He climbed into the truck and left.

The woman hobbled inside as if her legs struggled to support the extra pounds she carried. The screen door slammed behind her.

The old lady reminded Charley of her grandma, an accepting lady who always welcomed strays. There was a chance this old woman would help her.

She slipped from the woods, ran up the porch steps, and peered through the screen door as she rapped on it.

"Help! I need to call the police," Charley shouted.

The old woman walked with heavy steps to the door. She eyed Charley as if she had sprung up out of the river mud.

"Oh, my word. Get in here, Honey." She opened the door, tugged Charley inside, then shut and locked the door behind her. "What happened?" The woman put an arm around Charley, enveloping her in the scent of baked bread.

"A man is after me." Charley trembled. "If he catches me, he'll kill me."

"Ain't nothing going to happen to you here." The woman squeezed Charley's shoulder.

She led her to a wooden breakfast table and pulled out a

chair. "Have a seat. I'll lock the front door, then call the sheriff."

Charley sat on the edge of the chair. She watched the woman as she walked past her into the living area and locked the front door.

Charley didn't want to appear rude, but Tom could show up anytime.

"911 might be faster than the sheriff?" Charley's legs jiggled up and down.

The old lady raised an eyebrow. "He is 911."

She looked around the front room and scratched her head. "Now, where did I put that dern phone? Last time I had it, I was talking with Patty. That's my niece. Such a sweet girl. In fact, she's married to the sheriff."

She shook her head. "Not in here. Maybe I left it in the kitchen?"

Charley scanned the area.

"Is that it?" She pointed at the dark-green-vinyl-covered counters that topped the yellowed cabinets. "On the counter, next to the stove."

The woman smiled. "Oh yeah. I was in the middle of baking when she called."

She picked up her phone and a set of keys. "My husband is always on me about putting my keys up."

The woman hung the keys on a set of hooks on the wall between the breakfast area and the living room. "He gets tired of helping me hunt for the things."

She scrolled through her phone, tapped the display, then

held it to her ear. "Sam, this is Alma. We got a problem. Some man's threatening to kill a woman."

Alma frowned. "No, he ain't here now."

Her mouth fell open. "Thirty minutes? Can't you do no better than that? What about sending over Parker?"

She rolled her eyes. "Alright, alright. Just get here as quick as you can."

Alma hung up, then snapped her fingers. She turned to Charley. "My son works for the law in Houston. He's coming out this way to drop off something and promised to stop by here." She smiled. "Such a good son. I bet he can get here faster than the sheriff. I'll call him and see where he's at."

She tapped the phone screen, then pressed it against her ear. "Hey. How far away are you? We got some trouble here and who knows when Sam will show up."

Alma looked at Charley. "It's a lady. Some man is out to get her."

Charley peered out the breakfast window. Except for a few squirrels, nothing moved. Why was she worried? Tom didn't know where she was and the sheriff was on his way. Her legs relaxed. She sagged against the back of the chair and watched Alma.

"Uh-huh." Alma stared up at the ceiling. "So, about ten to fifteen minutes?"

She smiled at Charley. "We'll see you then. Love ya."

Alma motioned to her. "Come on, Hon. Let's get you a shirt."

Charley's legs throbbed as if she'd run a marathon. She

placed her hands on the table and pushed up out of the chair, then moved toward Alma.

The woman's eyes traveled from Charley's wet jeans up to her bare midriff. By the time she returned to Charley's face, her brown eyes had softened.

"I tell you what. You clean up in the bathroom while I find you something to wear."

Charley followed Alma down a darkened hall. Alma opened a door and flicked on the lights.

"Washcloths are in the cabinet."

"Thanks." Charley walked in and stared at the mirror. Mud streaked across her forehead and her cheeks. Her brown hair frizzed out in all directions. She turned on the water, cupped her hands, and drank the cool water, then splashed it on her face and blotted her skin dry with a hand towel. Her hair was a lost cause.

Alma appeared in the doorway with a red and green plaid button-up shirt.

"I can't wear this anymore." She smiled. "Gained a few pounds that I'll probably never lose." Alma handed it to her. "You can keep it."

"Thanks for all the help." Charley smiled.

Alma waved her hand. "Think nothing of it. I'll be in the kitchen when you're ready."

Charley shrugged on the shirt and buttoned it, then stepped into the hallway. The light from the bathroom hit on a picture frame. Charley recognized a thinner Alma with dark brown hair standing next to her husband who sported a head full of hair. She moved to the next framed photo and froze. *No way, no way, no way!* Her heart pounded loud in her ears as she stared at the smiling face.

"That's my son," Alma said.

Charley jumped.

"The good Lord only blessed us with one child, but what a blessing he is." She touched the photo and smiled, then looked at her watch. "He should just about be here. Come on. I'll get you something to drink." Alma grabbed Charley's arm and pulled her along.

It just couldn't be. Maybe Tom had a look alike. Alma said he had to drop something off. Had that something been Charley's dead body?

"Everyone in town likes Tom."

Charley's stomach clenched. She had to get out of there.

"He played high school football. Quarterback. Wasn't quite good enough to play college ball though."

When they rounded the corner to the kitchen, the hum of an engine sounded. Alma released Charley's arm and rushed to the window above the kitchen sink.

"It's Tom." She waved at him and headed for the back door.

Charley's head pounded. Black spots swam before her eyes. She pressed her hand against the wall sectioning off the living area from the kitchen. The keys hung just above her fingers.

As Alma turned to face the back door, Charley said, "I've got to go to the bathroom."

Charley grabbed the keys, slipped through the living room and out the front door, quietly closing it behind her. Flying down the steps, she flipped through the keys until she found one with the word Ford embossed on it.

Charley ran along the front and side of the house, then peeked around the corner. Sweat rolled down the sides of her face. She watched as Tom disappeared into the house. The screen door slammed shut. Charley ran low along the ground toward the minivan.

Alma's voice boomed out into the yard. "Tom, thank goodness you're here."

Charley cracked open the car door.

Alma's voice carried through the screen door. "She's in the bathroom."

Charley's hands shook. The keys fell to the ground. She ran her fingers through the grass. Sweat dripped into her eyes. She had to find those keys!

Tom's voice shouted, "Mom, she's not in the bathroom. When did you last see her?"

Charley's fingers hit metal. She snatched the keys and slid into the driver's seat. The screen door screeched. She shut and locked the doors, started the car, threw it into reverse, and shot out of the parking spot. Dust flew in the air. She shoved the minivan into drive and floored the accelerator. In her rearview mirror, she watched Tom race down the porch steps toward his truck.

Dust surrounded the minivan as Charley sped down the middle of the dirt road. She checked her rearview mirror. Tom's black truck broke through the fog of particles. Charley's heart raced.

She pressed harder on the accelerator. The minivan hesitated. His truck moved within a few feet of her bumper.

The driveway emptied onto a paved two-way street. It didn't matter which direction led to help; a right turn was faster. A quick glance as she turned showed an eighteen-wheeler barreling down the road toward her. Charley gritted her teeth and gunned it. The truck's air horn blared. Brakes screeched. Charley braced for the impact. She watched in the rearview mirror as the rig's cab swerved into the other lane and stopped. The semi stretched across both lanes. Charley smiled. That should stop Tom for a while.

A few minutes later, she checked the mirror again. Tom's truck went off-road around the eighteen-wheeler. She floored the accelerator. The minivan's steering wheel shook as the car strained to pick up speed.

Up ahead a flashing yellow light indicated a crossroad and a sign pointed left toward Trinity. The minivan swerved as she spun into the intersection, heading for the highway.

A car pulled in front of her. She swerved around it. The two-lane road turned into four lanes. Tom's truck raced toward her. Charley flew past convenience stores, a couple of gas stations, and a Dairy Queen.

Tom pulled in close behind her. With a car next to her, she had nowhere to go. A chime went off and the low fuel indicator flashed on the dashboard.

Charley hit the steering wheel. "Shit!"

She gripped the steering wheel. When the car ran out of fuel, he'd get her. There was only one way she had any chance of surviving. Charley slammed on her brakes and threw the car into park. Tom swerved. Horns blew. Tom's truck clipped her rear left bumper. Metal crunched. Charley's head hit the driver's side window. Everything went black.

Sirens wailed like a wake-up alarm in Charley's ears. She squinted. Behind her, two cars had crashed. Other cars were pulled along the side of the road.

Where was Tom? She turned her head. A sharp pain shot down her neck. Tom's truck straddled the other side of the road. As she watched, Tom opened his door, stumbled out of his car, and headed in her direction.

Her heart pounded against her chest. When the cops arrived, who would they believe? Tom had grown up in this small town. Charley was in a stolen car. Tom had a CIA badge. If the police called her boss, would he believe her story. He'd recommended Tom as her mentor.

People got out of their cars and rushed to help. Charley waved off any assistance, put the minivan in drive, and drove away.

Her left rear tire thumped down the road.

"Damn!" She turned onto a side street and spotted a boarded-up doughnut shop. Charley ditched the car behind it. Having only one shoe would slow her down but was faster than a flat tire and not nearly as noticeable.

Farther down the street, stood a restaurant. A parking lot away from it was a bar. Someone at one of those places would probably let her use a phone. She jumped out of the car and ran on the grass alongside vintage houses in need of paint and foundation repairs.

A siren wailed. Flashing lights headed in her direction. Charley gasped and slowed to a stroll. The police drew close. Charley clenched her hands until the nails bit into her palms. Sweat wet the back of her neck and soaked her hair. When the cop car disappeared around a corner, Charley bolted for the restaurant.

A silver metal roof topped the restaurant's blue siding. The white sign in front proclaimed its name in bold blue letters, The Blue Catfish. In the dirt parking lot, sat a silver Jeep and an old wood paneled station wagon.

As Charley approached the entrance, the smell of fried food greeted her. A "No Shoes No Shirt No Service" sign was posted in the window. She wondered if one shoe was enough.

Charley pulled on the glass door, but it didn't budge. She saw a couple of women cleaning in the restaurant. Charley rapped on the door. A slim woman with blonde hair hanging to her waist came toward her, pointed to the hours listed on the glass door, then walked away.

Charley didn't have time to argue. Tom's truck might be drivable. He could show up any minute. She ran toward the bar.

White letters on a grey background announced Bubba's Bar and Pool Hall. Darkened windows kept the scorching sun out and protected the privacy of customers. The siding was the color of a stormy sky before a tornado hit. A couple of pickups and ten or more motorcycles were clustered in the gravel parking lot. No rules were posted on the outside, only a sign about an upcoming pool tournament.

Visions of leering leather-clad men with gold chains around their necks playing pool and guzzling beer filled Charley's mind. She threw back her shoulders, inhaled a mix of cigarette and fish-fried air, then grabbed the door handle.

Charley opened the bar door. Cool air loaded with the smell of cigarettes, spilt beer, and body odor hit her. She shivered, wrinkled her nose, and slid into the bar.

Her eyes took a few seconds to adjust to the dark room. Garth Brooks belted out "Friends in Low Places" from the speakers. Lights hung low over four pool tables where men in jeans and t-shirts gripped pool cues waiting for their chance to play. Heads turned in Charley's direction as if a woman had never entered the hallowed walls of Bubba's. Charley ignored their leers and rushed up to the wood bar that faced the front door.

The bartender popped the top off a beer bottle, slid it to a bald guy sitting on one of the barstools, then looked at Charley.

"What can I do for you?"

"I've had some car trouble." Her eyes darted between the bartender and the mirror reflecting the entrance to the bar. "I left my phone at home. Do you have one I could use?"

Baldy turned toward her. "I know a few things about cars." He eyed her up and down as if to imply he knew a few things about women too.

Charley's stomach turned nauseous. She had had just about enough with men today. In fact, there was only one she could tolerate at the moment.

She forced a smile and said, "That's okay. My hubby is a mechanic." When she was desperate, lying came easy.

Baldy frowned and returned to his beer.

"We've got a phone." The bartender walked to the other end of the bar, next to the restroom entrance, and pulled out a landline phone from under the counter. "Here you go." He handed it to her and left to attend to other customers.

Charley picked up the handset. The only numbers she recalled were her mom's and Harry's. Between those two, Harry was the obvious choice.

Facing the front entrance, she watched the door while dialing Harry's number. The phone rang and rang. An ache stretched across her shoulders. She bit her lip. Only Harry could help her out of this mess. If he didn't answer…

"What's up Charley?" Harry's voice sounded rushed.

"Harry, I need you to come get me." She twisted the phone cord around her fingers.

"Where are you?" he asked.

"A place called Bubba's Bar and Pool Hall. I think it's close to Trinity." Charley watched as the front door cracked open.

Harry's voice took on a teasing tone. "Isn't it a little early to be drinking?"

"I haven't been drinking."

The front door eased open. She turned her back on the door. Charley watched in the mirror that ran behind the bar. She positioned herself so her reflection was hidden amongst all the booze arranged on the mirror's glass shelves.

Light seeped into the room. She wrapped the phone cord tighter around her fingers and increased the urgency in her voice.

"Just get here or I'll be the next dead body."

The sun backlit a build like Tom's standing in the doorway. Charley stretched the phone cord tight and edged toward the restrooms. Maybe there was a fire exit, a lock on the bathroom, or a window. Her heart pounded so loud she barely heard Harry speak.

"Call the cops. They can get there faster."

The man stepped inside.

"No cops. No time to explain. Just hurry." She dropped the phone in the base and raced toward the bathroom.

Someone called out, "Steve. Long time no see."

Charley turned around and watched as a pool player waved the man over. She exhaled, then debated whether to stay in the bar or hide in the bathroom. If Tom walked in the bar, he'd catch her. In the bathroom, she'd be trapped. She glanced around the room. Everyone was engaged in playing pool or throwing darts or downing drinks.

If everyone knew and liked Tom, then she couldn't expect help from anyone in the bar. If they didn't like him and Tom flashed his CIA badge at them, it might not go down so well. Big government didn't always fare so well in small towns, especially when a defenseless woman was involved. Still, the bartender might feel obligated to comply with Tom or call the cops. Once the police arrived, then she was in trouble. A stolen car and leaving the scene of an accident didn't exactly speak well of her character. The police might throw her in jail. She'd be safe, but what if they let Tom take her instead? It wasn't worth the risk. She'd find a hiding place outside.

Charley rapped her knuckles on the counter and smiled at the bartender.

"My ride will be here in just a few minutes. Thanks for letting me use the phone."

The bartender waved in her direction, then passed another beer to Baldy.

Charley cracked opened the door and checked outside. There was no sign of Tom or his truck. She darted out the door and searched for a place where she could see Harry, but no one could see her.

A dumpster sat between the restaurant and Bubba's. Images of rotten food, rats, and maggots filled her mind. She shuddered. No way could she hide in there. Then again, Tom wouldn't expect her to hide in a dumpster. It might not be so bad. She ran toward it, looked around, then lifted the lid of the shoulder-high container.

The stench of rotting food forced her head backwards. She gagged, covered her nose and mouth, then peered inside. Flies swarmed around the black and white plastic bags. The glassy eyes of fish heads stared at her from a burst bag. Hush puppies, corncobs, and coleslaw spread across the trash as if someone had tossed in a sack without tying it. Fish bones poked through several of the bags. Flattened cardboard boxes were stuffed in a far corner. Beer bottles were scattered about. The container was only about half full. If she squatted, the lid would close without any problem.

Once Harry rescued her, she would require a long hot shower and possibly a rabies shot. If Tom caught her, not even a shot could help her. She scrambled into the dumpster and closed the lid. Fish bones poked the soles of her foot. Goo seeped into her sock and squished between her toes. Bile rose in her throat. At least she still had the one shoe. She covered her nose and her mouth, but the smell had seeped into her hands.

Charley lifted the lid large enough for her to watch for Harry and get some fresh air. Flies landed on her arms, prickling her skin before continuing onto the feast awaiting them.

Charley looked up and down the street. Sweat rolled down her forehead and her back. Flies landed on her cheeks, her mouth, and her nose. She scrunched up her face, but they didn't seem to care. Her arms shook from holding the lid open. She closed it again. The heat, the smell, and the humidity almost sent her into a claustrophobic panic. High pitched squeaks sounded around her. She flinched. *Mice!* Her fingers ran across fish flesh and wet stuff until she felt the smooth contour of a beer bottle. She grabbed it, then used it to prop open the lid.

A door slammed. It sounded like it came from the restaurant. She didn't bother to check. It didn't matter. All that mattered was watching for Tom and Harry. Out of the corner of her eye, she saw the woman with waist-length blonde hair carrying a couple of trash bags. Charley held her breath. Maybe she was taking something to her car. The blonde moved past the parking lot and headed toward the dumpster. Charley searched for a cardboard box to hide under. Tires crunched on gravel. Charley's eyes flicked toward the sound. A black truck with a smashed bumper pulled into the parking lot.

42

Harry grabbed his wallet and raced from his apartment to his car. His eyes flicked to the far corner of the parking lot. The black sedan no longer sat there. Maybe the CIA was after Charley, but why? She had probably hacked some international secrets. Killing her for that seemed extreme, but two men were dead, one with a CIA badge and the other in Charley's trunk. She must have stepped into some serious shit.

He got in his car and keyed *bubba's bar and pool hall* into his GPS app - thirty minutes to arrive based on its calculation. Harry peeled out of the lot.

The skin on his knuckles paled as he gripped the steering wheel. If something bad happened to Charley, Harry would regret not calling the police. Buddy was a cop, but also a friend. He could trust him, couldn't he? Harry hadn't trusted him enough to discuss his memory loss, but that was more from a fear he'd lose Buddy's respect rather than a lack of trust.

The light up ahead turned yellow. Harry gunned it and passed under the light as it changed to red. Any cop would have a hell of a time catching him. They didn't call his Charger a Hellcat for nothing.

Harry entered the freeway. He weaved in and out of traffic. A white Lexus pulled in front of him. Harry blew the horn, switched lanes, and cut off a silver truck. The guy honked. Harry looked in his rearview mirror. The truck was right on his back end. Harry's heart pounded against his chest. He had no time for road rage.

Harry leaned back in his seat, gritted his teeth, and floored it, dodging between cars. The truck raced to keep up with him. A siren sounded and lights flashed. Harry didn't have time for a ticket either. He exited the freeway and flew through the intersection as the light turned yellow.

A glance in his side mirror, confirmed the truck never got a chance to exit before the cop stopped him. Harry grinned.

The GPS showed he'd shaved five minutes off the ETA. Harry turned onto Highway 19.

Fifteen minutes later, he fishtailed onto a two-lane road. "Bubba's Bar and Pool Hall" stood a few blocks down the street. Harry slowed as he pulled closer to his destination. He squinted at Bubba's parking lot. What the hell...

43

Charley froze as Tom got out of his truck. The blonde continued walking toward the dumpster with a trash bag in each hand. At her current pace, she'd reach the dumpster soon. Once she lifted the lid and saw Charley, she would scream, and Tom would come running.

If Charley hid in the back corner of the dumpster, the woman might not see her. She cringed at the thought of wading through the trash. Charley stretched across plastic bags, fish heads, and beer bottles until she reached one of the flattened cardboard boxes, then quietly dragged it over. Shoving aside a trash bag, she made enough space to scrunch down and pull the cardboard over her.

"Hey Susie, how are you doing?" Tom shouted.

Crap! He knew the woman.

A sugary-southern drawl answered. "Fine." Susie sighed. "Other than someone didn't show, so I had to come help mom." She paused. "What brings you into town?"

"I'm helping a family find their daughter. She's mentally unstable, wanders off sometimes and forgets how to get home.

I wonder if you might have seen her."

"What does she look like?"

"Wavy dark hair, about my age, slightly overweight. I've got a picture on my phone."

Where the hell did he get a picture of her? She didn't remember him taking a picture.

A clanging noise like bottles and cans hitting each other sounded as if Susie had dropped the bags on the ground.

"Yeah, she came by here earlier. We were closed so I didn't let her in." Susie paused. "You might check at Bubba's."

The clanging started up again. "Let me take those for you," Tom said.

Shit! Charley closed her eyes and tightened her arms around her legs.

"I wonder why there's a beer bottle propping this open?" Tom's voice carried a note of suspicion.

Charley clenched her fists. She had forgotten the stupid beer bottle. She tucked in tighter and held her breath.

The lid creaked. Flies buzzed around Charley as a bag dropped near her. The next bag bumped up against the cardboard, pushing it sideways off her shoulder.

Maybe they wouldn't notice her. Maybe she blended in with the trash. Maybe Tom would walk away.

The cardboard was knocked off her back. She closed her eyes, anything to avoid seeing his face.

Susie gasped. "Is she dead?"

"No, she's just playing dead." Frustration saturated Tom's voice. "Come on Charley. It's time to go home."

Charley wondered what he'd do if she stayed still. He couldn't shoot her in front of Susie.

"I don't think she's coming out," Susie said.

"She's coming out all right," Tom said.

Charley felt a tug on the back of her shirt. She started sliding toward the edge of the dumpster. Once Tom got her to the edge, he could pull her out. She uncoiled, jerked her shirt from his grasp, stood up and faced Tom.

Tom's eyes widened. Susie's mouth fell open.

"You'll have to come in and get me." She moved to the back of the container, avoiding fish bones that had pierced the bags or broken free. Flies swarmed around her legs and flew into her face. She swatted them away from her eyes.

Susie turned to Tom. "Do you want me to call the fire department?"

He shook his head and frowned. "I'll just get her." He grabbed the lip of the dumpster.

Charley looked around for a weapon. She picked up a fish head and threw it at Tom. It hit his forehead and slid down his face. She pelted him with hush puppies, corncobs, and beer bottles.

"Shit!" Tom glared at Charley.

She tossed a trash bag at him. He shrugged it off and climbed into the dumpster.

Charley spotted Harry's car pulling into the parking lot. She picked up a beer bottle and jumped out of the dumpster just as Tom closed in on her. She raced for Harry's car. A thud sounded, then footsteps pounded behind her. She clutched the beer bottle as she pumped her legs and arms. Tom grabbed her shirt. She tripped and fell face down in the dirt.

Charley rolled over and jumped up. She narrowed her eyes, held the beer bottle by its neck, and waved it in the air.

"Don't come any closer."

Tom laughed.

Heat rose in Charley's face. She tightened her grip on the bottle, pulled her arm to the side, then slammed it forward. Tom ducked, but it caught the crown of his head. He staggered sideways. She leaned toward him and with all her weight smacked the bottle on his forehead. The bottle shattered into shards of glass. Tom collapsed. Blood streaked his face and ran into his hair. Charley released the jagged neck of the bottle. Pain shot through her hand. Blood seeped from cuts in her thumb and index finger.

"What have you done?" Susie said her eyes wide.

Charley watched as Susie pulled out her phone, tapped on it, then held it to her ear.

"Send an ambulance to the Blue Catfish Grill," Susie's hysteria increased with each word.

Someone touched Charley's shoulder. She looked up into Harry's concerned eyes. "Are you okay?"

Charley looked at Tom's still form, then at her hand.

She nodded. "The bastard deserved it," Charley said. She kicked Tom in the side.

Tom coughed. Sirens sounded in the distance.

"We gotta get out of here," Harry said. Charley ran to the car.

44

Harry reached the car seconds before Charley. He yanked open the door and jumped inside. Charley slid into the passenger seat and slammed the door. Harry threw the car into reverse and spun out on the road. Dust clouded the air. He switched the car to drive and floored the accelerator. The car lurched forward. Harry slowed when he turned onto the main road.

"Why are you slowing down?" Charley asked.

Harry looked in his rearview mirror. "The last thing we need is a cop pulling us over for speeding." He wrinkled his nose and rolled down the window. "You smell like shit."

"Actually, it's fish." She smirked.

"Roll down your window." He frowned. "I'll never get the smell out of my car." He glanced at her. "What have you done now? I told you hacking would get you in trouble one day."

Charley glared at him. "I wasn't hacking." She paused. "It was work."

"What kind of work lands you in a dumpster in the middle of nowhere?"

Harry had enough trouble without Charley adding to it. No

doubt she had stepped on the wrong toes again.

"Forget it. I'll deal with it myself." She folded her arms and looked out the passenger window.

He recognized the stubborn set of her shoulders. "What the hell is going on?"

She turned her face toward him, her mouth set in a firm line. "Just drop me at my mother's house."

Harry must have really pissed off Charley. She would never recommend her mother's place. He looked at her baggy shirt, dirt-streaked cheek, and frizzed hair with bits of dirt and food in it. The smell alone was enough to put anyone off, even a mother.

"Are you kidding me? No way would your mother let you inside." He laughed. "We'd have to run you through the car wash. Twice."

Charley snickered. "It might be fun to see her face if I showed up like this." She paused and looked at Harry with sad eyes. "I can't go back to my apartment."

"What happened?" He looked over at her.

She bit her lip.

"And don't lie to me or leave out any details." He narrowed his eyes.

As she told the story, Harry's eyes widened. It sounded like something that would happen to him, not Charley. By the time she finished, they had reached the interstate and were headed toward Houston.

"Let me get this straight. You work for the CIA and so does Tom, but he's a crooked agent?"

"Not really an agent. He's a cryptanalyst like me."

"Why don't you call your manager?" Harry glanced at her. "Or do you think he's involved in all this?"

She shook her head. "If Derek was in on it, Tom would have let me call him, but Derek is the one who sent Tom to help me. He won't believe me over Tom."

"Is there anyone else you can trust?"

Charley shrugged. "I don't want to risk it." She paused. "At least not yet."

"What about the cops? We can trust Buddy."

She crossed her arms. "I don't trust anyone connected with the government."

Harry frowned. Buddy had come into money recently, moving into a larger house and a better neighborhood. When Harry teased him about a big raise, Buddy had laughed it off, but could he be on the take? Harry shook his head. *No way. Buddy?*

"What's Tom's last name? If you don't want me to call the cops, then I'll have to deal with him myself."

"Giles, but I don't want you to go after him. What if he kills you?" She pressed her hand against her mouth.

"Let me worry about that." Harry checked his speedometer and slowed to the posted speed limit. "It might help if I knew what the decrypted message said."

"Not much. Just listed a place, date, and time. I can't remember exactly." She stared out the window. "What do we do now?"

"We have to find a place to stash you until this blows over."

Harry turned on his blinker and changed lanes. "There's a motel I know that takes cash and doesn't ask for any ID."

He raised his eyebrows. "And I know a member of the staff." A vision of Sophia in her maid uniform flashed through his mind. His cheeks burned. He turned up the fan, flipped the vents open wide, and pointed them at his face.

"She can bring you anything you need. I'll give her a call." He exited the freeway, pulled into a Whataburger lot and parked.

Charley turned toward him and squinted. "How do you know this woman?"

"Just someone I met while working a job." He rubbed his chin.

"Hmm…" Charley raised an eyebrow.

"She's just an acquaintance." Harry rolled his eyes and grabbed his phone.

Charley shrugged. "Whatever you say."

He sighed and called Sophia. "Hi, it's Harry. A friend of mine needs a place to stay. She's had a bit of boyfriend trouble."

"Bring her to my place."

"The guy is crazy. The motel might be better."

Harry glanced at Charley. She frowned.

"No woman should stay there. Besides, I've dealt with crazy before." Her voice had a hard edge to it.

"This guy carries a gun and won't hesitate to use it."

"Remember, Smith and Wesson travel with me."

Harry cleared his throat. "How could I forget?"

She laughed. "I'm at home. Come on over."

"Thanks, Sophia. We should be there in about thirty minutes." Harry hung up.

Charley looked skyward. "Just an acquaintance. Right."

"She is." He didn't need to justify to Charley his relationships or lack thereof.

"I bet she's not hot either." Charley muttered. She pulled off her remaining shoe and both socks, stuffed the socks in the shoe, then handed it to Harry. "Would you toss this? I have to keep my clothes on, but I can, at least, get rid of my socks and shoe."

Harry didn't even want to touch the shoe, but maybe the stench in the car would diminish if he thew it away. It couldn't hurt. He grabbed the end of the shoe's lace, got out of the car, and tossed it in the Whataburger trashcan.

As he got in the car and drove away, he worried Tom would find Charley. Harry clenched his jaw at the thought of anyone hurting Sophia or Charley. Maybe taking Charley to Sophia's wasn't such a good idea. He glanced at Charley, but what else could he do?

45

Charley stood on the porch of Sophia's townhome. "Look at me, Harry."

She pointed to the ketchup, dressing, and grease stains on her shirt and jeans. "I can't go inside."

Charley looked down at her feet. "Who shows up at someone's house barefoot?"

She sniffed her shirt and wrinkled her nose. "And I stink."

Harry squinted. "I could drop you off at a homeless shelter."

"Very funny." Charley rolled her eyes and frowned.

"How are we ever going to explain this?" She waved her hand over her body.

"We don't need to explain it. If she asks, I'll come up with something." Harry rang the doorbell.

Charley smoothed her hair and pulled out a strand of cabbage. As she ran her fingers over the rest of her head, the door opened. She dropped her hands and smiled.

The woman in the doorway flashed a smile of perfect white teeth. Dark hair waved around her tan face. Her brown eyes held a glint of mischief. Dressed in tight jeans and a white knit shirt that clung to her body, Charley figured she was the kind of woman only dead men would ignore and only if they'd been dead for a while.

Charley glanced at Harry. His eyes were wide, taking in every square inch of Sophia. She wondered when he'd start drooling.

Sophia glanced at Charley. "What happened?"

Harry raised his eyebrows. "I told you her boyfriend was crazy."

"You weren't kidding." Sophia stepped aside. "Come on in."

Charley limped into the living area. Her feet ached. She longed to sit, but the sofa and chairs were white. Except for the dark wood floors and a deep purple throw tossed over the couch, everything was white, the furniture, the walls, the kitchen cabinets, and counters. Sunlight streamed through the window onto the flat screen TV. Not a fingerprint or smudge flawed the display. Charley wondered if the motel Harry had mentioned had a vacancy.

"I hate to put you out. I can stay at the motel."

"No way." Sophia turned to Harry. "You've slept there. Would you stay there again?"

Harry shook his head and frowned. "Let's just say it's not on my list of top one hundred places."

Charley sighed. "Thanks for taking me in."

"No worries. I've had my share of boyfriend trouble. Someone helped me." Sophia shrugged. "I'm just returning the favor." She stared at Charlie and her eyes softened. "I bet you're exhausted. Why don't you take a hot shower? I've got some clothes that will fit you."

Charley figured Sophia couldn't handle the dumpster smell any longer. Perhaps she should offer to pay to fumigate the townhouse once she was able to go home.

Sophia checked her watch. "It's close to supper. I'll order some food. Does Italian work for you?"

Charley's stomach gnawed at her insides. She thought about the dumpster full of rotting fish. Anything but fish sounded good.

"That would be great." She hesitated. "But I don't have any money on me." She tucked her hair behind her ear. "I can pay you back later."

Harry pulled out his wallet.

Sophia waved him off. "It's okay. I got it. It was a good day on the stock market." She smiled.

Based on the decor and the spaciousness of the townhome, Charley figured Sophia had more than one good day or perhaps her job paid well. However, the way they talked about the motel she doubted it.

"Will you be joining us, Harry?" Sophia asked.

Harry looked across the room to the window. "I don't think he saw my car, but I need to get out of here just in case he did." He frowned. "I won't return until he's no longer a threat."

Charley rubbed her forehead. She needed her phone, her wallet, and some clothes.

"How will I get my stuff?"

Harry shook his head. "He'll be watching your place. Anyone going in your apartment will be followed."

Charley's shoulders slumped. The last time she was this

isolated, she'd been a grounded teenager.

Sophia rested a hand on Charley's back. "Don't worry. I'll pick up whatever you need at the store."

"With any luck, we'll catch this guy soon," Harry said. "I'd better go."

Charley watched as Harry left and closed the door behind him. She wondered when she would see him again or if Tom would find her first.

Charley stood in the glass enclosed shower and inhaled the steam as water poured over her head. Some of the tension in her shoulders eased as bits of lettuce and purple cabbage made their way to the drain. She scrubbed her skin with a washcloth and the rose-scented body wash. As the dirt and stench washed away, she wondered when life would return to the way it was before she'd met Tom. What was she thinking? Even if Tom went to jail, his face would forever haunt her. She twisted the knob and stepped out into the steam-fogged room.

Wrapped in a towel, she stepped into the connecting guest bedroom. Plaid pajamas and socks lay on the bed's white comforter. Charley donned the pjs and socks. She'd have to go commando until her clothes were cleaned. The pajamas were tighter than what she normally wore, but probably hung loose on Sophia.

Like the living area, white dominated the room. Two grey decorative pillows and a pair of silver-based lamps were the only color in an otherwise sterile room. As she turned to leave, Charley caught her reflection in the mirror above the dresser.

Dark circles hung under her blue eyes. Her hair fell in wet ringlets. She moved closer to the mirror. A red scratch snaked across one cheek. She touched the raised welt and flashbacked to the woods with Tom close on her heels. Her reflection morphed into Tom's face, his eyes slits, his mouth a hard line, his expression as twisted as his personality. Her stomach churned and an ache throbbed behind her temples.

The doorbell rang. Charley jumped. What if it was Tom?

She rushed to the bedroom door, cracked it open, and listened. Voices floated up the stairs. The words were indecipherable, but one spoke in deep tones.

Charley closed the door and locked it. She looked around the room. The closet or under the bed would be the first places he'd look.

She ran to the window, pulled up the blinds, and looked down at the patch of grass. A jump from the second floor might break a bone. Pillows would soften her landing. She snatched them off the bed.

Footsteps sounded on the stairs. They stopped outside her door. Charley's heart pounded. She dropped the pillows, unlocked the window, and raised it. Hot air hit her face.

"Charley, the food is here," Sophia said.

She sagged onto the bed. "Thanks. I'll be right down."

Charley closed and locked the window, then went downstairs.

Charley sat at the dining table and stared at the chicken fettuccine on her plate.

"Are you okay?" Sophia said from across the table.

Charley picked up her fork and speared a piece of chicken. "Yeah. I'm just getting full."

Sophia broke off a piece of garlic bread. "How well do you know Harry?"

Charley shrugged. "Pretty well. We've been friends since elementary school."

Charley wondered what kind of relationship Sophia had with Harry. No way would Harry keep someone like Sophia as just an acquaintance unless she had rejected his advances.

Sophia topped off their wine. "What kind of work do you do?" she asked.

Charley rolled her shoulders and stretched. "I'm a cryptanalyst." Since no one ever seemed to know what that was, she added. "I decode encrypted messages."

Sophia nodded. "I've heard of those." She tilted her head. "It must be interesting." She wrapped the fettucine onto her fork.

"It is once you decode the message." At least it was until it gets you chased down by a nutter or killed. She took a sip of wine and wished it was tequila. Anything to help her forget the last twenty-four hours.

Sophia looked thoughtful. "You must work for the government." She raised her eyebrows. "Something exciting like the FBI or the CIA."

Charley realized she should have lied about her career. Between the day's events and the wine, she could barely think much less fabricate a job.

"I'm not sure how exciting it is." Changing the subject might distract Sophia. "What kind of work do you do for the motel?" Based on Sophia's looks and tastes in decor, she should be working in a high-end place and not the dump she claimed it was.

"I'm a maid." Sophia smirked.

Charley leaned back in her chair. Her eyes and mouth wide. "What?"

Darn. She shouldn't have reacted like that. Maybe she could blame the wine.

Charley looked around the room. Sophia must have done really well in the stock market to live in such a nice townhome.

Sophia laughed. "It usually surprises people." She shrugged. "There's little stress, no competition, and zero politics."

"I guess that's true." Charley lifted her glass. "I should consider it." She sure as hell didn't want to work for the CIA anymore.

"Won't your work miss you?" Sophia pointed toward the back of the house. "I have a computer in my study if you need to use it."

"It's okay." Harry had promised her that he would find a way to deal with Tom, but what about her boss? Harry told her to focus on remembering the message but how would that help her when she couldn't trust anyone in the CIA? Maybe she should reach out to her old boss. She'd worked for him for several years, but Charley doubted even he would believe her.

"I'm sure there are things you need." Sophia walked across the kitchen and pulled a pen and paper out of the drawer.

"Write down whatever it is, and I'll pick them up in the morning. There's a new toothbrush and toothpaste in your bathroom. I always keep them on hand for guests."

Charley wondered if one of those guests was Harry. "Thanks Sophia." She wrote down a list of items and passed them to her. "I really appreciate this. Not many people would take in a stinking stranger."

Sophia laughed. "Who knows? One day I may ask for your help." She tucked the list in her purse, returned to her chair, and resumed eating.

Charley imagined Sophia could handle just about anything, including Harry. She took another bite of fettuccine.

"If you think of anything else just let me know." Sophia pushed aside her plate.

"Is Harry dating anyone?" Sophia took a sip of wine.

"I thought he might be dating you," Charley said.

"We've been to dinner." Sophia raised an eyebrow. "He comes across as a player. You've known him a long time. Is he one?"

Charley shrugged. "He's dated a lot of women, but I'm not sure I'd label him a player."

Charley gathered the dishes. She had never liked sharing Harry with anyone. All the other women he dated had been losers in one way or another, but Sophia might just turn out to be a winner.

46

The sleep study room looked more like a room in a hotel than in a hospital. A navy-blue spread covered the wood frame king-sized bed. A couple of abstract pictures in tones of faded blue and white hung above the headboard. One bedside table held a lamp and the other held equipment for the study. A standing fan faced the bed, probably to help those who sleep with a constant breeze across their face or perhaps the sound provided comfort like waves lapping on the beach.

A plump woman directed Harry to the bathroom. "Go ahead and change."

Harry usually slept in his boxers. He hoped the grey and red plaid pjs he'd purchased wouldn't be too hot.

When Harry exited the bathroom, he grabbed a historical fiction book from his bag, then sat on the side of the bed.

The woman walked into the room with tape in her hand. "Let's get you all hooked up."

Harry wouldn't mind getting hooked up with some Johnnie Walker or a sleeping pill, but unfortunately, that's not what she had in mind. As she closed in on him, the smell of chocolate cookies enveloped him. He took a deep breath and remembered his aunt's cookies fresh from the oven. The chocolate sweetness had melted on his tongue and smeared his hands.

The woman peered at him. "They explained everything when you got here, right?"

Harry nodded. He didn't like any of it but had to do something about his night escapades.

"Do you have any questions before we start?"

He shook his head.

She rubbed her hands together. "All right lie down and let's get started."

The woman unbuttoned his shirt, applied adhesive paste, attached clips, tape, and electrodes to his scalp, the back and front of his head, the outer edges of his eyes, behind his ears, and on his chest. She wrapped a belt around his belly and stuffed tubes in each nostril. A clip hung from his finger. He lost count of the number of accessories. No way would he ever fall asleep. If he did, then what would happen to the electrodes when his sleepwalking-self attempted to leave? Or would he rip them off?

Dr. Worth had assured him they wouldn't let that happen. His shoulders relaxed. With someone watching him, he couldn't get into trouble tonight. Unless he killed the lady. His shoulders tensed as he looked at her motherly face. He hoped she would lock his door. It probably violated some kind of fire code. Still, he didn't see any weapons other than his bare hands and the electrode wires.

She hovered close to his face. When she opened her mouth, the scent of mint hit him.

"Did you bring anything to help you sleep, Sugar?"

He held up the book. "Just this." The pre-read material omitted liquor and sleeping pills from the list of what he could bring. Van always curled up next to him, but he wasn't on the list either.

She stood straight, then smoothed his covers. "Do you need anything else?"

He almost shook his head as an answer but didn't want to disturb her handiwork. "No, I'm sure I'll be fine." The word liar echoed through his brain.

The woman looked at him as if liar glowed on the electrodes attached to his head. "Just call me on the intercom if you need something." She flicked on his bedside lamp, turned off the overhead lights, closed the door, and left.

Harry opened Ken Follett's *Fall of Giants*. The words on the page merged together in his mind. Instead, names of suspects danced across the paper, but none made sense.

David or Emma might have killed Lisa, but why kill Chip? Yet, they were the most likely suspects for Lisa's murder. Tomorrow he'd follow up with them.

Then there was Candy, but what was her motive?

The mysterious Victoria might have murdered Lisa and Chip. If he could just talk to her, he might get some answers. He'd hit up Jack's Joint tomorrow night. At this point, he had nothing to lose. Drake already knew he'd been in the place asking questions. Besides, Drake couldn't arrest him for talking with people at the bar.

He read a paragraph, then stopped. The murders might not be connected at all. It seemed unlikely since Lisa and Chip ran in the same circles, but he should consider the possibility of two killers.

Harry returned to the page, finished it, and realized he didn't know what the hell he'd read. He read the first line again, but his mind strayed.

What about the stalker? The voice Buddy described sounded like Candy's, but she cared too much about Richie's money to threaten Dr. Worth over Harry.

Worrying over his problems wouldn't resolve anything. He needed more data, but for now, he had to sleep.

Harry focused on the page and read until the book fell from his hands.

47

The sound of the door opening woke Harry. For a moment, he wondered where he was. His shoulders tightened, then he remembered. Electrodes still clung to his body. Everything was intact. He relaxed. He had stayed the night.

After the technician removed all the equipment, Harry dressed and left for home. He wondered what the results of the sleep study would be. Whatever they were, he hoped Dr. Worth could fix him.

When Harry opened the door to his place, Van didn't greet him.

"Van, I'm home."

The apartment was quiet. He thought after a night away the cat might have missed him and come running. If nothing else, Harry represented a source of food.

He wandered into the kitchen and popped open a can of cat food. Within seconds, an orange blur raced into the room and twined around Harry's legs.

"At least you're consistent."

He dumped the food in a bowl, placed it on the floor, and scratched Van's head.

Harry watched the cat tuck into his food. "Unlike you, I can't eat and nap all day. I've got a killer to catch."

Today he wished he and Van could swap places, then an aroma of raw fish wafted by him. His nose wrinkled. Cat food. *Ugh.* Searching for a killer might be preferable after all. He sighed and headed for the bathroom.

Harry emerged from the shower. Someone was knocking on his door. Whoever it was could wait or just go away. His phone rang as he got dressed, but he ignored it too. He had a long list of things to do and didn't have time for interruptions.

The knocking grew more insistent as he tugged on his shoes.

"Open up Harry. I know you're in there."

Shit. Drake. Harry definitely didn't want to see him, but no doubt the man had already checked the parking lot and seen Harry's car. Maybe Harry could escape without Drake seeing him.

He glanced at his bedroom window. A branch thick enough to support him was within arm's reach of the glass panes. Harry raised the window and reached out to touch the branch. Leaves brushed against the tips of his fingers, but he'd have to stretch to grab a limb sturdy enough to support him. He leaned out and looked down the three stories. The view swam before his eyes. His breath came in short spurts. The memory of falling from a tree and the crack of bone as his arm twisted under his body rushed through his mind. He was only ten, but some events remained in his brain like the engraving on his grandfather's pocket watch: Amor Vincit Omnia: "Love conquers all". Harry doubted love could conquer his fear of heights.

He dismissed the tree-climbing idea and closed the window.

The banging on his door increased.

Drake would probably wait, hiding out of sight, until Harry left his apartment.

Van trailed Harry to the door.

"If only Drake was allergic to cats." He looked at Van. "When he comes in claw the shit out of him. He can't arrest a cat."

Harry opened the door. Only Drake stood on his doorstep.

"What are you doing here?" Harry asked.

"Where were you Friday night between ten and midnight?"

"Here. By myself." Harry glanced at Van. "Except for the cat." He tilted his head. "You want to interrogate him?"

Van looked up like he might oblige Drake.

"Let's see how funny you are when you're sitting in a cell." Drake scowled as if he might arrest Harry and Van.

Harry crossed his arms. "I haven't done anything." Fingerprints weren't enough to land Harry in jail.

"We found your fingerprints at two crime scenes. You haven't given us an alibi for the time of either death. I showed your photo around Jack's Joint, and you were in there asking questions about Lisa and Chip. Add it all up and it sounds like murder to me."

"Were my fingerprints found on the weapons?"

Drake looked at the ceiling. "Even you're not that stupid."

"You know what I think? You want me so bad you planted my fingerprints at both crime scenes."

Drake squinted. "Are you shitting me? You think I killed them just to get back at you?" He shook his head. "You're not making any sense. How would I get your fingerprints?"

"It's easy enough. Just pick up a glass I used at a restaurant or someone's house." Harry knew his accusation was a stretch, but he didn't want to admit to sleepwalking. If he did, Drake would have just cause for taking him down to the station, even charging him on suspicion of murder.

Drake shook his head. "You're crazy, Man. No one would believe that line of bullshit." He thrust his finger in Harry's face. "You're the killer and I'm going to prove it, then we'll see how well that pretty face fares in prison."

"Quit wasting my time." Harry leaned toward Drake. "If you're going to arrest me, then do it. Otherwise, leave."

Drake narrowed his eyes. "Once we have your motive for killing them, I'll be back to throw your ass in jail." He turned and left.

If Harry didn't find the killer soon, Drake would make good on his promise to get him one way or another. If Drake couldn't find a motive, he'd make up one. Harry needed to shorten his list of suspects, starting with David.

48

Harry waited for David to answer the door. He could have called him but chose to verify alibis in person. Lying face to face proved difficult for most people.

David opened the door dressed in casual clothes and wearing golf shoes.

"What's up?" David looked at his watch. "I have a tee time soon. Let's make this quick."

Quick worked for Harry. He just needed to know where David was the night of Chip's murder.

"Where were you on Thursday night between the hours of 10:00 and midnight?"

"The cops have already asked me this." David sighed. "I was at home in bed."

"Alone?"

David shook his head.

Harry forced himself not to visibly react. David hadn't wasted much time after Lisa's death before finding a new companion.

"Who is she?"

David's face flushed. He tugged on the collar of his shirt. "Rachel."

Harry narrowed his eyes. David wouldn't sleep with his wife's best friend. Would he? Harry might not know David as well as he thought.

"Lisa's friend?"

David raised his hands. "It's not like I'm cheating. She's single. We didn't fool around when Lisa was alive. Besides, it's not like Lisa didn't cheat on me."

He grabbed his golf bag and slung it over his shoulder. The clubs clinked against each other. "I'm going to be late. Anything else?"

Harry shook his head and left. He could cross off two possible suspects for Chip's murder. Unless they covered for each other, but Harry doubted it. Most people couldn't blush on demand.

With the list of suspects shrinking, Harry was rising to the top. He'd yet to find Victoria. She hung out at Jack's Joint, but it was too early.

Once Harry got in the car, he called Candy. She agreed to meet him at a local coffee shop. Candy didn't come across as a murderer, but her voice fit the description of the stalker's and she had known Lisa. Maybe she thought Harry was having an affair with Lisa as well as Dr. Worth. Would Candy kill Lisa just because she saw him watching Lisa? Or had a sleep walking Harry done more than just watch Lisa?

The smell of coffee and cinnamon rolls greeted Harry as he

opened the door of the Coffee Shack. People crowded around tables and stood in line at the register as the hum of conversations buzzed throughout the place.

Candy waved him over to her table. Harry weaved his way toward her, avoiding people carrying drinks.

She smiled. "I got you a coffee. Black, right?"

Harry took a seat across from her. "I'm surprised you remembered."

"Richard likes his the same way." She frowned. "The bastard."

"What's he done today?" He blew on the coffee, then took a small sip, testing the heat.

She rolled her eyes. "He woke up."

Harry laughed. "It can't be that bad."

"I don't like liars." She gripped her coffee cup.

Harry was a liar on occasion, but he had never lied to her. Never had a reason.

"Maybe he's telling the truth."

She leaned toward him. "Why would he hold a meeting at the Star when they have an office in the Galleria?"

Harry could think of several reasons, none of which Candy would like. He selected the least offensive.

"They might be considering investing in the Star." Harry shrugged. "He and his partners invest in retail stores. Why not motels and hotels?"

She shook her head. "Richard only invests in real money makers. That place is a dump."

"Did you recognize any of the men in the pictures I sent

you?"

From what Harry recalled, they were well dressed and probably all in their forties. Young enough to still take financial risks. Although, the Star seemed like a certain loss. Unless they tore it down and started again.

"No, but I've never met any of his business partners."

She sipped her coffee and looked at him over the rim of the cup. "I want you to keep investigating him."

Harry believed whoever killed Lisa also killed Chip. He needed to find what Candy did those nights, but he didn't want to raise her suspicions.

"I don't have a lot of time. It might help if we establish a pattern of his nighttime activities, then I'll know the best nights to tail him."

He lifted his coffee cup and pointed it at her. "Tell me what he's done from the Monday before Lisa's funeral until today."

Candy squinted. "Monday, I saw him before he left for work, but that was it. I was in bed before ten, so he came home sometime after that." She rubbed her chin. "Tuesday, he left town for some business." She cut her eyes at the ceiling. "Or so he said. He didn't return home until Thursday night." She rolled her eyes. "Friday and Saturday we know he spent time at that rundown motel."

"What did you do with all your free time?"

"Not much. I shopped." She smiled. "I've got to spend Richard's money while I can."

She took a sip of coffee. "Saturday, we had a girls' night out. I spent the night at a friend's."

"Anyone I know?"

She nodded. "Rachel." She looked out the window. "With Lisa's death, we regretted not getting together more often."

Harry bet Rachel didn't mention sleeping with David. Somehow, he didn't think Candy would appreciate it.

Candy had lots of free time for stalking Dr. Worth, but she didn't seem jealous of Harry, just upset with Richie. He'd try another approach.

Harry leaned across the table. "Do you ever think about us getting back together?"

Candy swirled her coffee around in her cup. "Sure, but then I think about Richard's money." She smiled.

If she held a grudge against Dr. Worth because of Harry, then she hid it well. Harry moved Candy to the bottom of his mental suspect list behind Victoria and Emma. He had to find Victoria.

"Do you know someone named Victoria? She was a friend of Lisa's. Hangs out at Jack's Joint."

Candy smirked. "Still searching for Victoria? And you call yourself a detective." She laughed. "I don't know any Victorias, and Jack's Joint isn't my kind of place."

It wasn't his kind of place either, but it was his next stop.

At five in the afternoon, only a couple of guys sat at the bar. One of them was Jim. The bartender from the other night was pouring drinks.

Harry sat on the barstool next to Jim. "Hey Jim."

Jim turned with a smile, saw Harry's face, and frowned.

"Cops were here. Showed me your picture. Said you don't have a sister." He narrowed his eyes. "I hate liars."

Harry held up a hand. "I had a reason for lying."

Jim gripped his beer bottle tighter. "Don't all liars?" He turned his back on Harry.

The bartender wiped down the bar in front of Harry. "What can I get for you?"

"Scotch neat." Harry turned toward Jim. "So, you've never lied?"

Jim turned and glanced sideways at him. "Maybe a few times." He took a swig of beer. "Difference is I didn't get caught."

The bartender laughed and placed the glass of scotch in front of Harry.

Harry pulled out his PI license and showed it to Jim and the bartender.

"Look, I'm a private investigator. Lisa Angel's husband hired me to find out who killed her. I know she hung out here with Chip. Did she hang out with anyone else?"

The bartender examined Harry's license. "She hung out with Victoria sometimes."

Harry's breath quickened. "Do you know how I can get in touch with her?"

"Nope. She comes in here a couple of nights a week, but I don't know much about her. How about you, Jim?"

Jim shook his head and took a slow draw on his beer, then pointed the bottle at the bartender.

"Were you here the night when Lisa got mad at Chip?" Jim

scratched his head. "I think it was almost two weeks ago on a Monday night."

That was the same night as Lisa's murder. Harry held his breath waiting for an answer.

The bartender shook his head.

"Anyway, it was the same night Lisa slapped Chip. I was passing by Chip's table on my way to the bathroom. A woman was shouting at him. The place was packed and noisy, so I didn't think much of it, but then she started pointing her finger at him."

Jim turned toward Harry and widened his eyes. "If it'd been a gun, he'd been dead. She looked just that mad."

Harry put away his license. "Did you hear what she said?"

"Like I said, the place was too loud to hear anything. Besides, I was on my way to the bathroom. I didn't have time to stop and listen."

"Do you know who she was?" Harry hoped it was Victoria.

Jim shook his head. "Never seen her before or after that."

"Can you describe her?"

"Light blue eyes. Really white teeth. Shoulder length brown hair. Blonde highlights. Tan."

Harry only knew one person who fit that description and had a motive for killing Lisa, but why kill Chip?

"Was the argument before or after Lisa slapped Chip?"

"Before." Jim scratched his head. "Come to think of it. Lisa, Chip, and Victoria were all sitting together when the woman stopped by their table." He rubbed his lip. "I'm pretty sure Lisa and Victoria left the bar together."

If what Jim said was true, then Harry figured Victoria went with Lisa to the hotel, but why would she kill Lisa or Chip? Harry pulled out two business cards and gave one to Jim and the other to the bartender.

"Next time Victoria comes in, give me a call. She might have some information that could help me catch Lisa's killer."

They took the cards, but he doubted either of them would remember to call. Once Harry caught the killer, then he could spend his nights at Jack's Joint and meet the elusive Victoria. Unless, she had committed the murders. Or worse, Harry had sleepwalked and killed them both.

49

The sun sank in the sky casting rays of light on Emma's house as Harry stood waiting for a response to the doorbell. He wondered how she was coping without Chip around the house. Some people took a long time to recover over the loss of a spouse. Some never recovered. While others, like David, bounced right back into another relationship. Harry sighed and shook his head.

Emma opened the door and looked at Harry with wide eyes. Her face was void of makeup. Her hair was tousled as if she'd just woken. The sash of her bathrobe hung loose around her body.

"I have some information on Chip's murder. I figured you would want to know."

Emma motioned him inside. "I was just making some coffee."

After he came in, she closed and bolted the door behind her. "You can't be too careful." She led him to the kitchen.

"Would you like something to drink?" She waved her hand at the counter filled with covered dishes. "Or something to eat?

Everyone's brought over so much food. No way can I eat all of it."

"I'll just take a water." Harry grabbed a seat at the bar.

Emma pulled a bottled water out of the refrigerator and handed it to Harry.

"So, what did you find out?" she asked.

"While on another case, I discovered Chip and Lisa Angel were having an affair."

He watched for her reaction. Her face remained impassive as she reached for the coffeepot and poured a cup.

"But I guess you already knew that."

She nodded, pressing her body against the counter.

Harry was running out of suspects and time, so he decided to lie. "The thing is. I was following Lisa. I saw you at Alessandra's the night she was murdered."

Emma shrugged. "So, lots of people go to Alessandra's for dinner."

Harry twisted off the cap of the water bottle. "But I saw you go in her room."

"If that were true, you would have told the police. They haven't mentioned it to me." She sipped her coffee and smiled.

She had him there. He searched his mind for something she'd believe.

"Thing is, I'm running low on cash." He took a swig of water, then wiped his mouth.

"Are you blackmailing me?" She shook her head. "I don't think so."

Emma placed her coffee cup on the counter, pulled open a

drawer, and brought out a gun. "I'm done with men. Killing you will save me a lot of trouble."

Harry's muscles tensed, then he forced a relaxed state he didn't feel. He loosened his grip on the water bottle and pointed it in her direction. "How will you explain my dead body?"

"I'll tell the police you came here to kill me. You chased me into the kitchen where I grabbed my gun and shot you." She aimed the gun at him.

Harry's heart beat hard against his chest. He held up his hand. "Wait a minute. Why would I do that?"

She shrugged. "Crazy people don't need a reason."

He shook his head. "I used to be a cop. They're not going to believe it."

Emma smirked. "They will when I tell them about Victoria."

"Victoria? What about her?" Harry wondered what Victoria had to do with any of this.

She waved the gun in front of his face. "How long do you think you can hide behind her?"

Harry decided Emma's brain bolts needed tightening or drugs had punctured a few holes in her mind.

"I don't know what you're talking about." Every second he kept her talking was another second added onto his life, another chance for him to escape.

"Don't play games with me." She frowned. "I caught Victoria with Chip at my house." She shot the words out like bullets. "Bad enough he cheated with Lisa. I figured if I killed Lisa, he'd come back to me, but no." She dragged the "no" out like it had multiple syllables.

Harry's shoulders sagged. At least, he knew he hadn't stabbed Lisa. Not that it mattered if Emma killed him.

"When I saw Victoria here. I figured Chip was cheating again. I couldn't let that happen. I knew the only way to stop Chip was to kill him. So, I strangled him." Her eyes watered and a tear slid down her cheek. "But he wasn't cheating."

Harry had to get out of there. If only he could distract her.

"What about Victoria?" Maybe nobody had seen her lately because Emma had murdered her too.

Emma put her finger on the trigger. "I'm going to kill her too."

Harry gripped the water bottle, threw the liquid in Emma's face, then ducked below the counter. The gun went off. The bang echoed around the room. Harry ran for the front door. Emma raced behind him.

He remembered she'd bolted the door. She'd shoot him before he could unlock it. He veered into the living room, grabbed the poker from the fireplace, turned and swung at her as she aimed the gun at him. She ducked. The gun shot wide hitting the wall next to him. Harry swung again. The poker caught the side of Emma's head with a crunch. She fell. Her head hit the marble-topped coffee table; a cracking sound assured Harry that she wouldn't get up anytime soon, maybe never.

Harry called 911 as blood gushed onto the table, adding a pool of color to the black and white marble swirls.

50

Charley opened her eyes and blinked. Sunlight peeked through the blinds creating a glare on the TV. The last few days flooded her mind. She cringed, then reminded herself to relax. No one except Harry knew she was staying at Sophia's.

She shrugged off her naptime drowsiness, walked to the kitchen and grabbed a can of Diet Coke. She looked at the spotless counter, the smudge-free-stainless-steel refrigerator, the dish-free sink. No appliances except for a toaster cluttered the countertops. So far, Charley hadn't found a flaw in Sophia except she was too neat.

Since Charley had arrived, she and Sophia had eaten take-out. Charley smiled. Maybe Sophia couldn't cook. Charley's mom always said, "The way to a man's heart is through his stomach." Perhaps, it was time for Charley to invite Harry over for some home-cooked meals. If she ever got to go home again.

Charley looked at the blank paper on the bar. If she could just remember the message, Harry could call the cops with the information. He could tell several cops. One or maybe even all of them he told could be trusted. She took a sip of soda and savored the sweetness.

Of course, Tom might have contacted the author of the message and changed the date, time, or place, thinking she would tell the CIA. However, she doubted it. No one would believe her over Tom.

Her boss must have tried to call her when she didn't show up for work. If he wasn't in on it with Tom, he must wonder why her phone went unanswered. Unless Tom gave him some explanation for her absence. If not, she would probably be fired.

She closed her eyes and visualized her computer monitor displaying the decrypted message. A clear image flashed into her mind. The numbers and letters fell into place. Her eyes opened wide. She scribbled the place and date on the paper. The only part that wasn't clear was the exact time. She shut her eyes tight and focused, but it didn't help.

Charley reached for her phone to call Harry, then sighed. Her phone was sitting dead in her apartment.

Charley looked at the time on the microwave. Wherever Sophia worked, she'd said she was pulling a double shift and probably wouldn't return to the house until sometime tomorrow. By then, it might be too late. Whatever was happening, was going down tomorrow at some place called the"Star".

She could ask a neighbor to use their phone. Charley peeked through the blinds. A white SUV and red sedan were parked at the curb across the street. Both were empty.

Charley walked toward the door. Tom's sneering face popped in her mind. She shook her head, but the image stayed. The soda gurgled in her stomach as if it wanted to escape.

No way would she let Tom intimidate her. She had been a prisoner long enough. With renewed determination, she flipped the deadbolt, then grabbed the doorknob. Her hand shook like a junkie needing a fix. She opened the door and stepped into the sunlight.

An engine revved. Charley looked down the street. A black truck appeared. She turned, raced inside, shut the door, and locked it. Her breath came in sharp bursts, her chest heaving.

She ran to the window, closed the blinds, then peeked around the edges. The black truck crept down the street. Charley gritted her teeth. Her hands trembled on the blinds. The truck passed by the townhouse slowly. She squinted and focused on the driver. Long blonde hair framed a woman's face. The passenger seat was empty.

Charley collapsed on the couch, her heart still racing. Some mindless TV might calm her. She picked up the remote and flipped through the channels until she found a comedy. As far as Charley was concerned, Sophia had a lifelong roommate.

51

Harry hated interrogation rooms. Everything in the room was grey except for the black chair that felt like a board against his butt. He looked across the table at Drake and Buddy.

Drake frowned. "So, you expect us to believe Emma killed her husband and Lisa, then you killed Emma in self-defense?"

Harry shrugged. "That's what happened."

"I'm not buying it." Drake leaned across the table. "Why were your fingerprints found at both crime scenes?"

Harry leaned closer into Drake's space. "It doesn't matter. Emma confessed to killing Chip and Lisa. If I hadn't hit her with the poker, she would have killed me too."

"We only have your word for that." Drake's eyes narrowed as if he could bore into Harry's mind and read it.

Harry's head ached and the fumes of garlic and onion emanating from Drake's breath didn't help. Drake should pop a mint in his mouth before an interview or perhaps it was part of breaking down the suspect.

Harry dropped back in his chair. He just wanted to go home. If only Charley had dug up something on Drake that he could use. Still, Harry had a name. He looked at Buddy and Drake.

"Have either of you heard of a Paul Ledger?" Harry asked.

Drake's face paled and his eyes darted around the room.

Buddy looked confused. He shook his head. "What does he have to do with any of this?"

"Just a name from another case I'm working." Harry sat on the edge of his chair. "Are we done here? Or do I need to call my lawyer?"

Drake stood. "That's it for now."

Harry had touched a nerve. Otherwise, Drake would have questioned him longer. Harry wondered what Paul meant to Drake. It didn't really matter whether Harry found out or not. He just needed a get-out-of-jail card in his back pocket. It wouldn't last forever but maybe it would be long enough for him to get everything sorted before he got charged with murders he didn't commit.

The morning sun split the sky over the police station as Harry walked out with Buddy.

"I'll give you a ride to your car." Buddy waved keys at Harry. "You look tired. I should just take you home."

Harry shook his head. "I'm fine." He looked at Buddy. "Do you think Drake believed me?"

"That Emma killed Lisa and Chip?" Buddy nodded. "I don't think he wanted to, but what choice does he have? With Emma dead, there's no one to disagree with your story and he doesn't have any evidence to prove otherwise."

They got in Buddy's car, a red Camaro, his latest acquisition.

Buddy ran through cars faster than Harry ran through women.

"Besides, I don't think Drake ever really believed you did it," Buddy said.

Harry snapped on his seatbelt. "He'd still like to see my ass in jail for both murders."

"Yeah, the man doesn't like you for sure." Buddy glanced sideways at Harry. "You might want to consider a different career. One that doesn't interact with law enforcement. Maybe leave town too."

Harry shook his head. "He can kiss my ass. He won't believe the truth about his sister but eventually he's going to have to stop blaming me and face the facts." He clenched his jaw. "I'm not letting him bully me out of a career choice or out of town."

Buddy smiled. "I didn't think you would."

He cranked the car and pulled out of the parking space. "That's two murders I don't have to worry about. Now, if I could just find Dr. Worth's stalker…"

Buddy signaled to enter the freeway. "What reason could the stalker have to tell Dr. Worth to stay away from you?"

"You got me. It must be another Harry, or maybe she said Larry instead of Harry. Dr. Worth was scared. She probably misheard the woman."

"It's possible. I still have someone watching Dr. Worth." Buddy exited the freeway, then a few blocks later pulled in front of Chip's and Emma's house.

Buddy turned toward him. "It's over now. Drake won't bother you anymore. At least not today. Go home and get some sleep."

Sleep sounded great. He hadn't sleepwalked in a while, but it would worry him until Dr. Worth knew the cause.

As Harry walked toward his car, he took one last look at Chip's and Emma's suburban home. A couple of squirrels chased each other across the yard. The sun sparkled on the windows the same as yesterday. Murdered or not, dead or alive, it didn't matter. The sun carried on and Harry figured he would too.

Harry reviewed his current status to keep himself awake while driving home. With both murders solved, he could concentrate on the three remaining mysteries in his life: his sleepwalking activity, Victoria, and the items left at his place. If he found Victoria, then number three might resolve itself. All the clues pointed to her as the culprit. If he confronted her, maybe she'd confess. After all, she owed him. He had saved her life today as well as his own.

As Harry pulled into his apartment parking lot, he glanced up at Charley's window. How could he have forgotten about her? That Tom guy wanted her dead. Keeping Charley alive was more important than anything else going on in his life.

His phone rang. He checked the display: Dr. Worth.

52

Janet had ordered a rush on Harry's sleep study results. Still, she had expected the results to take a week. So, when they showed up in her email inbox late in the day, she smiled and clicked open the attached file.

Janet studied each page. The brain waves showed a possible disruption in his sleep/wake cycle otherwise everything looked normal. Based on the documentation, she could rule out restless leg syndrome and narcolepsy.

She needed to meet with Harry to gather more insight into his sleep patterns and dreams or nightmares. While the study didn't provide conclusive evidence of what caused his unconscious activities, she could share with him the things the study eliminated.

Janet reached for her phone, then stopped. Her spine tingled. The memory of the stalker's attack and the voice saying, "Stay away from Harry" took her breath away. Thibodeaux recommended she follow that advice, but Harry was counting on her. It had taken her several months to gain Harry's trust. Another doctor would face the same barriers.

Harry didn't have time to waste. So far, no harm had come to him, but anything could happen.

She grabbed her phone and walked to the window. The man still sat in the black midsized car facing her building. Ever since the incident, she made it a priority to meet whoever Thibodeaux assigned to watch her. If she met Harry during the day at her office with someone watching her, nothing bad could happen. After all, whoever tailed her had a gun, and so did she.

A confidence she hadn't felt since the attack surged through her body. She punched Harry's phone number as if each number represented the stalker's face.

"Harry, the results from the sleep study came in. I'd like to review them with you."

"Great." He hesitated. "Wait a minute. Thibodeaux told me a woman is stalking you and she told you to stay away from a Harry. Just in case I'm that Harry, we shouldn't meet. Unless the cops have caught her. Have they?"

She wanted to lie but struggled doing so even on the phone.

"No, but Detective Thibodeaux has assigned someone to me so it should be fine."

"Did you mention to him that you planned to meet with me?"

"Not yet, but I will." She probably should let Detective Thibodeaux know, so he could warn her watcher.

"It might be better if you give me the results over the phone."

She needed to see his face, to judge his reactions. A video

call wouldn't capture all the body language and information she needed.

"It's really okay. Are you free tomorrow morning? 10:00? We can meet at my office. I'll let Detective Thibodeaux know so they can be extra vigilant. Who knows? This might help them capture her."

He sighed. "As long as you let Detective Thibodeaux know, then it should be fine."

Janet picked up her phone to call Thibodeaux, then put it down. She would meet Harry tomorrow. It didn't matter whether Thibodeaux liked it or not.

53

The scent of coffee floated into Charley's bedroom. Her nose twitched. She stretched in bed, shaking off last night's sleep. Either Sophia had returned, or a killer waited for Charley with a cup of coffee.

Charley got up and wrapped herself in the robe Sophia had loaned her, then headed downstairs. Sophia stood in the kitchen, holding a mug, staring at the paper on the bar.

"What's this?" Sophia pointed to the decoded message.

Charley bit her lip.

Sophia stared at her. Charley searched for an explanation. The AC hummed. In the distance, a siren sounded. Sophia tapped her foot. Still, nothing came to Charlie's mind.

Why lie? Charley planned on quitting the CIA anyway. Sophia would know Harry had lied about Charley having boyfriend problems. If Sophia couldn't handle Harry's fibbing, then she shouldn't date him.

When Charley finished telling the truth about what happened, Sophia stared at her as if Charley had morphed into an alien.

"Can I borrow your phone to call Harry?" Charley picked up the paper. "I've got to give him this information."

Sophia set her mug on the counter.

"Sure. It's in my purse." She walked to the coffee table, sat on the couch, and searched in a purse large enough to carry a laptop.

"I must have left it in the car. Let me check." She grabbed her keys and left.

Charley stared at the message she had decoded. What was the Star? A restaurant? A movie theatre? Probably one of those places that held special events. She poured a cup of coffee and took a sip.

Keys rattled at the front door. Charley watched as Sophia walked inside.

Sophia frowned and lifted her arms. "I guess I left it at work." She checked her watch. "I'll call Harry from the restaurant down the street, then run by work, and grab my phone."

How well did she know Sophia? Could she trust her to pass on the information to Harry? After all, Charley had trusted Tom. She obviously wasn't the best judge of character.

"I'll go with you," Charley said.

Sophia shook her head, then touched Charley's shoulder.

"Harry would want you to stay here." Her eyes softened. "Let me take care of this."

Harry trusted Sophia that meant she had to be okay, right? Charley handed the paper to her.

Sophia tucked it in her purse and left.

Charley locked the door and stared at it. She ran her fingers through her hair and wished she had never accepted the cryptanalyst position.

54

As Harry hung up the phone from talking with Dr. Worth, his phone rang again. Candy was calling. He didn't have the time or energy for her, but she would hound him until he answered.

"What's up, Candy?"

"I heard Richie talking on the phone. He's meeting someone at eight tonight at the Star. Would you follow him and see what he's up to?"

"I really don't have time."

"What's so important that you can't help me?"

Harry couldn't tell her about the threat to Charley. Fog had settled into the crevices of his brain making it impossible for him to dream up a lie. He checked his watch. Eight would give him enough time to gather information on Tom and figure out what to do next.

"I'll do it."

By the time Harry climbed the stairs and entered his place, he struggled keeping his eyes open. His shoulders and back ached. The pressure in his head warned of an oncoming migraine. He downed a couple of ibuprofens and took a hot shower.

He looked at Van stretched across his bed.

"I'll just take a quick nap." Harry dropped onto the bed.

55

Harry jerked awake and grabbed his phone off the bedside table. He checked the time: 6:30.

"Crap! I've slept all afternoon." He rolled out of bed. Van meowed.

Harry looked at him. "I don't have time to give you any treats. You'll have to wait for later. I've got to get to the Star."

If he left in the next thirty minutes, he could get there before Richie arrived so he could position himself to take pictures.

Harry dressed, grabbed his phone, and keys. Van rubbed around his legs and yowled.

"Alright, alright." He reached into the bag of treats, threw some on the floor, and left.

Harry arrived at the Star forty-five minutes before Richie's scheduled meeting. Only four cars were parked in the lot, each in front of a room. Either the Star was having trouble filling its rooms or everyone went out for the night. He parked in the back row under the shade of some trees. From there, he could see the lobby with his binoculars without drawing any attention. He hated surveillance, but he had promised Candy.

Harry killed the engine. After about five minutes, the cool air in his car depleted, forcing him to roll down the windows. A cool breeze flowed through the vehicle, bringing with it the smell of honeysuckle, triggering a memory from his childhood.

At his aunt's house, a honeysuckle vine climbed the wooden backyard fence. She taught him how to pull the stem through the pale-yellow flower and suck the nectar, a taste as sweet as honey, but a delicate flavor, light and fleeting. One summer, he almost took every bud off the vine. He smiled, shook his head as if to clear the mental vision, then returned to his task.

A sporty Black BMW pulled in front of the main entrance. A slim man exited the car. Both the car and the man looked familiar. As the guy headed for the lobby, Harry picked up the binoculars and zoomed in on the man's face. He recognized the narrow eyes, the tanned thin face, and dark hair as one of the men he'd seen with Richie previously at the Star. A few minutes later, he exited the lobby with a key in hand, drove toward a group of rooms, parked, and got out of his car.

Porch lamps cast a glow in front of each doorway, providing Harry enough light to make out the number of the room the guy entered: seventeen.

A few minutes later, Sophia walked past the rooms, carrying a couple of white towels. Harry smiled. He enjoyed seeing the swing of her hips, the glimpse of her shapely legs. She stopped at seventeen, then walked inside. Minutes passed and Sophia hadn't walked out of the room.

Harry frowned. "What the hell is she doing in there? It doesn't take that long to drop off towels."

Harry squinted into the binoculars, verified the number, then shook his head. Maybe Sophia paid for her townhome by providing extracurricular services. If so, Harry would mark her off his list of prospects. He didn't like sharing anything, especially women.

A limousine pulled into the parking lot. A man built like a bouncer at a bar got out of the driver's seat. He looked around as if scoping out the area, then opened the back door of the car. A short man barely five and a half feet tall exited. A dark tailored sports coat with a crisp white shirt graced his small frame. Whoever the short guy was he moved with confident strides toward seventeen. The door opened as if someone had been watching for him. The limo driver and Shorty entered the room.

Three men and Sophia? Something was up. Images and thoughts collided in Harry's mind: Sophia's expensive townhome, her unlikely occupation, her slipping something to a man in the parking lot. Harry had an idea about Sophia and if it were true, she could be headed for trouble.

Richie's silver Mercedes coupe slid into a parking space next to black BMW. Richie got out of his car, knocked on door seventeen, and walked inside.

Harry rubbed his forehead. "Holy shit! What the hell is going on?"

Although Sophia seemed able to handle herself, Harry worried with four men, she'd get hurt. He slipped out of his car, closed the door, and hurried toward room seventeen.

He crept close to the curtained window facing the porch, leaned against the wall, and pulled out his cell phone as if he were chatting. Meanwhile, he listened for sounds coming from the room. Muted voices carried through the windowpane, all deep tones, manly tones. No one screamed. No raised voices broke the barrier of the window.

A few doors down, a couple exited a room. Each lit a cigarette. They strolled toward him. As they grew closer, they smiled. Harry nodded, then resisted coughing when the smoke filled his nose and reached his throat. Cigarettes didn't tempt him. His aunt let him puff a cigarette once when he was a pre-teen. He decided then they weren't for him. Perhaps she should have let him try alcohol. The strong taste and burn might have put him off it too.

After the couple passed him, Harry moved closer to the window and peered in the sliver of light where the curtains didn't quite meet. Richie and the limo driver had their backs to the window. Sophia stood in the middle of the room facing them and talking. The limo drive moved toward her. She held her hands in front of her chest as if to stop him. Shorty and the other guy stood behind her. Based on Shorty's frown and pursed lips, he wasn't buying whatever she was saying.

Harry knocked on the door. The curtains fluttered. Richie's face appeared in the window. Harry waved. He had to think of some excuse quick.

The curtains closed. Harry heard some scuffling sounds. A few seconds later, Richie opened the door.

"Hi Harry. What are you doing here?"

"They're putting new carpet in my apartment. I couldn't stand the fumes, so I decided to spend the night at a cheap motel. I saw you drive up as I pulled into the lot." Harry pointed in the direction of Richie's car. "I figured Candy might have thrown you out for the night." He shrugged. "Some days it doesn't take much to piss her off."

She had never kicked Harry out, but he knew how to make her laugh when she got angry.

"Anyway, I thought you might want to go for a drink." He peered inside. "Unless you have company?" Except for the furniture, the room was empty.

Richie shook his head. "All by myself." He laughed. "Candy hasn't thrown me out yet. I'm looking at investment properties. This one was in the running." He looked around the room. "But after seeing the place…" He bit his lip. "It would take too much money to renovate."

"Shit!" The outburst came from the bathroom.

Harry pulled out his Beretta. Richie reached inside his coat. Harry cold-cocked him with the butt of his gun. Richie fell to the floor. Harry reached inside Richie's coat and grabbed the gun from his holster. Harry slid down next to the bed as he heard someone entering from the bathroom. He looked in the mirror on the opposite wall and watched as the man with the dark eyes and tan skin peer around the opening of the vanity area. The man glanced at Richie's body, then raised a 9mm pistol and scanned it across the room as he moved toward the motel door. Harry held his breath as the guy drew closer. Harry gripped his Beretta, aimed it, and shot the man's hand. The blast echoed in his ears. The man's pistol dropped to the floor. The guy grabbed his wounded hand. Blood ran through his fingers, dripping onto the beige carpet.

The limo driver moved into the opening. One muscular arm wrapped around Sophia's body, the other pointed a 9mm pistol at her head. A washcloth gag prevented Sophia from speaking. Her brown eyes were wide. A man's belt cinched her upper arms to her body. The man had a couple of inches on Harry in height, but Harry figured he could take him if it weren't for the gun pointed at Sophia. Shorty stepped out from behind the limo driver and pointed his gun at Harry.

"Put down the gun," said the limo driver as he jerked his gun closer to her face.

Once Harry released the gun, they wouldn't hesitate to shoot him. He'd probably kill Sophia anyway. Harry had to act fast. He dropped below the bed, slid to the end of the bed, and shot the limo driver in the shoulder. Sophia rammed her heel in the top of the man's foot. The man released her. As he reeled in pain, she turned and kicked him in the crotch. Shorty's gun went off. A bullet hit the window next to the bed. Bullets hit the wall above the bed as Harry rolled toward the headboard.

Another shot sounded. Shorty groaned. The air conditioner whooshed air through the vent. Tires squealed in the parking lot. Harry peered up over the bed. Sophia stood in the middle of the room. Her arm was bent at her waist just below the cinched man's belt. In her hand, she held the limo driver's 9mm pistol pointed at Shorty as blood stained the front of his crisp white shirt.

The door flew open. "FBI, drop your weapons." Glocks pointed at them from either side of the door.

Sophia and Harry walked out of the FBI Field Office. Harry had given the agents the details on what went down, but they had told him nothing. They ignored his questions as if he hadn't asked any.

Harry glanced at Sophia. "I don't know about you, but I missed supper. Want to grab a bite to eat?"

"Sure. As long as you're buying. There's a place just around the corner." She pointed a finger and moved in that direction. Harry followed.

He cleared his throat. "Seems like you should do the buying. After all, I saved your life tonight."

"I think the crotch kick and the shot to the short guy's stomach might have helped." She laughed. "Besides, I vouched for you. Otherwise, you'd be sitting in a cell along with the rest of them."

Harry smiled and nodded. "True. We make a good team." He arched an eyebrow. "I'm surprised the FBI didn't offer us a job." He watched her expressions and waited to see if she would confess.

Only a few people strolled on the sidewalk. The night was quiet except for the hum of the occasional car as it drew close to them. The air lingered like a damp blanket on Harry's skin.

"What were you doing at the motel?" Sophia asked.

"I was tailing Richie. His wife thought he was cheating on her." Harry ran his fingers through his hair. "Wait until she hears he's been arrested."

Harry glanced at her. "What were you doing in the room?" He wondered if she would tell the truth.

"I might as well tell you." She looked sideways at him. "If you're any kind of detective, you'll have already guessed anyway. I work for the FBI. The maid gig was just a way to infiltrate a drug ring that spans multiple states and countries. I had gained the trust of Richie and his crew, but when the short guy showed up tonight, he wasn't as trusting. His driver found the wire I was wearing."

"Why didn't you just bug the room?"

"The short guy wouldn't reserve a particular room. He wanted it randomly selected by whichever one of them arrived first."

They turned onto a street where a delicatessen sign flashed "Open".

"I hope a sandwich works for you." She glanced sideways at him. "I'm a cheap date. At least for tonight."

Harry controlled his reaction at the mention of "date". He didn't want to risk scaring her off by appearing too eager.

They ordered sandwiches and got drinks at the counter, then

grabbed a table close to the window.

Once they were seated, Harry asked, "What did you do for them?"

"They had a system. Someone called and made a reservation using a special code. When they checked in, they paid in cash. The drugs were waiting for them in the room. They stayed awhile so no one got suspicious. Before leaving, they submitted their next order and left the key and the order in a drawer in the room. I collected the orders and managed the distribution of the drugs."

She sucked on her straw, then swallowed. "No one ever notices a maid, so I was the perfect cover for the FBI and the drug runners."

From Harry's perspective, she was far from unnoticeable. He drank some of his iced tea and wished it was the Long Island variety. If ever a night called for alcohol, this night did.

She widened her eyes. "What about Charley? Have you dealt with her boyfriend?"

Harry knew the truth would come out sooner or later. He stared down the street. "There's a crazy man after Charley, but it's not her boyfriend. It's a guy she works with, Tom Giles." He turned and looked at Sophia. "Charley handles confidential information, so I had to make up a story."

Sophia rolled her eyes and shook her head. "Charley told me all about her job with the CIA. Will you ever stop lying?"

"Old habits are hard to break," Harry said with a smile. He raised his eyebrows. "It's not like you weren't hiding secrets."

She laughed. "I guess that's true."

Harry frowned. "Seems like the FBI would have shown up sooner."

"They were probably on their way when you knocked on the door."

The waiter placed their sandwiches and chips on the table.

Harry reached for a chip. "Since the Star takes cash and asks no questions, it was the perfect meeting place for them."

Sophia nodded. "That and Richard owns it."

Harry always wondered how Richie made his money. Candy would definitely dump him now. She would probably show up at Harry's place. He hated being the rebound man and he wasn't sure he wanted her back in his life. Besides, she'd just leave him for the next rich guy.

"Pretty smart." Harry took a bite of his sandwich, then wiped his mouth. "Why did the guy yell 'shit'?"

Sophia laughed. "I bit him. That's when the other guy stuffed the washcloth in my mouth."

"You still interested in detective work? Cause I could use a partner. The pay's not awesome, but the benefits are." Harry winked. "You could leave the FBI and work with me."

If Dr. Worth couldn't figure out what was wrong with Harry, Sophia's first assignment would be to follow him. Although, he didn't want to tell her everything. Who wants to date a crazy guy? The doc might have an answer for him tomorrow.

"I'll think about it." Sophia popped a chip in her mouth.

Harry picked up his drink and rattled the ice in it. "Why the FBI?" Sophia didn't look like the typical FBI agent. Maybe a spy in a James Bond movie, but in real life?

Sophia fiddled with her straw. "My brother overdosed on drugs."

Harry remembered the framed photograph of her family at her townhome and the sad look on her face when Harry asked about her brother.

She released the straw and stared into his eyes. Her jaw tightened. "I didn't just want the drug dealer. I wanted to take down the entire drug cartel responsible for his death." She smiled. "That short guy with the fancy suit? We've been waiting a while to get him. He's the top drug guy in Mexico. He gets everyone else to do his dirty work. He'll lawyer up, but this time he won't get away."

"Not many people would take revenge to the level of joining the FBI," he said.

Harry knew one thing for sure. He never wanted to piss off Sophia.

He rubbed his eyes. "I've got to figure out how to deal with Tom before he gets to Charley."

"You don't have to worry about that anymore. Tom was the drug cartel's inside man in the CIA. He's already in custody."

Harry sighed. The tightness across his shoulder blades eased a little. With Charley safe, he could focus on his sleepwalking and finding the mystery woman.

After the night's events, Harry's apartment was a welcome sanctuary. With a glass of Johnnie Walker in one hand and Van curled up next to him, his body relaxed. Harry would rather have Sophia by his side. Maybe one day… He sipped the scotch and savored the liquid gold as it warmed his throat. He leaned back on the couch. His eyes closed. Someone knocked on the door.

He didn't want to answer. His body ached and begged for sleep. The knock grew more insistent. He dragged himself off the couch and to the door. He checked the peephole. Candy stood on his doorstep.

Harry opened the door. Candy stomped inside.

"Can you believe that man was a drug dealer?" She shook her head. "I would rather he cheated on me." She turned and glared at Harry. "Do you know the FBI is already interrogating me?" She placed her hand on her chest.

Harry figured Richie was safer with the FBI than with Candy. Nothing could make this better for her. So, Harry chose the wise option. He kept his mouth shut and listened to her rant.

"You think I knew he was dealing drugs?" Her eyes widened.

Harry shook his head.

She raised her hands. "Of course not, but will the FBI believe that?" She plopped onto the couch.

Van ran out of the room. Harry wished he could.

She crossed her legs, leaned forward, and rubbed her forehead with her hand.

"What am I going to do?" She looked up at Harry. "Where am I going to go?"

Harry did a quick pro/con analysis. If she moved in with him, he'd have someone who could watch him at night, making sure his sleepwalking-self stayed out of trouble. He looked at Candy. She flexed her foot, showcasing the red soles of her Louboutin heels. The fitted form of her shirt and skirt shouted money. After dating her for over a year, he recognized the Louis Vuitton pattern on the purse she clutched. No one would catch her at the Star motel as an undercover maid. Candy was high maintenance: clothes, shoes, purses, emotions. He looked around his apartment. She would insist they move into some high-end River Oaks place.

Besides, maybe he wouldn't need a night sitter much longer. Dr. Worth might give him a solution to his sleepwalking when he met her in the morning. If she didn't, paying for a night sitter would be cheaper than Candy.

"I'm betting you stashed away some of Richie's money for yourself."

She smiled. "You know me too well."

Candy raised an eyebrow and looked him up and down. "Too bad you don't have loads of money."

He had inherited quite a bit from his aunt, but Candy could run through that in a couple of years, if not sooner. Besides, Sophia had cast a spell on him, one not easily broken.

She frowned. "I may have to go back to work." A smile crossed her face. "That's how I met my first husband." She ran a finger across her lips. "Quite a profitable venture."

Candy stood, then hugged him on the way to the door. "Thanks for listening. You always know how to cheer me up."

After she left, Harry realized Candy wouldn't pay him until she met her next conquest. He shrugged. It didn't matter. In spite of all her faults, Harry still liked her. If nothing else, she was entertaining.

56

Lamps glowing on end tables provided light in Sophia's darkened living room. Charley sat on the couch, listlessly flipping through channels, finally settling on an *I Love Lucy* show. Images flashed across the screen. The laughter of the TV audience fell flat in the silent room.

Why wasn't Sophia home yet? Charley walked over to the window and peeked through the blinds. Streetlights revealed someone walking their dog, and a couple of sedans parked at the curb. She ran her fingers through her hair, then returned to the sofa.

Sophia hadn't said she was coming home after picking up her phone from work, but she hadn't said she wasn't either. What if something had happened to her or to Harry? The front doorknob rattled. Charley stood and watched as the door opened.

Sophia looked at her and smiled. "Sorry, it took so long." She rolled her eyes. "Work." She shut the door and locked it.

"Did you get the message to Harry?"

Sophia nodded. "And you don't have to worry about Tom

anymore. They arrested him and his thugs."

Charley squinted. "How do you know?"

"I work for the FBI." Sophia dropped her purse on the coffee table. "Tom was involved in a drug ring we were trying to take down."

"What?" Charley's eyes widened. "A drug ring? The FBI? You're a secret agent?"

Sophia laughed. "I guess you could say that. Let me go take a shower, then I'll tell you all about it."

Charley moved close to Sophia and grabbed her arm. "What about Harry? Is he ok?" If anything bad had happened to Harry...

"Harry? He's fine." Sophia rubbed her bottom lip. "Very fine." She smiled.

Charley frowned. How could she compete with a quintessential James Bond babe?

As Sophia described the night's events, Charley sipped on a soda.

"So, Tom was supplying the drug runners with intel from the CIA. He also dealt with any messages intercepted by the CIA. Unfortunately for Tom, one got past him, the one you cracked. It gave us all the information we needed to catch them. Great job!" Sophia smiled.

"The whole thing is nuts." Charley shook her head. "I'm glad y'all are okay and Tom is in jail." She tilted her head. "Do you think my manager was in on it too?"

Sophia shrugged. "He's probably clean. They'll know more

after the internal investigation is complete." She looked at Charley. "You can stay here as long as you like, but there's no reason to hide anymore."

Charley smiled. "Thanks for the offer, but I'm going home in the morning. I need to find a new job. After this, I can't work for the CIA."

"I can probably get you a job in the FBI." Sophia grabbed the counter cleaner from under the sink.

"I'm done with government organizations." Charley crossed her arms.

Sophia sprayed the counter and wiped it with a paper towel. "What will you do then?"

"I'm not sure yet." She laughed. "Maybe Harry needs a partner."

Sophia stopped cleaning and leaned against the bar. "He did mention he needed one."

"You think I could do it?" Charley asked.

Sophia put away the cleaner, tossed the paper towel, then put her hands on her hips.

"You decoded a message that brought down an international drug ring and you survived a kidnapping. So yeah, I think you could do it. We just gotta get you a gun."

Charley eyes widened. A gun seemed extreme, but it sure would have come in handy with Tom.

Sophia opened a kitchen cabinet. "We'll go shopping for one tomorrow." She pulled out a mug. "You want some hot tea?"

Charley nodded. A vision of her pointing a gun at Tom flashed before her. She sat up straight and smiled. Tomorrow she would look into handgun classes, maybe a class in martial arts too. Next time, if there was a next time, she'd be ready.

57

Dr. Worth watched Harry as he took his usual chair near her. The shadows underneath his eyes had faded. His straight back and upright shoulders were a posture worthy of emulation. An energy radiated from him that projected optimism. She wondered if he thought she had answers for him. She hated disappointing him.

"How was the sleep study?" Dr. Worth asked.

"Took me a while to fall asleep, but I didn't leave the room." Harry smiled.

"That's good." Janet opened his folder and pulled out the sleep study results.

"The sleep study showed no sign of sleep apnea or restless leg syndrome. It might be the alcohol, but…"

Harry interrupted her. "When I forgot what happened, I had only had one or two drinks."

She questioned the truthfulness of his statement, but he had to know lying wouldn't solve his problem. At this point, he seemed desperate enough for answers to tell the truth.

"One or two drinks shouldn't cause any problems." She

frowned. "Unfortunately, nothing surfaced as an issue. Nothing that would explain the sleep walking and forgetting events."

Harry slumped back in his chair. "I can't live like this. How can I go to sleep at night when I'm wondering what I might do?"

His shoulders sagged, and the energy seemed to drain from his body. He leaned forward, gripped the chair's arms, clenched his jaw, and stared into her eyes as if determined to beat the beast within him.

"There has to be something I can do," he said.

"There are other things it could be, but we'll need to dig deeper into your past." She smiled. "I have something we can try, but it requires your complete cooperation."

Harry leaned back in his chair. "Of course."

She wondered if he really meant it. In the past, he had danced around sensitive topics or gave her smart ass answers to avoid revealing any emotion. "It may have something to do with your past. So, let's explore it."

He nodded.

"Let's start with your dad."

Harry crossed his arms.

Janet looked at her notes. "In a previous session, you said he hit you and your mother. Tell me more about this." She turned her focus on him. "A particular event you remember?"

He frowned. "One time…" He stopped.

She leaned toward him. "What is it?" If he wasn't forthcoming with answers, then she couldn't help him. Maybe she should try a different tactic.

A smile slid across Harry's face. He winked.

Janet squinted and dropped back in her chair. Was he coming onto her? She'd never gotten that kind of vibe from him in the past. If he turned out to be another erotic transference case, he would have to see some other psychiatrist. She hated losing him as a patient especially since he had proven to be one of her more interesting cases.

Harry's eyelids lowered. He rested his elbows on the chair arms and relaxed his shoulders. He crossed one leg over the other at the knees then swung one foot back and forth.

Those weren't Harry's normal mannerisms. Janet's heart quickened. She leaned closer and searched for other behavioral changes.

"You were going to tell me about a time your dad hit you and your mother?" she prompted.

Harry propped his arm on the back of his chair, then twirled a lock of hair around his fingers.

"He's not going to tell you." Harry's voice rose an octave and it dripped a southern accent. He looked around the room. "You got a cigarette? I could use one." He rolled his eyes. "Harry doesn't like them. I have to keep them hidden otherwise he would throw them out."

A shiver crawled up Janet's spine. She knew the voice. It was the voice of the stalker. She forced her breathing to stay even and her body and voice tone to remain neutral when she answered.

"Sorry. I'm not a smoker." She wanted answers but would

need to tease them out. "Where do you hide the cigarettes?"

He frowned. "If I tell you, you'll tell Harry."

"No, the cigarettes can be our secret. You know. Patient confidentiality."

Harry smiled and whispered. "I hide them and a pack of matches under the seat of his car. Just can't smoke in there." He touched his nose. "Harry has a keen sense of smell."

Janet wondered about the appearances of other unexplained objects in Harry's life.

"Did you give Harry the cat?"

He smirked. "Yeah, he needed something after our aunt died."

Janet wanted to get on his/her good side. She didn't want to trigger any anger and end up in a physical fight. If so, she'd lose. As an ex-cop, Harry had moves she didn't have.

"That was a nice thing to do."

"I try to help Harry." He sighed and threw up his hands. "I left him all kinds of clues to help him find Lisa's lover." He tapped the side of his head. "He's a little slow sometimes."

"You know my name, but I don't know yours." Janet smiled as she did when meeting someone for the first time.

He tilted his head. "Victoria."

Janet held out her hand. "Nice to meet you."

Victoria looked at Janet's hand, then shook it.

"How else have you helped Harry?"

"When we were little, I took most of the belt whippings and scoldings. He always wondered how he got the bruises." Victoria sighed. "Now, I just help him with his detective business."

"Harry's lucky to have you."

Victoria preened. "He is." She looked down at the floor. "Sorry I scared you."

She raised her head and locked eyes with Janet. "You were getting too close. I don't want him to know about me." She narrowed her eyes. "You better not tell him."

"Why not? Harry thinks something is wrong with him. If he got to know you…"

Janet had read about people with dissociative identity disorder who adjusted by accepting their personalities.

Victoria laughed. "It's not like we can talk with each other. It doesn't work like that."

Janet set aside the folder. "I could tell him."

Victoria shook her head, her eyes widened. "He won't like me."

"How could he help but like you? Look at all you've done for him."

Victoria raised her eyebrows. "That's true."

"It's really stressing him out not knowing. Is that what you want for him?"

Victoria's mouth and eyes turned into hard slits. "I said don't tell him." She shrugged. "He wouldn't believe you anyway."

Janet tried a different approach. "How have you helped him with his detective business?"

Victoria smiled. "I became friends with Lisa so I could find out about her lover. Even went with her to the hotel room, but I left before she was murdered. Didn't even see who did it."

She shook her head. All traces of her smile vanished.

"We were good drinking buddies. She didn't care that I only drank orange juice. I like champagne too. The bubbles tickle my nose." She giggled. "That's why Lisa ordered it that night at the Alessandra. She knows how much I like it." She nodded. "Lisa liked it too."

Victoria laughed, then frowned. "I miss her." She rubbed her lips and looked at the ceiling. "I went to Chip's to ask him questions, trying to get information for Harry. But I only got Harry in trouble with my fingerprints."

"Wait a minute. Harry only saw himself leaving on the video once."

"I was in a rush and forgot about that stupid video camera." Victoria cut her eyes toward the ceiling.

The stalker had only attacked Janet recently. Somehow Victoria had gotten out of Harry's place.

"How could you have followed me without the camera recording you leaving?"

She didn't use the word stalked. It sounded accusatory, even criminal. She didn't want to get on the wrong side of Victoria.

Victoria laughed and slapped the air. "I climbed out the bedroom window. Harry's afraid of heights, but I'm not."

Janet had enough information for Harry. It might not ease his mind, but it was an answer.

"I think we should tell Harry about you. How you've helped him."

Victoria gripped the arm rest, leaned into Janet's personal space and pointed a finger.

"I told you no and I meant it. Don't make me do something we'd both regret."

Victoria's eyes opened wide. "You don't really believe our parent's car crash was an accident, do you?" Her jaw tensed. "I would do anything to protect Harry." A sadness etched her face. "Too bad about our mom, but she should have stopped Dad from hitting Harry."

Janet had no doubt Victoria would act upon her threat, but Janet owed Harry. The patient confidentiality protected a patient's privacy, but how would the court view Harry's and Victoria's privacy?

Victoria moved to the edge of her seat. "We wouldn't want anything to happen to Harry either. I know him better than you. If he found out about me…" She looked out the window. "Our aunt's death almost pushed him over the edge. She was just one more person he thought he had failed."

She focused on Janet and snickered. "The trail of women's clothes kept him going."

"How did you do it? Get the cat and the clothes, then keep them hidden from Harry?"

Victoria grinned. "Our aunt has a storage unit." Her foot stopped swinging. "Harry doesn't want to deal with it. Can't face the memories." She twisted the watch on her wrist. "Anyway, the cat hung around there. I knew nobody wanted him with that torn ear and scruffy coat. I bought all the stuff the cat needed, then picked him up."

"Didn't Harry notice the charge?" Janet would be surprised if he didn't. What with Harry being a detective, he'd watch for any unusual charges on his card or any missing cash.

Victoria raised an eyebrow. "I have my own money. I sell stuff from the storage unit. Sometimes I panhandle. You'd be surprised at how much cash drunk people will fork over."

Janet doubted anything would surprise her after meeting Victoria.

"What about the clothes? Did you buy those too?"

Victoria shook her head. "Our aunt didn't believe in dressing like an old lady. She always had the latest fashions. And the lingerie…" She touched Janet's arm. "That woman believed in undergarments. Don't even get me started on the shoes." Her foot started swinging again.

"Anyway, our aunt's house sold quickly, and Harry only had enough time to throw everything in boxes and drop them off at the storage unit. She was a big boned woman and on the plump side. It's easy enough to squeeze into her clothes. She had big feet too."

Victoria looked at her shoes. "Harry's feet are on the small side. Still, it's a tight fit and heels are a bitch to walk in, but they look good."

Victoria smirked. "I pop in colored contact lenses to turn my eyes brown." She laughed. "No way would anyone mistake me for blue-eyed Harry."

"Did you leave the snake at my place?"

"Yeah, he was harmless. I saw a mouse in the storage room once." She looked up at the ceiling and shook her head. "And it's never just one mouse. Anyway, I caught the snake and kept him in the storage room to take care of the rodents. He did a good job." Her eyes widened. "I wasn't sure whether you were afraid of snakes or not, but figured it was worth a shot. So, I packaged him up and dropped him at your place." She inhaled. "I had just returned to the apartment and sat down in the recliner when Buddy called asking about the cat."

"And the book on my car?"

"I forgot to add the note telling you to stay away from Harry to the snake package, so I had to do something. I remembered the book in the storage room. I wanted to make sure you saw the note so I taped it to the cover." She shrugged. "I figured between the surprise of the snake and the book, you would drop Harry." She glared. "Instead, you met with him and even had him schedule a sleep study."

"The rain smeared the message. I couldn't tell what it said. Otherwise, I wouldn't have met with him."

Victoria hit the chair arm. "Don't lie to me. You saw Harry even after I pushed you into the sofa and told you to stay away from him."

Janet softened her eyes. "My job is to help people. I just wanted to help Harry."

Victoria sighed. "Now that we've met. I don't care how often you see him. Just don't say anything about me."

Janet wondered about Victoria's thought process. "If you don't want him to know about you, then why leave the Victoria's Secret clue?"

Victoria's eyes widened. "I guess sometimes I wish he knew about me."

"Then why not tell him?"

Victoria's body stilled. Her mouth formed a thin line.

"Don't tell him anything I've told you. Who I am or what I've done." Victoria leaned close to her.

Janet fought the urge to move away. She needed to calm Victoria down before the whole session derailed.

"I think he really likes the cat." Janet smiled.

Victoria sighed. "The cat did give me some trouble when he escaped from the Star." She rolled her eyes. "Luckily, he comes to me when I call. He doesn't scratch me like he does Harry." She shrugged. "I guess he trusts me. Anyway, I just took him back to the apartment with me. I needed to pick up a baseball cap and gloves so you wouldn't guess who it was rapping on your window. I thought that would be enough for you to give up Harry, but you're tougher than you look."

"I think Harry is tough too. He can handle the truth."

Victoria wrung her hands. "You're wrong. If you tell him about me, he'll spiral into a hole so deep that even I can't pull him out. Do you want to be responsible for that? He might even kill himself, anything to escape reality."

Janet doubted Harry would go that far, but if he did… Janet hadn't seen Harry long enough to know the validity of Victoria's statements. She couldn't tell Harry about Victoria if there was a chance it would cause him any harm.

Janet shook her head. "I won't tell him." She rubbed her chin. "How did you come up with the name of Victoria?"

A wave of sadness crossed Victoria's face. "We had a little sister, Victoria. Harry doesn't remember her or perhaps he has buried the memory of her. She died in the car accident along with our parents."

Victoria uncrossed her legs and pressed her back against the chair. She frowned.

"Now, what was I saying?" The southern accent had disappeared, and the voice had dropped an octave.

Janet closed Harry's folder. "It doesn't matter. I need to do some more research. Let's get together again next week."

Harry's eyes popped wide. "Next week? I can't wait that long."

"Just keep checking the video. If you see yourself leaving, give me a call."

Harry frowned. "I thought you wanted to talk about my past."

"After thinking about it, I realized there might be another solution, but it's going to take time and research. For now, I'm sure you'll be safe." Janet grabbed his folder and stood.

Harry got up from his chair. "You'll call me if you find anything - right?"

She smiled. "You can count on it."

As Harry reached the office door, he turned toward her. "Have they found your stalker?"

Janet couldn't tell him the truth. "No, but nothing else has happened."

Harry frowned. "Something might happen now, since we met today."

"I think I misunderstood her. I think she said Henry. He was an old boyfriend." She rolled her eyes. "One I don't plan to ever see again."

She would call Detective Thibodeaux later and give him some excuse to get rid of her tail.

After the door closed behind Harry, Janet stood at her office window and watched him walk to his car. She had wanted an interesting case and Harry had done it. A patient with a dissociative identity disorder would intrigue any psychiatrist.

Janet wondered when she'd see Victoria again. Or perhaps she'd meet someone new next time she met with Harry.

58

As Harry drove home, he mulled over Dr. Worth's abrupt ending of the session. He remembered struggling to recall a memory of his dad hitting him, then the next thing he knew the doctor had changed her mind. She might have something for him at their next meeting. At least, he wasn't sleepwalking anymore. Since that one incident, the video showed nothing but Van moving at night.

Harry's stomach grumbled. In his rush to see Dr. Worth, he'd skipped breakfast. He pulled into the Whataburger drive-through and ordered a burger, fries, and iced tea. As he waited in line, he drummed the steering wheel with his thumbs.

He still wanted to solve who left the cat, clothes, and card case. Almost two weeks had passed since the owner had dropped off Van. He doubted anyone would come and claim the cat. That was okay. Harry had gotten used to the varmint.

When he pulled up to the drive-through window, cool air pushed into his face and the scent of fries filled his nose. His mouth watered as he exchanged money for the loaded paper bag and iced tea. As he took off, he snagged a few fries and savored the salty carbohydrates. Everything looked better with burger, fries, caffeine, and a clean slate. Without another case, he could focus on finding the mystery woman. He figured she held all the answers to a lot of his questions.

He smiled as he pulled into the apartment parking lot. No more worrying about Drake lurking nearby to arrest him for murder or anything else. He grabbed the bag and Styrofoam cup, then climbed the stairs to his place. As he unlocked his door, he wondered if any surprises waited on the other side.

Van greeted him, winding around his legs. Harry put everything down on the counter and scratched the cat under the neck. Van jumped up on an end table and started batting something with his paw, then swatted it onto the floor. Metal clanged as it hit the floor. Harry picked it up, then eyed the key. A chain ran through the keyhole. On the other end of the chain, black letters covered by a plastic label identified it: Storage Unit.

Harry looked at Van. "How did this get here? I thought it was in my bedroom drawer." He laid the key next to his wallet on the counter.

He ate his food and sucked down enough caffeine to replenish his energy. Van jumped on the counter and knocked the storage key on the floor again. Harry picked up the key, then tightened his fingers around it.

"I've put it off long enough. Dr. Worth's right. It's time I went through my aunt's things." Harry grabbed his wallet and headed for the door.

About the Author

Helen Wills is a retired IT Project Manager and a resident of Trinity, Texas, where she lives with her husband and three cats. Originally from Mobile, Alabama, she spent years reading mysteries before deciding to write one of her own.

In her debut book, *A Past Best Forgotten*, Helen introduces Private Investigator Harry Bennett, an ex-cop, who has the connections and skills to solve crimes. If only his past would quit interfering...

Visit Helen Will's website at www.helenwillsmystery.com.

Printed in Great Britain
by Amazon

48407276R00208